THESE THORNS ARE SHARPEST

M. R. PRITCHARD

Cover Art and Interior Art: Stockphotos from DepositPhotos. Elements, Filters, Fonts and digital manipulations with Canva. Photographs by M. R. Pritchard.
Edited by: Kristy Ellsworth

Midnight Ledger Publishing
14391 Spring Hill Dr. Suite 203
Spring Hill, FL 34609
MidnightLedger.com
First Edition December 2025
ISBNs: 978-1-957709-83-3 (Hardcover), 978-1-957709-84-0 (Paperback)
Printed in the United States of America

About "These Thorns are Sharpest"

M. R. Pritchard

Bound by lies and forbidden desire, their secrets may shatter the Veil itself.

Angels are not pure, demons are not mindless, and even gods keep dangerous secrets. The Veil of Shadows spans Heaven's kingdoms, Hell's burning caves, the mortal Earth, and forgotten realms where lost souls drift.

This novel follows Teari, a pure-blooded Angel haunted by her father's hidden crimes, and Chel, the last surviving Hellion warrior, scarred by war and survivor-guilt. Ordered to take a vacation, Chel lands on the Earthen plane with a fake honeymoon cover that quickly turns into a secret mission. Teari joins him, and their pretend marriage soon blurs into something real.

Expect forbidden love, slow-burn passion, and gothic peril as old prisons crack open and new threats rise. Familiar faces from the Veil of Shadows—Meg, the Raven King, Rue, Dacre, Evelyn, Remington, Layla, Thrush, Shay, Jed, Jasper, and the ever-watchful cat Lucipurr—return as the Veil itself begins to thin.

Dark, romantic, and charged with destiny, 'These Thorns Are Sharpest' is a story of love that defies realms and the sharpest thorns of all: the ones we inherit.

A warrior bound by duty.
An Angel haunted by her bloodline.
The only way to survive is together.

Chel never asked for time off but when the Queen of Hell demanded he take a "vacation," the Hellion warrior found himself stranded on the Earthen plane. What should have been rest quickly became a hunt, chasing the strange creatures crawling out of the ocean. And then there was the little lie he told the grocery clerk... about being on his honeymoon.

A forced vacation.
A fake marriage.
And the one Hellion she can't resist.

Teari has spent her life carrying her father's sins, silenced by secrets too heavy to name. Now benched from her post as Gabriel's healer, she's sent on her first "vacation" but shadows are stirring, the Veil is thinning, and the truth she's buried refuses to stay hidden. She might run from fate, but she can't run from him.

Bound together by lies, desire, and the unraveling Veil, they'll have to decide whether to risk their hearts—or lose the ones they love most.

Perfect for fans of forbidden love, winged guardians, cursed devotion, and slow-burning passion set against gothic peril.

Bound by lies and forbidden desire, their secrets may shatter the Veil itself.

THESE THORNS ARE
SHARPEST

M. R. PRITCHARD

Chapter 1

Blood was thicker than water. But Angel blood? That was closer to the inky water of the Black River in Hell than anything else.

There was a real reason why Teari left her father's kingdom to serve the Archangel Gabriel. She didn't dare speak of it because in her world silence was survival. There was a time when power was bought with secrets. Times had changed, but that change didn't stretch far. Some secrets were soul deep. There was a time when the Archangels and the Deacons conspired to rule all. They gave off a holy impression, but Teari knew what had gone on behind closed doors. There was no holiness in what the Archangels were doing. Meg had put a stop to most of it and when Alastor and Lucifer killed the last Deacon just before the war, the glass castle had shattered.

Babylon no longer held all the power. It had been restored to its rightful deity; a White Horse who resided on the Earthen plane.

Still, Teari was a black sheep deep down. She'd always been too soft, too curious, too unwilling to look away, and too willing to stand up for what was right. Although, sometimes she had been eager to stand for the wrong thing. There was a time when she'd nearly made Meg, the Queen of Hell, her enemy. That was before she had all the details, before she realized Sparrow would be out of her reach and nothing more than a friend. A girl could dream but an Angel could not mingle with that omen.

Now she was a healer and simply that. She had been a soldier briefly; it was part of her training to stay in Gabriel's kingdom. He didn't want a healer who could not protect themselves. Her hands were far more useful putting bodies back together rather than breaking them apart. Her stint in the Legion was quick, but enough to bury her deeper into Gabriel's kingdom, enough to give her cover and respite. She had made a commitment to Gabriel, and it gave her enough distance from her father's rule to pretend she'd carved out a life of her own.

She hadn't.

Not really.

She was still caught in his shadow. He still called upon her to clean up what he'd stained.

Think what they'll say about you, her father had said. *They'll banish you. They'll strip you of your gifts. And you'll come crawling back home.*

Home.

Teari shuddered. That wasn't home. That was the gilded cage where she was raised. Where she'd come into her healing powers. Where she'd first seen what true corruption looked like when tucked under divine skin.

She would never be like the creature that made her.

Her father, for all his radiance and scripture-wrapped powers, was not pure. He was far from it. Archangels could not lie but they could deceive; they sinned. The murk was thick. They murdered their mistakes and scrubbed the blood away with her hands.

Teari had taken that role as soon as they realized her worth.

And it was breaking her. She'd take a thousand years serving the crown of Hell as a healer over the corruption she couldn't escape.

Even here, behind Gabriel's gates, she felt the old rot creeping beneath her skin. Her father's claws were long and patient and rooted deep within her. Every time she tried to pull away, he yanked her back with veiled threats. The weight of the unspoken, of children who never received names, of women left hollow and grieving, of sins buried under marble and incense. It all hung on her like the heaviest of chains.

And while Teari kept her chin up and her mouth shut, it was taking a toll. There was only so much she could take, only so much she could see. There was too much blood on her hands. Too many last breaths. Too many gravestones.

Archangels were not pure. Their souls were not divine. They still did bad shit. Awful shit. Teari's father was still using her to hide his sins. He was using her to sop up his mess and it was never ending.

Her bloodline hid a secret she could never escape. And as long as her father lived, she would never escape what the Archangel Raphael had done–and continued to do. The judges of Babylon looked away for a few souls of payment.

Archangels were not holy.

They were propaganda with white wings.

She would never escape her father. He would continue to send messages sealed in gold. He'd never say what the mess was. He didn't need to. Teari always knew.

It was always the same. She'd never forget the place where she'd first learned how to hold a dying child. She'd never forget finally understanding the lengths some Archangels would go to keep their hands clean and their bloodline pure.

Even now, she could feel the pull like a hook beneath her ribs.

The air shifted behind her.

"I wondered where you'd disappeared to," came the familiar voice of the Raven King. Sparrow had come for a visit. He was once Gabriel's Legion commander, a cursed man, and now he was the King of the deceased Archangel Remiel's land.

Teari didn't turn. "You could call or message me."

"You never answer these days."

Teari glanced out of the corner of her eye. Sparrow was beside her, hands tucked into the pockets of a long black coat; typical vampire brooding male. His black wings were tucked so close against his back she barely noticed them. Those had gotten him the title of the Raven King; the only King in the Seven Kingdoms of Heaven with black wings.

He was trouble bottled in scars and beauty. He was one of the few beings in this realm she trusted. Him and Meg. Chaos and fire, both of them. But at least they were honest about it.

"You've got that faraway murder-glow in your eyes," Sparrow said, giving her a once over. "Having a bad day?"

Teari sighed. "Just... thinking."

He nudged her shoulder and a light trill of birdsong escaped his lips in a soft whistle. "You don't have to stay here."

She was standing at the edge of a shallow garden behind Gabriel's southern cathedral, bare feet pressed into the soft earth. Golden sunlight spilled across the marble paths. She was here looking for peace.

"I must stay here," she replied to Sparrow with a sigh. "I won't go back to my father. Or, maybe I should run off and join Hell's kitchen crew. You all need a new chef down there?"

"Your cooking sucks." Sparrow laughed. "Meg would take you in a heartbeat though. You know that."

Teari crossed her arms. "I'm not sure where I belong anymore."

Silence stretched between them, broken by the distant sound of cathedral bells from Babylon.

"Our fathers were monsters," Sparrow said.

"Mine is still alive."

"You are not your father, Teari," Sparrow said. There was something in his voice; knowing.

She looked up.

Teari pressed her lips together, emotion burning under her ribs. She wished she believed him. But the truth was ugly—the things she'd done, the cover ups. No matter how far she ran, she was still the pure blooded child of the Archangel Raphael. And Archangel blood never let go.

Chapter 2

The castle in Hell had always felt like home to Chel. The Hellion barracks were better than the hovel he'd grown up in. The Hellion lair reserved for Hellions of high standing, including himself, was even better with high ceilings, leather furniture, old wooden tables, and plenty of blood in the bar fridge. He couldn't escape the memories from before the war. Every time he stepped foot in the lair there was a flood of images of battling Alastor and his chaos that had taken the castle. In the end, Chel was the only one who survived.

Now, he stood near Meg's office, arms crossed, boots still streaked with Helldust and sweat from training. Smoke clung to his clothes, sharp and bitter.

Meg opened the door and ushered him inside.

"You're limping," she said, sharp eyes assessing him.

Chel shrugged. "It's nothing."

"You're leaking." Her tone came to a pitch.

He looked down. His leathers were torn through the thigh. Blood soaked the edge of the fabric. The wound had sealed, but barely. It might scar. Another one to add to the tally.

"Flesh wound," he said, unimpressed.

Meg stared. "That's Hellion talk for impaled."

He half-smiled. "Gotta be tough."

"I wish you'd take care of yourself better. You're the last one, Chel." Meg's expression softened.

Chel's smile disappeared and his jaw snapped shut.

The others were gone; Tukka, Klaus, Skeele. They had died fighting. All for Meg. And he had lived.

Meg stepped closer. "You've given me more than I had any right to ask for."

A large hand covered his heart. "It is my duty as a Hellion. My birthright. Protecting this throne, you, the young ones, it is all I know and all I will ever know."

One dark brow rose on Meg's face as she turned away from him and walked to a nearby chair. She sat and kicked out the club chair across from her, motioning for him to sit.

"You're tired." Meg threaded her fingers together.

"No. I never tire. As Sparrow would say, unpossible."

"Sit." She nodded to the chair.

"I'm not sure I should." Chel had a queasy feeling in his stomach.

"Don't be afraid." She slouched, very un-Queen like. "Rue says you've become attached to her kitten."

Chel shrugged. "Lucipurr is cute." He finally moved closer and sat across from Meg.

"My son says you're moody."

Chel scowled.

"You've been drinking. Drawing even. I didn't know you could draw, Chel."

He pressed his lips together, remembering the night a few weeks ago when he'd had a bit too much to drink and it sent him into a downward spiral. Despair didn't look good on a Hellion.

"That was an accident." Chel's back straightened. "It won't happen again."

"You were bred to be a Hellion." Meg looked away. "But you've become something more. You're loyal. We've been through some shit."

"Part of the job."

"Maybe." Meg leveled her stare on him. "Maybe that was the old way things were done."

Meg had brought plenty of change to Hell after she took the throne. She'd battled Lucifer for peace. Her rule had brought hope to the creatures of Hell. She challenged the old ways of thinking.

Chel's back straightened again when he started to understand where this conversation was going. "It is my duty to protect you, your family, this throne. Nothing more. I have nothing more in my life."

"I don't need you to do it anymore."

That landed deeper than he expected. His mind went completely blank with shock.

Meg must've seen it in his face, and her tone gentled. "I know you've been trying to connect with someone."

"There is no one." He didn't want to admit that all his calls had gone unanswered. All his invitations to the balls and celebrations were ignored or a halfhearted excuse was given. Rejection did not suit him.

"There is a house on the Earthen plane. You've been there before," Meg reminded him. She reached into her pocket and pulled out a set of tarnished keys. They jangled on a keyring with a plastic pink flamingo. "Go there. Rest."

"I am not tired."

"Take a vacation then."

"Are you firing me? There is no greater disgrace to a Hellion."

"I am not firing you." She jangled the keys out to him again. "You'll still be a Hellion. I'm simply asking you to take some time for yourself."

Chel growled before swiping the keys out of Meg's hand. "I can't believe you're sending me away."

"You might enjoy retirement." She smiled.

"Doubt it."

"If there is a problem here I will call you back," Meg promised as she stood.

He looked up, a sinking feeling in his chest.

It was disgrace.

"Oh Christ almighty," Meg finally said. "I am not firing you. I am not even forcing you to retire. I'm simply asking you to take a rest, find peace, get a tan." She spun around. "Find a girlfriend, get laid, and stop moping around this castle."

Chel's eyes went wide.

"I need you to stop and see the White Horse in Montana before you go to Florida."

"And ask permission?" He stood and followed her to the door.

"She's expecting you. She asked for you, actually."

Chel's brows rose this time. "What is really happening here?"

"You're going on vacation." Meg smirked. "But you might be going on an undercover mission." She clicked her tongue. "I still want you to rest."

"I'm not sure about this. I have not spent much time on the Earthen plane."

"You'll be fine. Rue said you fit in just fine on campus when you filled in for her bodyguard last year."

Chel swallowed hard, remembering how he'd damaged her tiny apartment just by walking through it.

Meg turned to him, settled her hand on his big arm. He went still. The Queen of Hell didn't like to be touched and rarely touched others.

"Thank you, Chel." Meg looked up at him. "I can never thank you enough for everything."

Chel nodded even though the awful feeling spread throughout his chest. He didn't like the idea of being sent away. He sighed and absently rubbed his aching wrist—an old injury that never seemed to heal right.

"You'll be just fine." Meg opened the door. "You deserve this."

Chel nodded as he left.

As he packed, Chel wondered if he should stop and tell his mother he was leaving Hell. He wasn't sure if she needed to know.

A flood of memories hit.

Then...

During the reign of Lucifer, Demon children were not to be seen and not to be heard. Breaking either rule would result in severe punishment. It felt awful at the time but Chel would learn it was to prepare him for life under Lucifer's thumb. Chel learned early how to hide in the shadows. He learned how to avoid the light. Bred to be a Hellion and serve the throne, he spent his childhood years in training. It was the only thing that made his father proud. The only time he'd heard his father utter a whisper of delight was the day he'd completed his training. There had been no joy in the family household for years prior.

Chel would never forget that day because there should have been four people at the dinner table, but his sister's seat remained empty, as it had for nearly two years since she'd gone missing. It was the first moment in a long time that anyone uttered an emotion besides despair.

Demon women weren't known for their longevity. Many died in childbirth or defending their young from rage-filled fathers. It was a family dynamic like nothing else. Lucifer's reign kept his subjects in a constant state of dread. It trickled through day-to-day life like a dark tap left to drip and drip and drip.

Yelena was three years younger than Chel. She spent almost all of her time with their mother. Raised to be nothing more than a breed horse, she spent her time learning how to survive childbirth and motherhood. One day she was sent to the nearby stream to collect water for washing laundry and never returned. She was never found and it was assumed that she was murdered. A dark lull hung over Chel's family ever since. And Chel found he harbored an extreme dislike for any man who could harm a female.

His family was bred to be Hellions but something changed when Lucifer died and the new Queen took over. There was a shift in the edge that drove Hellions to violence. They held back, anticipated, contained their rage for only necessary times. They slept lighter and trained harder. New concepts had been taught like compassion and delayed reaction. Chel was not the same Demon his father was.

Chel would never forget when he stepped through the

threshold, the familiar sights and sounds of his childhood greeting him with a bittersweet embrace. The air was still heavy with grief, the weight of loss palpable in every corner, especially the kitchen where his mother spent most of her time.

Chel's mother hadn't spoken much during dinner, her eyes hollow with sorrow. She sat in silence, hands clasped tightly in her lap as if trying to hold on to the fragments of her shattered world. She'd been like this since Yelena went missing.

His father was a brooding figure in his favorite lounge chair, radiating an aura of simmering anger, his jaw clenched with unspoken fury. Chel remembered the same Demon from childhood. He hadn't changed a bit.

"Utter bullshit," his father slammed a fork down. "I didn't send my only son off to be a pussy in the ranks." He reached across the table and grabbed Chel by the collar of his uniform. "You listen to me, you smile and nod, but deep down understand that mentality will not save a soul. You need to be quick, exact. You need to kill. That is a Hellion's duty."

"Yes, sir," Chel had nodded and stared into his father's red eyes until the moment of rage passed.

There it was. The rage that drove previous ages. They were going to be different, better. Sparrow's teaching and guidance was always inspiring, but Chel didn't tell his father that. He finished his dinner and came to the realization that this might be the last time he visited his parents.

Chel's mother stood and began clearing dishes. She left the dusty plate at the setting next to Chel. Yelena's seat. She'd never cleared the place setting after all these years. It was like she was expecting Yelena to come running back home and burst through the door for dinner. She never came, she would never come. Yelena had been gone for years; kidnapped and murdered by wrath-filled Demons.

Chel's gaze shifted to the empty space where Yelena once sat, a void that echoed with the haunting absence of her presence. The ache of her loss weighed heavily on his heart, a reminder of the fragility of life and the cruel whims of fate.

As the evening wore on, Chel found himself grappling with a revelation that gnawed at the core of his being. His father's violent outbursts and callous disregard for Yelena's death stirred a wellspring of conflicting emotions within him: a potent brew of anger, sadness, and a dawning realization that threatened to shatter his sense of identity.

In a moment of clarity, Chel realized that he could no longer ignore the toxic legacy of his father's behavior. He could not condone the cycle of violence and indifference that had plagued his family for far too long.

He was not his father, and he refused to allow himself to become a reflection of the man who had brought so much pain and suffering into their lives.

"Do you have any news of Yelena's body being found?" Chel asked his father.

"Who cares?" his father shouted. "She's gone. Just

another damned Demon woman, they make more every day."

"Yelena was more. Your wife is more. Do you not give a fuck about either of them?" Chel challenged the Demon. He spoke of the love and warmth that Yelena had brought into their lives; cozy evenings reading, dancing, picking flowers. The memories were a stark contrast to the darkness that his father's rage had wrought upon their family.

His father's anger boiled over and Chel stood his ground, refusing to back down. "I'm going to be better than you and if I ever have a wife or daughter I will love them more than you have ever loved anything."

"Get out of my fucking hovel with that mouth. You're nothing but a piece of shit. Hellions in my day didn't give a fuck about women or children. You were bred to serve the throne. Wait and see where this new ideology takes you all. You'll be dead in no time, and well deserved. Fuck off." Chel's father stormed off, disappearing to a room in the back of the hovel and slamming the door.

His mother hugged him. "You're a good Demon." There were tears in her eyes. "Yelena would be proud. I'm proud." She was taking off her apron and threw it aside. "I'll be leaving here now."

"I'll take you elsewhere. You can't stay here," Chel said.

She pulled a bag from under the sink. "I have only stayed this long for you, but I don't think you'll be back."

Chel shook his head. "I'll never see him again."

His mother nodded, wiping tears from her face.

"There's a place I can go." She was shaking her head. "It's safe. Private."

"Good." Chel reached for the door. "Let's get you out of here."

His mother walked outside and Chel grabbed his gear and belongings. He closed the door to the hovel, taking one last glance at his family home. "Goodbye," he whispered.

Chel turned to face his mother. Walking closer, he wrapped his arm around her narrow shoulders. In that moment, Chel realized that he was not defined by the sins of his father, not bound by the chains of past Hellions. He was a warrior, a protector, and above all a son who refused to let the darkness of his father's legacy extinguish the light of hope that burned within him.

They walked down a dirt path. The sounds of furniture breaking and angry shouting came from the hovel. As they moved on, Chel vowed to honor Yelena's memory by forging a new path; one guided by empathy, tenderness, and the unwavering belief that he could be the change that his family so desperately needed.

The reign of Lucifer was over, the darkness that had infiltrated every corner of Hell was slowly dispersing.

CHEL SHIVERED AS HE STUFFED A PAIR OF PANTS into his duffle bag. He didn't have many belongings to bring with him.

He paused and decided that maybe he'd send his mother a letter instead of going to visit her. If he saw her, he'd be plagued by memories of Yelena for weeks. It seemed grief didn't pass when the innocent met malevolence.

He would send a letter. He rubbed his wrist. It had been aching a lot these days. Maybe he'd have someone write the letter for him.

Chel sat in a chair too small for someone his size, knees angled awkwardly, arms crossed like he might break something if he moved too quickly.

The bookstore was quiet; the kind that made you realize how loud you were just by breathing. Damn, he breathed loud. He needed to fix that.

Chel had exited the portal in the back only to immediately be asked to babysit a bookstore for a few hours.

He glanced at the clock. It had been a few hours too long.

Dust filtered through shafts of sunlight, catching on motes in the air like ashfall. The scent of paper and floor polish wrapped around him. A bell above the door hadn't made a sound since Layla and Thrush had left. Probably because he'd locked the door and flipped the sign to "Closed."

He wasn't used to this. There was no way in hell he

was going to try and use the computer and deal with money. Nope. Instead he tried to enjoy the peace.

There were no screams in the air. No roars of Hellions. No weight of orders cracking through the back of his skull. Just... books. Hundreds of them. All spines and ink and strange titles.

He reached for one, out of curiosity. Something about ravens and riddles. The pages crackled like firewood as he flipped through, skimming a passage about lost sisters and prophetic dreams.

He didn't expect to like it. But he found himself leaning forward.

By the third book, he was stretched out on the little loveseat beneath the window, boots on the floor, flipping through a history of curses carved into bones.

No patrol. No reports. No blade at his side.

Just silence. And stories.

What the fuck am I supposed to do with this? he thought looking up at the wall.

He hadn't had time like this since—well, ever. His days had always been war and training, weapons and fire, endless lines of enemies and duty. He didn't know what it meant to fill a day without the rhythm of battle and hum of protecting others.

And yet... he wasn't bored.

He was unsettled.

By the time the shadows reached across the hardwood floor and the sky outside turned amber, Chel had gone through five books—three closed halfway through, one upside down, and another he kept re-reading the same paragraph of for twenty minutes. If Layla could see him now. He could read and he could read quickly. It was something Skeele had taught him—speed reading he'd called it.

He heard whispers and a crackle from the back room. Someone was coming through the portal.

Chel stood. He heard Layla's voice, then Thrush's.

Layla stepped out first, cheeks flushed, curls springing loose from behind her ear. She was already talking rapidly about the Peabody library and the Angel they'd met.

Thrush moved closer, listening.

Chel had met the guy ages ago...

THEN.

An Angel descended, his presence commanding yet puzzled. His wings spread wide, casting a golden glow over the chaotic scene. With a wave of his hand, the Demons were obliterated, their bodies disintegrating to ash. The Angel's eyes swept over the room, taking in the devastation and those who remained standing.

"What do we have here?" the Angel asked. "A Hellion. A Nephilim." He leaned to the side and focused on Rue and Remington. "Those two are something different." Then he stared at Shay. "And you're barely human."

Magic prickled in Jed's hands. He drew on it, ready to blast the Angel to another planet. He had zero trust for

Angels of any kind. They'd only hunted and tried to kill him his entire life. He wouldn't let this one do the same.

"These children," the Angel said, his voice resonant and powerful, "who are they, and why do they bear such auras?"

Jed took a deep breath, his voice steady despite the turmoil and urge to kill. "They are under our protection. Their mother left them with us to keep them safe. We will protect them from everyone and everything, including you."

The Angel's eyes narrowed, his gaze shifting to Shay. Recognition flickered in his gaze and he took a step back. "You," he said, his tone wary, "are part Crossroads Demon. Somehow. But you weren't born that way."

Shay lifted her chin, her eyes defiant as she swiped blue hair away from her face. "Yes, I am."

The Angel took a step backward. "No deals." He shook his head.

"This is not a crossroads," Shay clarified. "But that doesn't mean I won't kill you." She tapped the fire poker on her palm menacingly.

The Angel crossed his arms and he gazed quickly around the room. "You're all leaving?"

"That seems the smartest choice," Jed said.

"Can I stay here if you're leaving?" the Angel asked. "I need a place to hide." The Angel was surveying the library. "And I get the feeling you all can't stay here, not after this." He opened his arms to the piles of ash all over the floor.

"We don't own this place," Jed warned.

"I'll take care of it," the Angel promised.

"I have never met an Angel that I've trusted," Jed said. "Why should I trust you?"

"I've already fixed the wards." The Angel moved his hands to his hips, real proud of himself.

"I think we should take the deal," Chel suggested. "This piece of flying garbage could fend off more Demons who come here looking for us."

"Hey!" the Angel shouted. "I offer help and you insult me?"

Chel shrugged, unafraid and unbothered.

"I apologize for my friend," Shay said. "But we have yet to meet an Angel who hasn't tried to kill first."

The Angel toed a pile of ash before focusing on Jed. "Not all Angels are of the old ways. Some of us just want peace, just like God intended."

"You can stay here," Jed finally said. "We'll collect our things."

The Angel smiled with relief. He turned his back to the grouping and began picking up pieces of the broken chairs and tossing them in the fireplace.

NOW.

Layla spotted Chel and blinked. "Hi! You didn't destroy the bookstore. Thrush was worried."

"Tempted," he said, then nodded toward the stack of books on the table. "But I got distracted."

Her brows lifted in amusement. "By reading? I am glad you're not illiterate."

Chel shrugged, but his mouth twitched. "Don't tell Meg." He exhaled a big breath. "So you finally met Jasper at the Peabody Library. What's he up to these days?"

"He was very strange. Said he was restoring the building and cataloging books." Layla shrugged.

"He seemed lonely," Thrush said. "Guy needed some sunlight. Or a date."

"He's been alone there for over ten years." Chel stood and walked closer to his duffle bag that he'd tossed on the floor. "Poor guy is just sitting around and waiting for someone."

"Who?" Layla asked.

Chel shrugged. "That's beyond my pay grade."

Thrush gave him a sidelong look. "We were going to drive you up to the ranch. Shay should have dinner on soon."

Chel glanced out the shop's front window.

"I'll walk," he said.

Layla blinked. "It's at least an hour."

"I've walked worse," Chel replied.

Thrush didn't argue, just held his gaze a moment then nodded.

Chel grabbed his jacket, hesitating briefly before tucking the smallest of the books under his arm. He didn't know if it was allowed, but no one stopped him.

As he stepped into the cooling evening, he felt something unfamiliar settle low in his chest.

The door to the bookstore clicked shut behind him, and for the first time in centuries Chel wasn't headed to battle.

Lame Deer's main road stretched out in front of him, quiet and empty. He was the only creature out at this hour it seemed.

He walked until he reached the turn to head toward Colstrip. Jed and Shay's ranch wasn't far off Route 39. Warmth spread in his chest when he thought about seeing Shay again. It had been weeks. He'd missed her at the castle, her visits became less and less since they'd moved to the ranch. A cool breeze chilled Chel's skin and he remembered that she was probably canning and preparing for the winter months. She talked about it often enough that he should have remembered. She'll tuck in for the winter with Jed. The northern land of the Earthen plane would slow to a trickle of activity once the snow started piling up.

The seasons weren't as severe in Hell. That realm was a dark reflection of the Earthen plane and the snow never accumulated around the castle like it did in other parts, due to the burning caves underneath.

Chel noticed a sign for Crossroads Ranch and turned.

The gravel path turned to dirt a few yards down, curving past a run of trees and dipping low where the earth sloped into fields. The sun had nearly slipped below the horizon, and the world had gone gold.

The stillness pressed in. Cicadas sang in the tall

grass. A bird wheeled overhead. In the distance tiny lights flickered: lightning bugs. Somewhere far off, a screen door creaked and slammed. No monsters. No horns. No sharp teeth. His tongue brushed his own. Well, *he* had sharp teeth. He glanced over his shoulder. It was strange not seeing his wings. They weren't present on the Earthen plane, not when there was balance between the realms. No wings could be seen here.

Chel didn't know what to do with the quiet.

Every step took him further from the life he knew, from the fire and the edge of a blade. He'd never been given time to feel the weight of his own thoughts like this.

Now, they crowded in. Every memory he'd repressed was fighting for his attention; Alastor's brutal attack in the Hellion lair, Yelena, his mother, seeing his Hellion brothers come back from the dead to fight in the war against Lucifer.

Every time he blinked, he saw them. All teeth and loyalty and... dead. They were dead. Replaced with new recruits over the years. It had never been the same.

And what did that make him now?

A relic?

A weapon without a war?

He dragged a hand through his hair and exhaled hard. Dust puffed beneath his boots as he crossed a rickety wooden bridge over a small creek. Water rushed quietly underneath. Somewhere nearby, a frog chirped like it didn't know anything about the end of the world or Hellions on vacation. That made two of them.

Chel slowed.

He'd never been to Montana. But this... this wasn't what he expected. It was raw in a way that didn't ask anything from him. All scars were exposed for twilight and no one cared. He could get used to the feeling and suddenly understood why Shay and Jed had settled here.

He passed a tree where someone had carved a name into the trunk.

He didn't know why that hit him so hard. Maybe it was the memory of chasing Yelena through the forest when they were children.

He paused to lean against the trunk for a moment, fingers brushing over the jagged letters. Someone had wanted to be remembered. Maybe that was all any of them really wanted. He'd left marks on the tree near the river where she'd been stolen from. He pushed the thoughts away and kept going.

The ranch came into view, its porch light glowing like a lantern in the dark. Something smelled divine and the thundering of hoof falls echoed in his ears.

"Hellion," he heard Nero's voice. "You look lost." The giant black horse trotted closer to him in greeting and nodded his head. "You're just in time for dinner."

"Hello, Demon horse. You look quite at home in these fields," Chel brushed a hand over Nero's neck. "Quite at home for a beast of the underworld."

Nero made a noise that sounded like a laugh. "This is

some of the last true land you'll find on this plane, it doesn't care where I'm from." Nero nickered and pawed his hooves at the ground. "Want to race?"

Chel dropped his duffle bag and cracked his knuckles. "I had a standing chance with wings but now I only have these old knees." He tapped his thighs once before taking off in a sprint.

Hellion and Crossroads Demon horse racing on the Earthen plane was a sight for anyone. There was no winner because Chel's knee gave out five-hundred yards in and he grabbed Nero's tail, causing the horse to twist and fall to his flank. He'd spent too many hours sitting around that bookstore today. Or at least that's the excuse he gave Nero as they limped toward the ranch house.

CHAPTER 3

Chel didn't like the small clearing where Nero had brought him. He looked far off in the distance and notice a half burned house. Something had happened here. And it was either the lingering energy from the event that burned the house in the distance, or the approaching White Horse that gave him an uneasy feeling.

The trees were pale here with bone-white trunks, silver leaves, and bark that shimmered when the wind blew.

He stepped between the stones marking the path.

The White Horse moved closer and Nero stood beside Chel like a guard.

He'd never seen a creature like the White Horse. No reins. No saddle. Just muscle and silence and knowing eyes. Her coat was the color of freshly fallen snow, gleaming in the soft light as if it had been crafted from the very essence of purity. Her mane and tail flowed like liquid silver, and her eyes were filled with a calm intelligence. She glanced at Nero and nodded. Then her gaze settled on Chel.

He could feel magic in the air, a subtle hum that seemed to resonate from the White Horse itself. It was a creature of some other kind, it was something more—something ancient and powerful hid beneath its gentle exterior.

For a long moment, he simply stared. A sense of peace washed over Chel.

An owl broke the moment with its echoing hoot.

"I'm here," Chel said flatly. "You can thank Meg for that."

The horse regarded him for a long moment. Then, without sound, she stepped forward and circled him once.

Chel held still. There was something about this damn horse that made his skin tighten. It was reading him cell by cell.

Finally, she spoke. Calm and certain.

"You've been carved hollow."

Chel didn't answer.

"But not empty."

"You're not very subtle," he muttered.

"And you're not as tired as they think you are."

Chel exhaled slowly. "I'm not tired."

The horse tilted its head.

"Even rest can be part of the battle."

Chel looked away. "I don't know what that means."

"You will."

The horse stepped closer, breath soft against his chest. Its eyes were like mirrors, reflecting not just his face, but pieces of himself he didn't want to see. Regret. Guilt. Hope.

"You'll help more than you think," it said.

Chel's brow furrowed. "How?"

"You're going to Meg's house in Florida?"

He nodded. "That's what I've been told."

"It's nice there, the gulf waters are really something." The White Horse glanced at him quickly. "Remember water is a conduit on all planes. That body of water is the biggest portal between the realms."

"Okay," Chel dipped his chin in understanding.

"Something has gone wrong near Perdido Key. I don't want it infecting the whole panhandle."

Chel went still. This definitely didn't sound like a vacation or retirement any longer.

"Infants have disappeared." The White Horse lowered her gaze. "In unusual ways. And their mothers too. I want you to investigate it."

Chel's head was buzzing. He wasn't an investigator. Nor was he skilled in interacting with humans. "Some more details would be wonderful."

"Something is coming out of the gulf. I want you to figure out what it is and stop it before the Veil thins and war begins."

Chel nodded. "Where would you like me to start?"

Her lips moved like a smirk. "You'll know where to start when you see it."

By the time Chel reached the ranch, the porch light was glowing and the smell of roasted garlic and fresh bread saturated the air.

He knocked once, but Shay was already opening the door before his fist hit wood again. "Come in, come in. Boots off unless you're tracking demons."

Chel hesitated. "They're clean."

Shay looked pointedly at the dust clinging to the soles. "I watched you walk from the northern pasture. Off with them."

He grunted and kicked them off. There was a hole in his sock that he hadn't wanted her to see.

Inside, the house was warm and lit with soft yellow lamps. A cast-iron pot bubbled on the stove, and the dining table was already set with mismatched plates and a few empty chairs. A jar of canned tomatoes sat beside a basket of biscuits.

Jed stood by the sink, drying his hands with a towel. He nodded once at Chel. "You made good time from the bookstore. The kids called when you left. Layla was afraid you'd scare the locals."

"Didn't see any." Chel was hesitant to walk through the house—he didn't want to accidentally destroy anything. Although, the boar head mounted on the wall in the living room drew his attention.

"That so?" Jed turned toward the hallway. "Well, the guest room's empty if you want to stay the night."

Chel's stomach had started growling halfway through the walk and hadn't let up since.

Shay waved him over to the table. "Wash up and sit. Flu season's coming and I am not catching it this year."

Chel blinked at her. "I've never had the flu. No one in Hell is ill."

"That you know of," she replied, eyes narrowing. "Illnesses are weird. You get one scratchy throat and suddenly you're hallucinating shadow demons."

He snorted but made his way to the sink, scrubbing his hands under warm water. "Hellions don't get sick." The soap smelled like pine and something sweet, probably homemade judging by the wildflower bits floating in it.

Back at the table, Shay was pouring cider into mismatched mugs.

"I've been canning for weeks," she said, gesturing to the shelves lining the far wall. "Winter's gonna hit early, I can feel it in my bones."

Chel nodded, unsure what to say.

Jed handed him a steaming plate. "The White Horse is going to let you stay?"

Chel glanced up. "Seems it."

Jed raised a brow.

Chel shrugged.

Shay smiled around a mouthful of stew. "Sun and saltwater. That house will feel so much bigger without us and Meg's kids there."

Chel was nodding. Before the war, Jed, Shay, Rue and Remington and himself were in hiding at the beach house. It was definitely cramped.

Jed's mouth twitched like he wanted to say something but he didn't.

Chel took a bite of the stew. It was rich, spicy, filled with slow-roasted root vegetables and something that might've been venison. His stomach sighed in relief. For a hot second worry flashed through him. He was used to living off bagged blood. He stirred the stew, wondering if food like this would keep him satiated.

"You'll need transport," Jed said after a few minutes of quiet. "Take my bike."

Chel looked up, surprised.

"You ride, don't you?"

He nodded. "It's been a while."

Jed wiped his mouth with a napkin. "Good. It's got a full tank and some rune work to keep it off the radars."

"I appreciate that."

Jed leaned back in his chair. "You got cash?"

Chel reached into his jacket and pulled out a black credit card. "She gave me access to one of her accounts here."

Shay whistled low. "Must be nice to have the Queen of Hell for a boss."

Chel didn't answer, just took another bite of stew.

For a long time, they sat in companionable quiet.

But outside, the wind picked up.

Chel hadn't been on the open road in years, not without a mission, not without a weapon strapped across his back and a dire prediction choking his every move.

Now he was riding south on Jed's motorcycle with a packed duffel, a half-charged phone, and Meg's money.

Hell's dime, human earth.

What a strange thing freedom was.

He didn't rush. He could have made it to the gulf in two days, easy. But Meg hadn't given him a deadline, and the White Horse hadn't exactly laid out a tight schedule. So he gave in to curiosity and, to his own surprise, hunger.

At the first gas station just outside Billings, he filled the tank and stared at the candy aisle like it was a weapons rack. He left with a pack of sour gummies, a bag of jerky, and something called "pickle chips" that he ate just to prove he could.

They were awful and he couldn't get the taste off his tongue.

By Missouri, he was stopping at every roadside diner and food truck he passed.

Pancakes the size of his head in Nebraska. Churros in

Kansas. Fried catfish in Mississippi, so spicy he had to breathe through his teeth. He sampled pie in three different towns.

His phone's battery dropped steadily over the trip because he forgotten to turn off the navigation app and the screen brightness was at full. He kept checking it to figure out what the hell grits were supposed to be. He was still unsure of their origin but he now knew they tasted best with brown sugar and milk, not tomatoes and butter.

By the time he hit the Florida line, the battery was red and gave up entirely.

Chel rode the rest of the way in the dark, wind warm off the gulf and salt thick in the air. The road narrowed as he neared Perdido Key, the trees thinning into sea grass and dunes.

He pulled up to the beach house just past midnight.

It was small but sturdy, white-painted wood weathered by salt and storms, just like he remembered. The porch light flickered as he approached, but the wards on the windows glimmered faintly with Jed's touch; subtle, protective. They were strong enough to protect Meg's children years ago. He ran a finger over the etching and made a mental note to deepen the carving on the few that the salt and sandy wind had eroded away.

Chel unlocked the door to the beach house and stepped inside.

It smelled like sea air and old pine, like no one had visited here in a while but the house hadn't minded. The floor creaked beneath his boots. The furniture was simple: a worn couch, a bookshelf half-stocked, and a kitchen. All familiar.

Chel plugged in his phone and watched it flicker back to life.

He walked the perimeter of the house. The bedrooms seemed smaller. And he was sure he hadn't grown any bigger.

The beach lay just beyond the back porch, moonlight streaking the waves silver. It was peaceful. He stood there for a while, letting the wind blow through his hair and tug it out of the knot he had it tied up in.

"Something is coming out of the gulf. I want you to figure out what it is and stop it before the Veil thins and war begins."

Chel squinted in the distance. There was nothing but waves and boats in the distance–shrimp trawlers headed out for the morning catch was what he'd heard at a nearby diner when he'd stopped to eat.

He coughed once and a burning feeling flooded his chest. Chel coughed again then over and over until he could barely catch his breath. He bent, hands landing on his knees and he coughed harder, so hard he was sure the sausage patties and jalapeño omelet were going to come flying out of his stomach.

They didn't.

But blood did drip onto the white sand.

Chel sat with a thud. He suddenly felt exhausted. His

chest hurt, his head hurt, and his skin felt like it was on fire.

"What the..." he muttered to himself, head spinning.

He had to crawl back to the beach house. Weakness had overcome him quickly and he didn't think he'd make it. He thought about rolling into the dunes to sleep off whatever was wrong with his body.

Maybe it was the food. He hadn't eaten a volume of food like that ever in his life. And, he'd had no blood. Maybe it was the lack of blood?

Chel dragged his body past the motorcycle. He made it to the door and found enough energy to crawl inside and kick the door closed.

"It's fine," Chel mumbled to himself. "This is nothing. Just... something." He looked to the countertop where his phone was charging and defeat thudded in his gut. A hundred feet suddenly felt like a thousand yards. He couldn't make it. He closed his eyes and tried to ignore the throbbing in his head.

CHEL WASN'T SURE HOW LONG HE'D BEEN ON the floor.

His skin was cold and damp then burning, an endless cycle. The front door was still closed, sand had blown in by the wind. His head felt filled with cotton. Muscles seized. Skin felt too tight. Breathing felt shallow and taut, like every inhale scraped the inside of his ribs.

He tried to push himself up and collapsed with a grunt, forehead smacking the cool wood floor.

"Fuck," he hissed, barely a whisper.

The fever had him pinned.

He blinked through the haze, searching for his phone. It lay a few feet away, face-down near the leg of the couch, the charging cord ripped out in his fall.

How did it get there?

He clawed toward it, dragging himself an inch at a time. His limbs shook with the effort. He coughed, deep and ragged—pain blooming sharp in his chest. When he reached the phone, he nearly dropped it three times before unlocking the screen.

He hit Meg's contact first.

It rang.

And rang.

And rang.

Then voicemail.

"Meg. I... something's wrong." His voice cracked. "I can't breathe. I think I've been cursed. Please call back."

He didn't expect her to answer. She was likely elbow-deep in some demon's chest or reigning hellfire down on something that deserved it. Or her fangs were buried deep in the Raven King's neck.

He scrolled, vision swimming, and found the next name.

Teari.

He hesitated.

He hadn't spoken to her in months. Not properly. Not since she told him to stop calling. But she was the only healer he trusted, the only one who might know what was happening to him.

He hit *call.*

It rang.

Then voicemail.

He tried again.

And again.

And again.

No answer.

He left a message, breath ragged and broken between syllables. "Teari. It's Chel. I—I think I'm sick. Really sick. I've never felt like this before. I can't think straight. If you get this... please."

He hung up, stared at the screen, then typed out a message with trembling hands:

> Chel: I'm not exaggerating.
> Something's wrong. I need help.

THE THREE DOTS DIDN'T APPEAR FOR A LONG time.

Then finally a message came through.

> Teari: You'll be fine. Sleep it off.
> Probably a man-flu. You're not dying.

. . .

Chel stared at the reply.

The phone slid from his fingers and thudded softly against the floorboards.

Chel didn't try to reach for it again.

He just lay there, cheek pressed against the cool wood, sweat slick on his skin despite the way his bones felt like ice. The ceiling above him tilted in and out of focus, like the house itself couldn't decide whether to let him stay conscious.

He tried to breathe deep and failed.

Each inhale was a struggle like pulling air through wet cloth. His lungs rattled, tight and wrong, and every time he coughed it scraped like stone grinding inside his ribs.

His vision blurred.

Maybe from fever.

Maybe from the sting in his eyes.

Not dying, Teari had said.

Just sleep it off.

His throat burned.

She didn't believe me.

That thought gutted him more than the fever ever could.

He'd faced down princes of Hell, creatures with too many eyes, a hundred blades to the gut without flinching, but this?

This helplessness?

This quiet, hollow unraveling?

He didn't know how to survive that.

Chel had always known what to do with pain; push through it, bleed and keep swinging. But this was different. This was his body betraying him in slow motion. No enemy to cut down. No weapon to raise. Only himself.

He didn't know how to fight this kind of battle.

He blinked, sluggish, and stared at the ceiling fan barely spinning above him. The rhythm was uneven, like it might fall. He wanted to laugh. Or curse. Or cry. The White Horse was going to be so disappointed.

Instead, he whispered into the empty house, "Meg, I don't know what to do."

The words barely made it past his lips.

He squeezed his eyes shut.

You're the last one.

Meg had said it like it meant something. Like that should give him strength. Like it should mean survival.

If this was how he went out, face down on a wooden floor in some tiny beach house, lungs filling with salt and blood, would anyone even know?

Would anyone care?

He clenched his jaw, trying to shove the thought away, but it settled deep in his chest like a stone.

I should've died with the others.

He hated the thought.

His hand twitched toward the phone again but stopped halfway. What was the point? No one was coming. Not tonight. Maybe not at all.

The darkness pulled at him—quiet, painless, seductive in its weight. Just close your eyes. Just stop trying. It sounded so easy.

Close.

Your.

Eyes.

Not like this. He deserved to die on the battlefield.

Chapter 4

The mirror was still cracked. Teari had hit it weeks ago when she could no longer look at herself. She stared at the fracture running down the center of the glass. It split her face in two. Fitting.

Her fingers trembled as she set down the washcloth, water dripping from her wrists to the edge of the porcelain sink. She had barely slept in days. Between the injured Angel Legion guards Gabriel kept throwing her way and the silent screaming inside her own chest, rest felt like a language she no longer spoke.

Her phone buzzed against the counter.

She wiped her hands and picked it up.

MEG.

She answered. "Please tell me no one is bleeding."

"Have you heard from Chel? He's not answering his phone."

Teari blinked. "He called me a few times the other day."

Meg's tone sharpened. "Did you answer?"

A beat passed.

Teari looked away from her reflection. "I've been busy."

"Teari."

"He's a Hellion," she said quickly, defensively. "They heal. Eventually. Give him a little blood. He probably just got a stubbed toe or something and panicked."

"He's supposed to be at my beach house on the Earthen plane. That stretch of coast is practically deserted this time of year. Could you just go make sure he isn't dead?"

Teari closed her eyes and pinched the bridge of her nose. "I can't?"

"Well, I'm in negotiations with a shrimp farmer in the south peninsula and also trying to keep an exiled banshee from melting half the north gate. Forgive me for asking for some help ensuring the last of my original Hellions isn't dead."

Teari sighed.

"Maybe you're due for a vacation too," Meg offered, voice a little softer. "Get some fun in the sun. Maybe have a few margaritas. Touch grass. Put your toes in the sand. Swim with the sharks. Do something different."

"I can't." Teari's fingers tangled in the back of her cropped hair. "I've never had a vacation."

"Maybe you should."

"I just don't think it's a good idea."

Meg sighed. "Teari. Humor me. No one ever lived a happy life by working themselves into a grave."

The words hit harder than they should have. Teari stared at her reflection—at the cracks and hollows beneath her eyes, the too-pale skin. She didn't look happy. She wasn't.

"There are things you don't know," she said quietly. "Even if I *did* try to take a vacation, it would be interrupted. Gabriel, you, Sparrow, your... kids."

She bit off the last part. Her gaze dropped. She didn't want to bring Rue or Remington into this argument. She'd do anything for them.

"It's just... highly unlikely there will be any relaxing." Teari leaned against the sink.

There was a long pause on the other end.

Then Meg spoke, voice raw, "Teari. There was a time that I saved your life. I'm calling in that favor. Please take a vacation as repayment. Please go check on Chel and make sure he's not dead. I have no one left to ask."

Teari swallowed hard and looked at her packed bag in the corner, the one she hadn't dared to open in years. The fast-Zombie war flared behind her eyes. The dead, blood, a circle of faces around her hospital bed as she healed from the unhealable. She'd been abandoned on the Earthen plane at a human hospital with her arms cut off just below the elbows.

Meg had been there. Meg had left her there. But she had to. By the time Meg had returned to collect Teari, she'd had so many transfusions of human blood that she'd lost her healing powers. And more. But Meg fixed that. She'd lost her will to...

"Okay," Teari whispered into the receiver. "Fine. I'll check on him."

"Thank you," Meg said.

The line went dead.

Teari stood in the silence.

Outside, the wind howled against the windows of her cabin. She didn't know why her chest felt tight. She didn't know why her hands wouldn't stop shaking. But she reached for her travel satchel anyway.

CHAPTER 5

THE DOOR CREAKED OPEN AS TEARI STEPPED inside, the scent of salt and sickness hitting her like a fist. The house was dim, thick with the kind of stillness that meant something had gone very, very wrong. Or someone was dead.

"Chel?" she asked.

Silence.

Her boots scuffed against the wood as she crossed the room.

Then she saw him sprawled near the couch like he'd fallen mid-crawl. Pale. She'd never seen a Hellion that pale before.

Her breath caught. She was across the room in seconds.

"Chel, what the hell—"

He groaned, barely conscious.

"Angel?" It was a rasp, cracked and dry, like sandpaper. Blood crusted his lips. "Don't tell me I died and went to Heaven."

"Definitely not Heaven," she said quickly, dropping to her knees beside him. "What happened?"

His brow twitched. "Didn't... want to call. Know you don't like it when I call you." His head lolled to the side.

She pressed the back of her hand to his forehead and hissed. "You're burning up. Idiot. You should have called days ago."

"Did," he muttered. "You said man-flu."

Teari froze, just for a second. Guilt stabbed deep. She did say that and then she ignored him. For days and days. How long had the dumb-dumb been lying on the floor like this? Christ, she would never be able to lift him. And she knew that rattle in his chest with every shallow breath he took was not a good sign.

"You didn't sound this bad," she said, even though she knew he had. She hadn't listened. "Can you move?"

He groaned and tried to roll.

"Stop." She scooted closer to him. "Just, stay still. I'll try it this way."

She rubbed her hands together then spread her palms over his chest. Her magic flowed into him in pulses, slow and steady. It wasn't enough to burn him out, but enough to stop him from swirling in the toilet bowl of death.

It wasn't just sickness tearing through his body. She felt something tangled beneath the fever, some human illness he'd never been exposed to before. What had he walked into?

"Where have you been since arriving here?" she asked.

"Diners." He licked his lips. "Gas stations."

"Please tell me you didn't eat gas station food."

She sighed; she couldn't fix him in one session. He was too big and too sick. This was going to take days to bring him back to life.

She wiped her palms on her jeans and exhaustion hit her from the healing magic dump.

He opened his eyes. They were bloodshot.

He probably contracted every virus between Florida and whatever portal he'd come through to get to the Earthen plane.

"I feel a bit better," Chel coughed out.

"Let's get you to bed."

Chel's body went stiff. "I'd rather get to the shower."

Teari took a good look at him. "Just how long have you been slowly dying on the floor?"

"Seven days."

"Oh my god. Seven days!" she groaned. "How are you even alive?"

"Hellions are a hearty breed."

"Come on," Teari motioned for him to move. "I'll help you up."

Chel groaned as he sat up. Teari pushed at his shoulder, noticing the firm muscle under his shirt, at least he hadn't lost that while he'd wasted away on the floor, but

Christ he was heavy. She would never have been able to lift him. He rolled to his knees and used the nearby couch as leverage to stand.

"I smell like a corpse."

She hesitated, then braced his arm across her shoulders. "Corpses smell better. Come on. Let's get you cleaned up."

Chel grunted but didn't argue. His steps were clumsy, his weight heavy against her as they staggered down the hall toward the bathroom. Every few feet he paused to cough. At least it was a dry cough now; the rattle had left his chest and he hadn't coughed up blood.

Teari kept her arm firm around his waist and gripped the waistband of his jeans. She could feel the tremor in his body, like a storm still rolling through him even though the worst had passed. The guy was sick.

Inside the bathroom, she guided him to the edge of the tub. "Sit. You're not going to make it standing on your own."

He sat, panting. His eyes flicked up to hers. "I can do the rest."

Teari arched a brow. "You can barely hold your own weight."

"I don't need a nurse."

She crossed her arms. "And I don't want you collapsing and cracking your skull open. Let me help."

He cursed under his breath, but didn't stop her as she turned the knobs, steam quickly filling the small space. She tested the temperature, then turned back to him.

He was hesitating.

"Come on. You don't have anything I haven't seen." Teari muttered as she began searching for washcloths and towels. "Gabriel employs me to heal all of his Legion Angels. You know how many asses I've seen?" She made a gagging sound. "Just get under the water."

Her gaze dropped as he unbuttoned his shirt with stiff fingers. His hands shook. He paused midway through, fingers fumbling.

"Teari..."

"Sorry. That was crude. I'm a healer," she said evenly. "I've seen everything. Don't be embarrassed."

"I need help with the buttons."

"Oh, of course." She moved in front of him and unbuttoned his shirt right down to the waistband of his jeans. Then she reached around his waist and pulled it up to untuck the tail of his shirt. Her face was so close to his chest, she could feel the heat radiating off his skin. She felt his breath fan her shoulder. He was looking at her. She moved away and helped get his arms out of the shirt.

"Slowly," she warned him. "Don't tip over."

"This is not how I'd planned on spending my vacation."

She blinked. Vacation?

But then he shrugged the shirt off and let it fall to the floor.

Teari sucked in a quiet breath.

Scars. So many of them spanned across his ribs, his shoulders, and a brutal slice across his abdomen that had healed ugly and deep. And beneath all that damage, bulging muscle. Dense, functional, unforgiving strength was carved into his frame like war had sculpted him by hand. She knew Hell had sculpted him. Chel came from a long line of Hellions bred to serve the throne.

She let her magic flare briefly in her fingers, almost unconsciously, scanning for damage that was still lingering. Her hand hovered near a gash at his side, an old wound. She cursed Meg for not having a formal healer in her realm.

"You're held together with grit and a prayer," she murmured, sensing a wound on his thigh.

He smirked faintly, the corner of his mouth twitching. "Mostly grit."

"Take off your pants," she ordered. "You have a wound festering. I can smell it."

He groaned but stood. "The last time a female told me that..."

Teari sighed and rolled her eyes, turning as he reached for the button of his jeans. "Why do I get the feeling you are held together with meat glue?"

He sucked in a breath and Teari turned again. She didn't need to search for the wound, he was already inspecting the bright red slash across his thigh. It was weeping yellow pus.

"What happened here?" she asked.

"One of the new recruits caught me with their blade during training."

"When?"

"A few days before I got here."

Teari sighed. "Do you have a death wish?"

He was quiet for a moment. "I glued it. Figured that was enough."

She shook her head. "This might hurt." She laid both palms on his thigh and pressed inward toward the wound. Pus drained out. "You're going to need to wash this out good. When it's clean I'll have to stitch it closed." She used the towel near her to catch the drainage.

He didn't reply. When she looked up she noticed his eyes were closed. She was going to have a discussion with Meg and Sparrow. Their Hellions didn't deserve to be held together with glue, even if that's what they preferred.

She reached out and touched his chest lightly, healing magic pulsing once. "Do you want me to fix these?" She motioned to the scars.

Chel inhaled sharply. "No. Don't burn out on old wounds."

Teari narrowed her eyes. "I'm fine."

"When's the last time *you* slept?" he countered, but his voice was fading again.

She ignored the question.

"When's the last time you had blood?" she asked quietly.

He glanced toward the shower, jaw tightening. "Before I left Hell."

"Chel—"

"I didn't think I'd need it."

"You're a Hellion. Of course you need it."

"I can survive a long time without the blood," he said. "It's not ideal but I've done it before. Plus Meg never brought it up. I didn't intend to stay here very long."

She didn't like that answer. Not one bit.

"You were coughing up blood before," she said. "You just came here, to a different realm, expecting everything to be fine and easy and quick and bloodless?"

He looked away. "I didn't plan for this."

"You think?" She stepped back to give him room. "Get in the shower. I'll grab more towels."

"Teari—"

"I'm not looking," she said, already moving toward the door. "Unless you faint, then all bets are off."

He chuckled once, dry and low, but it turned into another cough as she slipped out of the bathroom and leaned her back against the hallway wall.

Her heart was pounding against her ribs like never before.

Why him? Why was she standing in this tiny beach house on the Earthen plane with him? She exhaled a breath. The guy was persistent as heck. He'd been calling her for years, flirting, asking for dates. She couldn't drag him into her drama. The image of him standing half naked in the bathroom flashed through her mind. Christ almighty. Hellions weren't really her type but... he did have a nice body. He wasn't terrible to look at. Most Hellions resembled monsters but he'd been spared most of the severe features. His skin wasn't red or dark, just a hint of color to it like a summer tan. He had a regular head of hair, no horns or scales, although he'd grown it out the past year and kept it tied up in strips of leather like a manbun. He needed it cut. He looked better with it short. Even without the Hellion wings he'd get a lot of stares on the Earthen plane. He was probably over seven feet tall. He towered a full foot over her. And his bulky muscles made him look like a bodybuilder on steroids. At least he wasn't as crude as most Hellions. And he was persistent. At least he was with her.

THE SOFT SOUND OF WATER STOPPED. A moment later, the bathroom door creaked open.

Teari looked up from where she sat on the edge of the couch, a cooler beside her. Chel stepped into the hallway with a towel slung around his neck, wearing a clean T-shirt and boxers and worn sweatpants slung over his shoulder.

She didn't say anything at first, simply focused on the leg wound as he walked. His pain tolerance must be high or he was good at hiding a limp.

He looked less like death. Still rough, but upright. Alive. No longer half-dead on the floor. Damp hair hung over his brow and shoulders. His skin, while still pale, had some of its color back.

Chel raised a brow. "You're staring."

"I'm trying to figure out what to heal first, since superglue has been your primary healing method."

He shrugged.

"You could have died."

"But I didn't."

"You were halfway there and being very dramatic about it."

He gave a dry huff and lowered himself onto the opposite end of the couch with a wince. "I'm never going to live this down, am I?"

Teari smirked, though her eyes still scanned him with healer precision. "No. And your lungs are still recovering. I'd suggest not doing anything heroic for a few days."

"I'm off duty, apparently," he muttered.

"Meg told me."

They fell quiet for a moment.

The only sound was the low hum of the old refrigerator in the kitchen and the faint hiss of the waves through the open window. The room still smelled like lavender and salt.

Chel leaned his head back against the couch and exhaled slowly.

"Thank you," he said, not quite looking at her.

Teari blinked. "For what?"

"Not letting me die face down on a beach house floor."

She shrugged, more flippant than she felt. "It would've ruined the hardwood."

Another silence stretched between them.

Chel turned toward her, elbows on his knees. "You could've ignored Meg's call too. You didn't."

"No," she said, quietly. "I didn't."

"I wasn't sure you would come."

"I wasn't either."

He studied her face like he was trying to read the parts of her she never spoke aloud. "Why did you?"

She hesitated, fingers curling around the edge of the couch cushion.

"Um," she said finally. "Meg called in a favor. A big favor."

Something passed between them.

He looked down at his hands. "It's strange."

"What is?"

"This," he said. "No blade. No Hellion Lair. Just... this."

She nodded, the tiniest smile tugging at her lips. "You're terrible at resting."

"Working on it."

They sat like that for a while.

Eventually, Teari stood. "You should eat something."

Chel raised an eyebrow. "Are you cooking?"

"Do you want to die *again*?"

He laughed low and hoarse.

She motioned to the cooler on the floor next to her. "There was a special delivery while you were in the shower."

She wasn't sure how Meg had gotten the cooler to the Earthen plane so fast. But she did, and it was filled with the bagged blood that the Hellions consumed on a daily basis. Only bagged blood for them, and Teari knew why. Fresh blood turned a Hellion wild; it would ignite the Bloodlust.

She got up and grabbed her med kit off the floor where she'd dropped it when she'd arrived. "You want a glass for the blood, or are you going to suck it out of the package like a heathen?" She opened the cooler and pulled out a bag of blood then tossed it to him. "Are you going to have that before or after you get your stitches?"

She heard a crumpling sound and looked at him. He was crushing the empty bag in his hand.

"That was quick."

"Can I have more?" He wiped the back of his hand across his mouth.

Teari tossed two more bags of blood to Chel and he caught them midair and consumed them before she'd walked across the room.

"Greed doesn't look good on you," Teari teased.

"Please excuse my manners, Angel, I haven't eaten in a week." Chel grumbled about wanting more blood as he scooted down on the couch. "I've never had stitches before. Glue has always worked just fine. Will this hurt?"

"That's obvious." Teari sighed as she found a needle

for stitching and sutures. "I'm guessing this will hurt less than most of these old scars."

She moved closer and kneeled next to him to get a better look at the slash across his thigh. The edges of his skin were bright red and inflamed. She held her left hand over it and cleared the infection.

Chel sucked in a breath.

"Does it hurt?" Teari asked.

He tipped his head back on the couch cushion. "Was that fresh blood in the bag?"

"No idea."

Chel grabbed a nearby pillow and pressed it over his pelvis and closed his eyes.

"You want me to numb the wound?" Teari asked.

"No," he grumbled.

Teari threaded the needle and went to work stitching. Chel didn't move a muscle as she worked. When she knotted the sutures and clipped them, she looked up. His eyes were still closed and his nostrils were flared. He wasn't asleep, but appeared to be holding something in. She sighed and shook her head. Hellions. She didn't understand them. She reached for a bandage and secured it over the sutures. "Keep this clean for a few days. The bandage can come off tomorrow and the stitches should be removed in about five days or so."

"Will you remove them?" he asked.

"If you'd like me to." She stood and moved away, packing up her medical bag and setting it on the counter-top. She glanced at Chel, who was still as stone, eyes closed, pillow pressed over his hips. She realized that he wasn't in pain—it was fresh blood and he was probably fighting for his life to control the Bloodlust. She turned around and looked out the kitchen window and made a mental note to send Meg a nasty-gram later.

She ran her tongue over her teeth.

She opened the fridge only to find it empty. She got the cooler and arranged the bags of blood in neat rows. "I'll go to the store for food. You want anything special?"

"No," Chel's voice sounded pained. "Wait. Steak."

"Sure." Teari walked toward the front door and as she reached for the knob she said, "I'll be back in a little bit. Try not to die while I'm gone."

"I didn't think you cared." His voice was like gravel.

She didn't reply as she reached for the door. A large hand slammed it closed. Teari felt heat behind her. She gasped as she turned.

Chel was off the couch and very close, his pupils huge like he was high as a kite. He licked his lips.

"That was fresh blood," he warned, inching closer until Teari's back was pressed flat against the door.

"You'll pull your stitches," she warned as her heart fluttered.

"I don't care about the stitches." He leaned closer, his free hand hovering over her hip. "Angel..."

The way he said the nickname made her want to collapse. She'd always liked Chel, heck she'd always found him attractive for a Hellion but he was too good for her;

too compassionate, too eager to protect the innocent. She would simply disappoint him.

Damn he looked good like this though; arched over her, muscles bunched, fangs pressed against his lower lip, and the heat radiating off him. She swallowed hard, remembering the way he looked as he was getting ready for the shower, the way he messaged her incessantly, the way he always invited her to every ball, every get together, everything. He always invited her and she always said no or brushed him off. Teari's hands moved, hovering over his chest.

"Chel?" she asked, searching his eyes. "It's the blood," she warned him.

He shifted his weight, pressing his body flush to hers. "No." He sighed. "I want you. Badly. I always have, Angel."

Teari nodded and leaned her forehead against his shoulder. This was fast. Too fast. But they'd known each other for years. Would it be so bad? She hadn't been touched in years, she found it too hard after the wars. Her hands had never truly felt like her own after they grew back. She had a difficult time touching others and allowing them to touch her.

Chel gripped her waist, his other hand sliding down the door and behind her neck. She could feel every inch of his hard body pressed against her. No one had hugged her or held her like this in ages. It felt good. She relaxed into his embrace.

"Don't bite me," she warned. "You've had enough fresh blood."

He nodded. "Tell me to stop. I can't stop myself." He groaned and pressed against her harder.

As Teari's hands slid up his arms and across his shoulders, she tipped her head back and looked up. "It's okay," she whispered, knowing fully that this would complicate things a hell of a lot more than anything.

She rose on her tiptoes and pressed her lips to his.

Chel groaned loudly as he wrapped his hands around her hips and lifted. Teari wrapped her legs around his waist and kissed him deeper. The blood that lingered in his mouth tasted good, ignited a desire inside her as well. She wasn't a Hellion; she didn't need blood to survive but it was part of life. Although, Angels were more cautious about consuming it. She'd been raised to be wary of it.

Chel moved toward the couch, carrying her. He sat, bringing Teari down on his lap. He reached for the buttons of her top and started undoing them—or attempting to. Teari stopped his hands and moved them to her thighs as she worked the buttons open.

Chel's eyes were half-lidded as he watched, then wide as she opened her shirt. His hands were on her again, smoothing over her waist and her breasts as his thumbs slid over her nipples. He leaned forward, kissing and licking her skin until his mouth latched over a nipple. Teari threw her head back and sucked in a breath. She rocked on his lap. Chel's hands roamed to the button of her pants, and he tugged, impatiently popping it. Large hands slid between her waistband and skin and over her ass, pushing the jeans away. She held onto his shoulders as he moved, feeling the sharp drag of teeth over her breast.

Her hands moved to both sides of his head, stilling him.

"Don't bite me," she reminded.

He growled and flipped her sideways. Suddenly Teari was on her back and the couch cushion dipped under her shoulder as he positioned himself above her. He tugged on her jeans and pulled them down then threw them across the room.

"Let me see." He kissed her lips. "I've been waiting forever to see you."

Teari felt her cheeks flush as she straightened her legs then opened them.

Chel sucked in a breath then muttered something in Hellspeak. She didn't know the language but it sounded like appreciation or a prayer even. He moved down her body, mouth dragging as he kissed and nipped and sucked on her skin. Teari shuddered as her body over-heated. She wasn't sure how much of this she could endure. He nipped her hipbone, then his hands slid to her inner thighs and pushed her legs further apart to make room for his shoulders. Teari hissed as he licked up her center and growled.

She'd never been with a Hellion before but the heat, the teeth, the sounds he made was doing it for her. She couldn't control her hips from moving when his tongue pressed into her, probing and laving. And that was all it took for her to throw her head back and lose it. Teari saw stars as her eyes squeezed shut and her gasps hit a crescendo. Her hands were gripped in his hair, pulling and tugging. He licked her softly until she came down from the high and then he was crawling up her body, pressing open mouthed kisses to her skin. Searing kisses. The scrape of his teeth made her heart flutter.

Teari watched him, feeling boneless and empty.

Chel kissed her hard, his tongue pressing between her lips. Her hands slid across his scarred abdomen, fingers skirting the angles and planes and resting on the waistband of his boxers. His arm slid under her back and tugged her down the couch, lining up their hips.

Teari reached into his boxers and wrapped her hand around his length. Chel hissed and pressed his hips forward.

"This won't last long," he warned. "And for that I apologize."

Teari was shaking her head. "It's fine." She was just as impatient to feel him as she pushed the waistband away. She glanced down and got a good look at him. Christ he was big.

"It's the blood," he warned. "I'm trying my best not to lose control."

Teari was nodding as she watched him slide inside of her body. "Oh, god." Teari closed her eyes and tipped her head back. Her nails pressed into his shoulders.

Chel was moving slow, giving her time to adjust to his size. His arm slid under her back and he gripped the nape of her neck, holding her in place and giving him leverage as he began to move, hips thrusting and gyrating against her. He sensed when he'd thrust too deep and pulled back, an apology whispering off his lips. His hands were smoothing over her skin, worshipping her body like she was a goddess. He was whispering to her in Hellspeak, against her ear and against her skin as his mouth dragged across her throat and clavicles. His voice was deep and the words he was saying were erotically foreign; he could have been repeating a grocery list for all she cared. She didn't want him to stop talking or moving against her.

If she had known he'd be like this she wouldn't have blown him off for all these years. Hellions weren't known for being good in bed. Not that many had dared to be with one. She glanced away. But they weren't in bed; maybe it was just couches.

She felt him grind deeper and he seemed to swell inside her. His hand moved down her belly to press the soft spot between them. His mouth latched onto her nipple.

It all happened so fast. She felt his teeth, the pressure in her belly, the fullness and stretching of her body to accommodate him, and then the world exploded. In the distance she heard a growl, felt the press of fingers on her hip and neck.

He was whispering something against her ear when

she came back down from oblivion. Then he was pulling out of her body in a slow drag that drew an exhale from her throat.

Teari's cheeks flushed. Oh, no. What did she do? She didn't have time to think because Chel was moving her, sliding her to the side as he positioned them together on the couch. One minute his arms were tight around her back, the next, his entire body relaxed. She glanced up at his face and realized he was fast asleep.

Her thighs ached. This was a bad idea. She moved his arm, but before setting it gently against his leg, she noticed a silvery scar around his left wrist. She traced it with her fingertip and frowned. He never mentioned losing a hand. Teari held up her arm and studied the thin scars just under her elbows.

Seems they had a little something in common. She searched his face. No, it wasn't enough.

CHAPTER 6

The fever came back and Chel drifted in and out of sleep for a day and a half; barely lucid, lips cracked, and breath wheezing. Every time he stirred, Teari was there pressing a cool cloth on his brow, murmuring words he couldn't quite make out.

The second night, he blinked awake to find her kneeling beside the bed. She wasn't praying but she was studying him, her hand hovering over his chest.

"Angel, you're still here?" he rasped.

She didn't look at him. "Someone had to keep you alive. Seems you've got more bugs than a virology lab. After this you should be immune to every infection between all the realms."

"Do I get a prize for that?" His lips twitched, almost a smile.

"Chel," Teari's voice was serious. "Don't ever get this sick again."

He nodded. "I'll do my best."

"Are you hungry? There's blood." She swallowed hard. "It's not as fresh now. It should be easier for you to handle."

"Yes."

She stood and walked away. Her footsteps quickened as her phone rang in another room.

Chel groaned as he rolled to his side and rubbed his face. He had to get out of this bed. He needed to move but the gnawing sense of weakness had returned. His arms and legs felt like rubber.

The last thing he remembered was Teari stitching up his leg and he'd done his best to control a raging hard-on after drinking the bagged blood. After she'd left to go to the store, he'd put on his sweatpants and moved to the bed. But his dreams were filled with images of Teari. Her large eyes as she'd inspected his body. Her warm hands. She still looked divine even without her wings visible on the Earthen plane. He wanted to touch her but she'd been so avoidant. She wasn't ready, but he'd wait until she was. He'd wait forever for her to finally warm up to him because he couldn't see himself with anyone else.

Later, when the fever broke again he managed to sit up on his own. Motion in the corner of the room caused him to jump to his feet and raise his fists.

"Slow down, Hellion," Teari's voice was filled with humor. She rose and handed him a clean shirt and said, "You should get some fresh air."

He changed, slowly, joints stiff and sore. When he

came out, she had made toast and poured blood into a chipped mug.

"Thanks," he said, accepting it with a nod.

"Don't mention it," she replied, already turning away.

He glanced out the window and realized the sun was setting.

"Let's get you outside." She motioned to the door. "I brought chairs out to the beach earlier."

"I could have done that. You don't need to move furniture." He sipped from the mug.

"They weren't heavy and you can barely move your-self." She held open the door but he waited for her to go through first, then shut it behind them.

He followed her down the porch steps and past the motorcycle.

Waves lapped against the shore in slow, lazy breaths, pulling foam back into the gulf.

Chel was afraid he'd break the beach chairs Teari had brought out, so he sat in the sand with his knees drawn up, arms resting across them, T-shirt sleeves tight against his biceps. The sea breeze had cooled as the sun dipped lower, casting the sky in shades of burnt orange and amethyst.

Beside him Teari stood barefoot, her hands tucked into the sleeves of her light sweater, watching the horizon.

Neither of them spoke for a while.

It was the kind of silence that felt intentional, not uncomfortable.

Chel finally broke it. "Do you like the beach?"

Teari didn't answer right away. "It's nice."

He turned to glance at her.

"I never had the time to figure out what I liked," she said, voice quiet. "A lot was decided for me."

Chel didn't push. He just nodded, gaze drifting back to the sea. "It was similar for me."

"You're healing faster now," she added.

"You sound surprised."

"I'm not," she said. "You're a Hellion. You're not easy to kill."

He gave a soft huff. "Still nice to have someone around who knows what the hell they're doing."

A gull cried overhead. The sun kissed the edge of the water.

Teari shifted, digging her toes into the sand. "I should tell you... I won't be here much longer."

Chel didn't move, but his jaw tightened. "You're leaving?"

"I have to," she said. "I have a job to do. I wasn't supposed to stay this long."

"You make it sound like you overstayed your welcome."

She looked at him. Her blue eyes were sharp in the fading light. "You don't need me. I'm just... interrupting your vacation."

He didn't argue. He just looked away and nodded once. A sinking feeling flooded his chest.

"I'll come back if you need me," she added. "You can call. I'll answer next time."

His gaze flicked to her. "You promise?"

Her mouth pulled into something almost like a smile. "Don't push it."

A faint buzz interrupted the moment–her phone vibrating in her pocket.

Chel glanced toward the sound. "Are you going to answer that?"

Teari froze, hand hovering over her pocket.

Then, just as quickly, she let her hand drop and turned her eyes back to the horizon. "It's nothing."

The lie hung between them like fog.

Chel didn't press, though the corner of his mouth twitched with something unreadable. "Alright. Keep your secrets."

They stood in silence again as the sun slipped beneath the waves, shadows stretching long behind them.

For just a moment, it felt like the world was holding its breath. And neither of them said what they were really thinking.

Chel's voice broke the silence like a stone dropped into still water.

"Did I ever tell you I lost my sister?"

Teari turned slowly to look at him. "No. I didn't know that."

He was watching the horizon. His hair had begun to

slip loose from its bindings, wind pulling strands across his cheek.

"We were just kids," he said. "She went to the river alone. She liked to watch the stars reflected in the water. I told her I'd meet her there but I didn't make it. I don't even remember what I did instead."

Teari didn't breathe.

Chel's voice dropped lower. "She never came back."

The waves rolled in. The wind picked up.

"I searched for days. Weeks. My father was the type of demon who didn't care. My sister was a burden. But me and my mother searched, every day. Someone took her. And they killed her." His jaw clenched. "That was the end of my family."

Teari stepped closer, her voice barely above a whisper. "I'm sorry to hear that."

"I don't usually tell people," he said, still not looking at her.

She moved across the sand and sat next to him. Her hand found his.

It wasn't much, just a touch, the light pressure of her fingers against his knuckles. It grounded something in both of them.

"Thank you for trusting me," she said.

He looked down at where her hand rested against his, and something in his expression softened.

"I just want you to know," he said, voice low and raw, "that you're not the only one who lost something and kept going like it didn't tear you in half. The ones we fail never leave us."

Teari's breath caught.

For a moment, they sat like that; quiet and still, with grief curling between them like sea mist.

Her phone rang again.

"I must go." Then she said, "I'll come back. If you need me."

He nodded.

"Just, one thing." Teari cleared her throat.

"Sure." He was watching her lips.

"Wash your fucking hands and stop eating at suspicious roadside diners."

He laughed, couldn't stop until he was leaning back in the sand and holding his stomach.

Teari made a little noise in her throat and a memory came flooding forward. Him and her on the couch in the beach house. He was high on fresh blood. He'd put his hands on her. A memory flashed of her underneath him, of her sighing, throwing her head back and making sweet noises in her throat.

Chel blinked and looked at Teari. "I'm sorry."

"For what?"

"Did I hurt you?" He looked away, rubbed a hand over his face. "I don't typically drink fresh blood. You know it's very hard for a Hellion to keep control."

A soft hand settled on his arm. "Chel, nothing happened that I didn't want. It was great." She patted him. "Don't think of it. We can move on."

Move on?

What if he didn't want to move on?

Chapter 7

Chel wasn't built for rest. When the fever broke and his limbs were back under his command, something in him still twitched beneath the skin. Restlessness. Or instinct. Or the nagging memory in the back of his mind from the White Horse. Maybe all of the above. Either way He needed to move.

The ride into town was short, the roads damp from the night's salt-fog. The engine of Jed's bike purred beneath him, comforting in its familiarity. He pulled into a mostly empty gas station, the kind with faded signage and a convenience store that smelled like fried chicken and old lemon cleaner. He knew better now, he wouldn't try the fried chicken. He wouldn't eat a single item from the gas station. He filled up the tank then drove down the road to the grocery store.

He needed toothpaste, steaks, and, apparently, coffee. He'd never drank much of the stuff but Meg had left a supply in the cabinets and Chel had taken to experimenting with his free time. He liked it sweet but the creamers upset his stomach.

Chel pushed open the glass door of the small-town grocery store, the bell overhead jingling like it was trying to sound cheerful and failing. The place was the same kind of quiet as the rest of Perdido–too clean, too still, the shelves half-stocked but meticulously neat.

He made a slow pass through the aisles, grabbing what he could stomach; some fruit, bread, cold cuts, the biggest steaks he could find in the cooler, and a bag of chips he'd never seen before that claimed to taste like "spicy crab fire."

He didn't trust that but was willing to try it. Lastly he found oat milk for the coffee. It was worth a try.

As he approached the register, the woman behind the counter straightened. She had light brown hair pulled into a messy bun and clear hazel eyes that flicked to his face, widened slightly, then settled into something like amused recognition.

"Well I'll be damned," she said, smiling. "You're back."

Chel blinked. "I am?"

"You don't remember me?" she asked, hands already reaching for the scanner. "It was over ten years ago, but I remember you. You were in here with a blond guy and a woman with blue hair, plus two kids. Teenagers almost. They cleaned out the freezer section and disappeared before I could ask how one of the boys managed to grow a foot in a few months."

Chel froze halfway to setting down a bottle of iced tea. "You've got a good memory."

"A man your size is hard to forget," she said, eyes twinkling. "Especially when he's—oat milk?"

He didn't know what to say to that so he gave a stiff shrug.

She kept scanning his items. "Nice bike, by the way. Last time you all drove a Jeep Grand Cherokee. I'll never forget watching you climb out of the back seat."

He nodded. "Yeah."

"But a motorcycle now. You in a gang or something? How does the gang feel about oat milk? We never sell that stuff. It always expires."

Chel coughed. "No motorcycle gang."

"I figured. You aren't wearing a jacket or have biker tattoos." She tilted her head, clearly not buying his discomfort as coincidence. "What happened to those kids you were with? Did they go off to college?"

Chel hesitated. "They... grew up." He couldn't tell her that Remington was a prince of Hell and learning his duties. Or that Rue was an archeologist up near Maryland, studying ancient runes and trying her best to uncover hidden family secrets. No, he definitely couldn't tell her any of that information.

The clerk laughed. "Well, yeah. Time does that."

He nodded again. This time a bit too firmly, like he could nod his way out of the conversation.

"Got a girlfriend?" she asked casually, bagging a loaf of bread.

He opened his mouth, paused. "No."

"Hmm. Shame," she said, then grinned. "Biker bar down the road, you know. Good wings. Rough crowd. You been there?"

He shook his head. "No."

She raised her brows. "Then what *do* you do with your life?"

Chel blinked. His mind raced for something plausible; anything that didn't involve blood, fire, or the shriek of collapsing realms.

Before he could stop himself he said, "I brought my new wife here. Honeymoon. Always liked the beach."

The clerk's hands froze over the receipt printer.

"New wife?" she echoed.

Chel nodded, slower this time. "Yeah."

"Oh." She glanced around, as if expecting to see a woman appear from behind a display of bananas. "Is she with you?"

"She's... on the beach," Chel said quickly. "I'm bringing her lunch."

The woman's face softened. "Well, aren't you sweet? Look at that. Big and romantic. Is the oat milk for her?"

Chel said nothing. His ears burned.

She handed him his receipt and winked. "You tell her she's a lucky woman. And congrats, seriously. I can't wait to meet your new wife."

"I'll... let her know," Chel said, backing toward the door like the building might explode.

"Take care of her," the clerk called after him. "New brides need that. And come by again!"

Chel stepped into the sunlight, groceries in hand, heart pounding for reasons that had nothing to do with danger and everything to do with whatever the hell *that* was.

His bike was waiting, warm and humming like it hadn't just watched him fumble his way through a fictional marriage.

He muttered under his breath as he climbed on.

"Great. Now I'm married. And apparently being harshly judged for buying oat milk."

Chel kicked the door shut behind him and dropped the grocery bag onto the counter with a grunt. He was hungry, but food would have to wait.

He pulled out his phone and scrolled to Shay's number, then hit call. She answered on the third ring.

"Hey, big guy." Shay's voice lit up and he heard the sound of a chopping board in the background.

"I need help," Chel said.

A beat. Then, "What kind of help? Crossroads Demon kind of help? Because if that's so, you're supposed to summon me without the cell phone."

He rubbed a hand down his face. "No Crossroads Demon. Not today. Yet, at least."

Shay sighed. "Alright. How bad?"

"I accidentally told the grocery clerk that I was here on my honeymoon."

There was a pause. "You what?"

"She asked if I had a girlfriend. I didn't know what to say. It just came out."

"Who *is* this imaginary wife?"

He hesitated. "I didn't tell her. But she remembered us from years ago. Lady has a spectacular memory. She remembered your blue hair, and Rue and Remm. Maybe she thinks you're my new wife?"

Shay made a sound like she'd just spit out water. "Oh, wow. We're starting strong."

"I panicked," Chel muttered.

"Okay. Okay. Don't worry. I can fix this. I'll put together a believable backstory. Allergic to shellfish. Former ballet dancer. Terrible at karaoke."

Chel walked out onto the front porch while she rambled, the phone pressed to his ear. He wondered if she needed to know about the oat milk for the story.

The breeze off the gulf was stronger now. The tide was higher than it should've been, even for evening. As he scanned the shoreline and Shay continued talking, he stepped down from the porch and began walking the sandy path to the beach.

He heard Jed's laughter in the background as Shay told Jed what Chel had done.

"Do you think I should go down there with him?" Shay asked, her voice sounding far away as she spoke to Jed.

"Absolutely not. You are not vacationing with Chel."

"You wanna come with?" Shay asked Jed.

"That will confuse the locals. Chel got himself into this mess, let himself get out of it."

"Thanks, guys." Chel sighed. He did create the mess.

He saw movement in the water. Strangely, he didn't see anyone walk into the ocean, nor did he notice someone swimming out there alone in the dark.

A tall figure with pale hair plastered to their skin walked *out* of the water.

"Shay," Chel said quietly.

"Yeah?"

"I'm going to have to call you back."

"Okay, hang in there, big guy. Maybe one of the local ladies can pretend to be your wife. Although, I'm not sure how the White Horse will feel about that. She's lost enough humans to Hell."

He hung up and moved across the beach, eyes locked on the figure emerging from the gulf. They walked slowly, barefoot, trailing water as they crossed the sand and headed inland toward a narrow row of houses tucked beneath the dune line.

Chel followed.

He kept his distance, steps silent, body alert.

The figure, tall, lean, and strange in the way their movements were *too fluid*, approached a small beach rental. They disappeared inside for a few minutes. When they emerged, they wore clean clothes: jeans, a button-down shirt, and sandals. Human enough.

But Chel knew better.

He could *feel* the wrongness now, the grace buried just beneath the surface. This wasn't a possessed local or a creature of Hell.

It was an Angel. He was damn sure of it.

Chel watched from behind a low fence as the figure walked down the road, passing a few blocks before walking up to a house and knocking on the door.

A woman answered. She was brunette, mid-thirties, barefoot. She smiled. Innocent.

Chel's stomach turned.

The woman slipped on a pair of sandals and reached for a purse then stepped out and locked her door. They spoke briefly. Then, casually, like it was planned, the two of them walked together down the road toward town.

A date.

Or something that looked like one.

Chel tailed them until they reached a local restaurant, the kind with a neon marlin sign and paper menus. The two were seated near a window, chatting over glasses of water and breadsticks.

Chel waited across the street. Twenty minutes. Thirty. Nothing happened. Just two people having dinner. Maybe he was nuts. He pressed a hand to his forehead. His skin didn't feel feverish. He shook his head and cursed himself. This was stupid. He started to walk away.

As he passed behind the restaurant, the sound of low voices stopped him.

Two guys stood behind the dumpster, smoke curling around them as they leaned into a conversation.

"...yeah, she quit the day after," one said. "Bailey said she couldn't look at him anymore."

"Damn."

"She said it wasn't his fault, but you know how that is. The baby was born dead. Full term. Just gone. And then he shows up with a new girl two weeks later, like nothing happened."

Chel went still.

"That sounds fishy," the other guy said between pulls on his cigarette.

"She moved up north somewhere," the other man continued. "Said Perdido made her sick. Bailey said all she did was cry. She's in a hospital up there. They locked her up and won't let anyone talk to her."

"Damn," the other guy flicked his cigarette. "She was too sweet for this place." He glanced toward the back door of the restaurant. "Can you believe that jerk coming back here with another date?"

"It's fucked up, man."

Chel turned toward the glowing windows of the restaurant.

The woman sitting across from the Angel was smiling. She probably didn't know he was an Angel. Probably thought he was simply tall and handsome and rich.

And suddenly, he got an uneasy feeling about what he was looking at.

The White Horse had said, "*Something is coming out of the gulf. I want you to figure out what it is and stop it before the Veil thins and war begins. You'll know where to start when you see it.*"

Wars had been a frequent occurrence in Chel's life. Only since Meg took the throne had there been peace. Power was gained from collecting souls from the Earthen plane but that had stopped after the last war. Mostly. The blatant collection of souls from the White Horse's realm, the Earthen plane, had stopped. There was always some sneaky shit going on under the curtain.

He'd heard plenty of stories about male Angels and their preferences for human women. Now he wasn't so sure that had stopped completely. Meg and Sparrow had been working endlessly to put an end to the skin trades in Hell and stop the flow of humans for their blood. Now he wondered if the Angel was here for blood or money or lust. It didn't matter. He didn't belong.

Chapter 8

The sun was just starting to rise when Teari stepped up onto the porch of the beach house. She knocked twice and turned to listen to the ocean.

There was a groan on the other side of the door and heavy footsteps then muttering in Hellspeak. The door swung open and Chel was there, shirtless. Just loose shorts sitting low on his waist.

"I didn't call," he said, looking confused.

"I know. After last time I figured you wouldn't. So I just came. It's been five days. The stitches need to come out."

He stood there taking up the doorway, eyes wide, like he'd seen a ghost.

"Can I come in?" Teari asked with a laugh.

"Please." He motioned for her to enter and closed the door softly behind her.

Chel had clearly been sitting at the table, planning

something medical. Teari noticed the towel and scissors and rubbing alcohol.

"What are you doing?" she asked, arching a brow.

Chel looked away. "I was gonna take the stitches out."

"I said I'd check your stitches. I'm punctual." She held up a small leather pouch. "And I brought better tools than whatever filthy scissors you're using."

He shrugged and sat, tugging the leg of his shorts up so she could see the wound she'd stitched together.

She set her kit down on the table then touched his thigh lightly, inspecting the healing cut. The wound was mostly closed. The edges were clean. A few stitches still clung where his skin hadn't quite knitted back together but it would close completely in a few days.

"Good progress," she murmured. "But you've got too much scar tissue building. I'll fix it."

He tilted his head slightly, watching her. "You always this gentle?"

"Only with the ones who whimper through fevers."

He smirked, but his pulse gave him away. She felt it under her fingers.

As she snipped and tugged out the first stitch, he winced.

"So what have you been up to all week?" Teari tried to distract him with small talk.

He sighed. "Lots of walks on the beach. I found a gym down the road but it smells weird."

"That's good, Chel. Playing human like the best of them." She pulled another stitch.

"I did have one strange interaction. The clerk at the grocery store around the corner remembered me from years ago when I came here with Jed and Shay. Rue and Remington were still kids."

Teari's brow lifted. "That long ago? Good memory."

"Yeah." Chel shifted slightly. "She asked a lot of questions. And then asked if I had a girlfriend."

Teari snorted. "I'm already worried about where this is going."

"I panicked. I told her I was here on my honeymoon."

Teari blinked. "You what?"

Chel coughed. "I might've said I had a wife."

Before she could respond her phone buzzed. She glanced down, her expression hardening.

"I have to take this. It's Gabriel." She set her suture removal scissors on the table and turned.

"I'll be right back," she said, stepping toward the porch. "Don't... bleed out. Or reach for the glue." She winked.

Chel watched her go, frowning.

She answered on the third ring. "Sir."

"Teari," Gabriel's voice was calm, clipped, and unbothered as always. "Meg and I had a conversation."

She stilled. "Oh?"

"She's asked me to grant you an official leave of

absence. I've agreed. Starting immediately. No assignments. No summons. One month."

"Sir, with respect, I have three patients still—"

"They've been reassigned."

"You didn't even ask—"

"You've never taken leave," he said, "in all your years of service. This is not a punishment, Teari. You're being given time. Take it."

"But I—"

"Take it," he repeated, voice final. "Meg insisted. And I agreed."

The line went dead before she could argue further.

Teari stared at the phone in her hand, blood prickling beneath her skin. A month of silence sounded nice on paper but that wouldn't stop her father. When he needed her, he'd call. And she'd answer. Because she always did and if she didn't she'd be dragged through the mud.

She stepped back into the house.

Chel hadn't moved.

"You were saying," she prompted, picking up the suture scissors and getting back to work removing the stitches.

He looked up, eyes curious. "Everything alright?"

"No." She snapped. "Apparently, I'm on vacation."

His brow rose. "Seriously?"

"Gabriel and Meg decided it for me. I've been benched."

"You good with that?"

"No," she said truthfully. "But it's happening so I gotta suck it up."

She turned to face him. "So. You told the grocery clerk you were on your honeymoon?"

He nodded slowly. "Yeah."

"You don't have a wife."

"Nope."

She looked around the cozy kitchen, then out the window at the soft pink haze settling over the water.

"Alright," she said finally.

Chel blinked. "Alright?"

"We'll pretend."

He blinked again.

She shrugged one shoulder, like it didn't matter. "You already started the story. Might as well play it out."

"You don't answer my phone calls or my invitations to the spring ball but you'll pretend to be my wife?"

"I'm being forced to take a vacation," Teari said, voice edged with both humor and bitterness. "Might as well make it weird." She pulled the last stitch out and stood.

Chel grinned. "Weird is my specialty."

She rolled her eyes and moved toward the pantry, muttering something about needing real coffee. But behind the casual tone, she felt the weight of the lie settle around her like silk threads tightening at the collarbone.

Because no matter what Gabriel said, no matter what Meg promised, a month away didn't mean freedom from her own demons.

CHAPTER 9

CHEL HAD FACED SHAPESHIFTERS, DEMONS, AND the devouring dark between worlds, but walking into a beachside market with Teari on his arm pretending they were married?

That ranked disturbingly high on the list of things he didn't know how to survive.

The bell over the market door chimed.

A few locals glanced up as they entered. The grocery clerk from the other day, Anna as her name tag read, straightened behind the register the moment she spotted him.

Her eyes flicked to Teari.

Chel cleared his throat. "Uh, hey. This is my wife." The words sounded strange coming out of his mouth.

Teari didn't even flinch. She slid her arm casually through his like they did this all the time. "Hi," she said, smiling with unsettling charm. "We're just grabbing a few things for lunch."

Anna's brows rose. "Wow. She's gorgeous."

Chel blinked. "Uh. Yes. She is." Her soft curves pressed up against his body. She was so warm.

"Very lucky," Anna added, clearly to Teari, clearly teasing.

"And you're both so tall." Anna clicked her tongue. "You should've honeymooned in Miami, this town is too boring for people looking like you two."

"Oh, I know," Teari said smoothly. "He brings me coffee every morning. Makes the bed. Rubs my feet—"

"Okay," Chel cut in. "That's not entirely accurate."

Teari leaned closer to him, lips near his ear. "You told her we were married, Hellion. You started this. Pretend to be a newlywed. A human newlywed."

He muttered something unintelligible and moved toward the produce section, dragging her with him. He was sure the tickle of her lips against his ear was going to cause his head to explode. Or his pants. One or the other. He needed a distraction.

"Why do you look like you want to chew glass?" Teari whispered as she picked through avocados, a teasing lilt in her voice.

"This is awkward."

"You're doing fine. Just don't make the face."

"What face?"

"The one where you look at me like I have five heads."

He rubbed his face. It was hard not to look at her that way. He'd wanted to touch her and take her out and be with her for years. And now here she was, playing along.

She handed him an avocado. "This is ripe. Buy it."

He stared at it like it might detonate.

They worked their way through the small store, grabbing sandwiches, chips, and a lemon soda Teari insisted was "for research." Chel was keenly aware of how they looked, how her hand occasionally brushed his when they reached for the same item, how she laughed too easily, how they moved together like maybe this wasn't just some cover. She was a good actress.

At checkout, Anna leaned over the counter again. "So when was the wedding?"

Chel opened his mouth.

Teari beat him to it. "Last week"

Anna giggled. "Straight to the honeymoon."

"Yes, we're taking the whole month together," Teari said sweetly, elbowing Chel in the ribs.

He smiled, rubbing his side.

Anna bagged their food and handed it over with a wink. "Enjoy your lunch, lovebirds."

Chel took the bag, nodded stiffly, and practically marched out the door.

Outside, the wind was lighter and the sun was just beginning to haze the sky gold.

Teari followed, sipping her lemon soda.

"That wasn't so bad," she said.

"You're going to be the death of me."

"No, Hellion, not washing your hands will get you there."

"I'm not sure she believed us."

Teari looked at him. "You can manage that, can't you?"

He stared at her, expression blank. Memories of the bloody Hellion Lair returned, his friends dead. "I've never held someone's hand without blood on mine."

She blinked.

He looked away.

She didn't press.

Instead, she took his free hand in hers. Her skin was soft and warm. He'd always wondered what she felt like.

"Then consider this practice," she said. "For next time."

Chel looked down at their joined hands, then out toward the road.

He didn't say it out loud, but the thought rang through him all the same:

I could get used to this.

Even if it was all a lie.

CHAPTER 10

Teari had taken the guest room farthest from Chel's. The house wasn't large but it put the greatest distance between them. She lay on the bed, eyes open in the dark, phone screen lighting the ceiling in brief pulses as it vibrated against the nightstand.

Raphael (3 missed calls).

Raphael (4 missed calls).

Raphael (5 missed calls).

She pressed ignore and turned it face-down.

She wouldn't answer. Not tonight. The Archangel Raphael could call someone else to clean up his mess. She wasn't going to deal with his drama tonight. Not while Chel slept in the other room, unaware of the horrors she carried, ghosts braided into her bones.

Let me rest for once, she thought bitterly. *Just this once.*

She closed her eyes.
Sleep came quickly.
But peace didn't.

Then...

Teari stood in a room carved of gold and light, one she remembered far too well—Raphael's inner sanctum. Silent. Pristine. The air smelled of blood and incense.

Her hands glowed bright with healing light.

There was an infant in her arms.

Barely formed. Blue. Still.

"Fix it," her father said, voice sharp behind her, cold and ancient. "Erase it."

Teari shook her head. "It's already gone."

"Erase the evidence."

"I—" Her hands trembled. She didn't want to take a pure soul. This was wrong. "This isn't healing."

Her father stepped closer. "This is loyalty. You can't stop now, not after all these years."

The baby disintegrated in her hands, its body turning to light, then to nothing. Her magic devoured it like fire devours parchment.

Barely a year later, another infant was placed in her arms.

This one had eyes open, so blue. It blinked once.

Then it, too, was gone.
Six months. Again.
Two years. And again.
Nine months. And again.
Each one was snuffed out under her touch.
She screamed, but no sound came.
Only her father's voice.
"You were born for this."
"You exist to clean up after us."
"You want to save lives? Save our reputation."
She fell to her knees.
The blood on her hands didn't wash off—it soaked in, staining up her arms and across her chest until her wings turned red and cracked.
She wasn't a healer anymore.
She was the graveyard.

Teari woke with a sharp gasp, breath punching out of her lungs like she'd surfaced from drowning.

She sat up, drenched in sweat, her body rigid, heart galloping against her ribs. She coughed, feeling the bile sliding up her throat.

The room was so dark. And for a moment, she thought she might still be in that chamber, her father standing just behind her, breath cold and demanding against her neck.

But she was alone. In the beach house. In a borrowed room that smelled of salt and lemons. Still shaking, she swung her legs over the side of the bed and stood. Her hands tingled with phantom magic, remnants of dreams she wished she could forget. The floor creaked under her bare feet as she padded to the kitchen.

It was empty. Dimly lit by the moonlight slipping through the curtains, a glass sat on the counter. She filled it at the sink, drank, and noticed that the water out of the tap was never really cold here. Strange. She leaned there for a long moment, forehead resting against the cabinet. The glass in her hand trembled slightly as she set it down on the counter.

The silence stretched.

Her phone was still in the other room, vibrating again.

But she didn't go back for it.

She couldn't answer him.

Not now.

Maybe not ever.

She wasn't shaking anymore, not exactly. But her limbs still felt wrong. Her breath still came too shallow. Her thoughts moved too fast and then not at all.

Tired, she told herself. *Just tired.*

She turned away from the sink and leaned into the silence. Outside, the gulf hissed against the shore.

And then, a flicker of movement just beyond the window caught her eye.

Her spine snapped straight.

There it was again.

A shape in the dark, tall and still, just past the edge of the porch light, stood where the dune grass met the back of the house; half in shadow, half in moonlight.

Her heart surged into her throat.

The old fear came fast; primal, trained, inescapable. Someone had followed her. They'd have crossed the realms. Her father? A hunter? Someone who knew what she'd done.

Who she'd let die.

She stepped back from the window slowly, her eyes locked on the shape.

Her fingers reached for the knife block by the sink without conscious thought. Her hand closed around the handle of the chef's knife and she took a steadying breath.

Then the porch steps creaked.

The doorknob turned.

Her body moved before her mind did, stepping forward, knife raised in defense, eyes wide and burning.

The door swung open and Chel walked in.

He stopped short the instant he saw her.

They froze.

Chel; barefoot, hoodie hanging loose around his shoulders, holding a bag of chips. Teari, wild-eyed and clutching a knife like she was ready to carve fate in half.

"Teari," he said, slowly, carefully, "please don't stab me. I don't need more stitches."

The breath rushed out of her.

She dropped the knife onto the counter with a sharp clatter and pressed a shaking hand to her forehead.

"Christ," she whispered. "You can't just walk in like that."

"I'm living here right now," he said gently.

She gave him a look. "Okay. Sorry. It's fine. You just scared me."

He crossed the kitchen slowly and set the chips down, watching her. "Are you alright?"

"I thought someone was outside."

He nodded, quiet. "I was just patrolling. Hard habit to break." He shrugged. "It's a Hellion thing."

She blinked. "Sure."

Chel shrugged. "I've been in bed a lot this week. Can't sleep."

She sank into one of the kitchen chairs.

Chel glanced at the knife, then back at her.

"I'd rather you keep the knife by the sink than in my chest," he said. "But I get it."

She huffed a laugh. "I wouldn't have stabbed you."

"You would've."

"...Maybe a little."

They sat in silence, the moonlight soft through the window.

"You want to go for a walk?" Chel asked. "It's really nice outside."

Teari took a breath. She didn't want to go back to sleep, and she didn't want to look at her phone. "Sure." She nodded.

CHAPTER 11

Teari's brows lifted. "This is just a normal walk, right?"

He reached for the doorhandle. "You're wide awake. So am I. Might as well take a walk."

She gave him a skeptical look. "Are you suggesting this as some kind of romantic beach thing, or are we pretending to be on our honeymoon again?"

"Sure," he said, already heading toward the door. "Let's call it that." He winked. "The humans might be watching. And word gets around Perdido Beach quickly. We can't break cover."

She didn't move right away. He could feel her hesitation behind him.

But then she rose, slowly, and followed.

The sand was cool underfoot, the tide low now.

Chel walked just ahead, hands in his pockets. Teari

moved beside him in silence, the wind playing with the ends of her sweater sleeves.

She glanced at him once. "You're doing that thing again."

"What thing?"

"The silent brooding."

"It helps me think."

"You don't have to think. You're on vacation."

Chel's lips quirked, but he didn't respond.

Truth was, he wasn't just walking. He was watching, listening, and feeling for that pressure in the air, the twist in the sand, the shift in the surf, the moment things turned sideways without explanation.

They passed a broken fence half-buried in the dunes. Farther ahead, a row of beach houses stood dark and still, some with windows boarded, others just... empty.

"Meg said she purchased a few blocks worth of houses around the beach house. For privacy." Teari said as she stepped closer to him, her arm brushing his. "You're scouting," she said softly.

Chel didn't answer.

She sighed. "You could've told me."

"You needed air."

"You needed backup."

He glanced at her, hiding a smile. "I know you trained with Gabriel's Legion for years. No one better to have for backup."

They walked a little farther, silence folding between them like a shared cloak.

"I think there's something moving along the coast-line," Chel finally said. "It's not just the missing women. It's the way people look away when you ask. Like they know and can't say something."

Teari glanced toward the surf. "You think it's coming from the water."

"It is." He cleared his throat. "You should know that I'm not entirely on vacation. The White Horse asked me to investigate something strange going on in this town."

She looked at him sharply.

"I overheard something the other night. One of the locals said a young woman lost her baby. It died, full term. And the boyfriend was still around. She left after he started seeing someone new. Moved away. Couldn't look at him. No one has been able to contact her since."

Teari went very still. "Sounds like some small town, Earthen plane bullshit."

Chel turned toward her, his voice low. "I saw the guy come out of the ocean. It was an Angel. I followed him to a house down there." He pointed. "And he met a woman and took her to the little Italian restaurant on the main drag."

The wind picked up again, colder this time.

Teari wrapped her arms around herself and stared out into the waves.

Chel didn't touch her, but he didn't step away either.

"We're not done pretending yet," he said quietly.

She glanced at him, confused.

He nodded toward the houses. "Not just for the

clerk. For the whole town, they're all watching. I hope you're a good actress."

Teari met his gaze. "Challenge accepted, Hellion."

"Have you ever danced under the full moon on the beach?" Chel's heart had never beaten so hard. She'd rejected him so many times.

Teari raised a brow. "Is that a Hellion tradition or just a personal fantasy?"

He smirked, but his throat was tight. "Little of both."

She paused, then smiled. "I have never done such a thing."

Chel lifted his hand toward her. The wind tugged at the edges of her sweater.

To his surprise, Teari reached for him.

Her fingers slid into his palm, cool and steady. He tugged her gently toward him, pulled her close with one hand still joined in hers, the other settling around the small of her back.

She didn't pull away.

The world narrowed to just the two of them in the hush of surf and moonlight.

Chel hummed under his breath, an old Hellion tune from his earliest years. Others used to whistle it before battle; a lullaby twisted into ritual, made warm only by memory.

Teari stilled in his arms. "Make sure you're not calling demons to come find you. I recognize that song."

He chuckled, low and rough. "It's a hunting song. Not a summoning."

"Oh, well then. Comforting. We don't want Nero and Shay popping in for a deal."

He laughed harder.

They moved slowly, weightless on the sand, the tide lapping at their feet.

She smelled like salt and lavender, something clean and sharp beneath the ocean air. His heart beat too hard, too fast—not from fear, but from the realization that this might be the closest he'd ever get to something normal.

Teari tilted her head against his shoulder, just for a moment. Just long enough to shake him apart from the inside out. He wanted to ask her to stay forever but he didn't want to ruin the moment.

Instead, he whispered, "For what it's worth, you're better at pretending than I am."

"I've had more practice."

His arm circled tighter around her waist. "I like this."

She looked up at him, eyes darker than the sea. "That could be a problem."

Neither of them spoke after that but something wilted in his chest. He should've known better. He could sense there was something dark and hidden in Teari he hadn't noticed before, but he was picking up on it now. She carried a darkness in her soul, something that hurt.

They kept moving, slow steps in rhythm with the waves beneath a watching moon. The sand was cool beneath Chel's feet, soft and shifting with every slow step. Teari moved with him gracefully, like she didn't notice the heaviness in the air.

The lull of his humming had faded into silence now. But neither of them had pulled away.

The ocean whispered behind them. The town was asleep.

"You know," he murmured, eyes never leaving hers, "your phone rings all the damn time."

Teari huffed a soft breath. "It does."

"But you never answer."

She glanced away, the moon catching in her lashes. "Sometimes I do."

Chel tilted his head, still guiding their slow circle in the sand. "You don't have to tell me who it is."

"It's my father."

Chel's step faltered. "Do you want to talk about it?"

She was quiet for a beat, the rhythm of their movement never breaking. Then she said, "He drags me into his drama. Always has. He doesn't fix things, he buries them. I'm the one with the shovel. It's an inherited problem."

Chel's jaw tightened, but he said nothing.

Teari's gaze dropped to their joined hands. "When he found out I could heal, he dragged me deeper into his circle. But only so I could erase things. Accidents. Consequences. Inconveniences. I was never allowed to be a daughter. Only a tool."

Chel's grip shifted slightly, firmer without being forceful. "That's not what you are."

"You don't know him," she said, voice barely audible over the surf. "Archangel. Pureblood. Reputation older than most gods. And I'm his. His blood. I've spent my whole life trying to get away but his claws are deep."

Chel was quiet for a long time. "When I last visited home, my mother had bruises and she would barely talk."

Teari's eyes snapped up to his.

"My father was a demon of the old ways. Lucifer's ways. He was not kind." Chel's voice was steady, but low. "He was always violent. Always thought if you bled, you learned. He never cared that my sister died."

He exhaled through his nose, gaze distant. "I helped my mother leave. I took her to a mountain town where nobody knew her name and he couldn't find her."

Teari's mouth tugged upward, faint and sad. "I'm glad she got out."

"I am too." He looked back at her, eyes gentle. "You don't have to deal with him."

Her throat worked and she nodded once, still guarded.

Chel gave her a small smile. "Family can be sharp, you know. Sharp like the thorns of a rose. Or a hawthorn. Or a damn bloodvine."

She raised a brow. "Are you listing Hellion flora now?"

He chuckled. "Maybe. The thorns of the family, these thorns are the sharpest. The ones you're born from," he finished, softer now. "The ones that think they have a right to grow inside you. They hook us, bury inside so deep we'll never really be free."

Teari didn't speak, just stepped closer, resting her forehead against his chest.

They stayed like that as the waves curled around their ankles and the moon carved silver along the surface of the water. No pretending now. Just breathing. Just being.

He felt wetness on his chest and looked down. She was crying, tears falling from her eyes with no sound. He moved her hand to his waist and wrapped both arms around her tightly, holding her.

Teari's voice was weak when she finally said, "Sometimes I wish I'd been born here."

"You want to be human?" he was confused.

"No. Just... I don't want to be like *this*."

He rubbed her back and let her cry, worry spreading in his chest. He'd known Teari for years but he'd never seen this side of her. She was battling something dark inside. He wasn't surprised. He had his own demons he dealt with on a daily basis. But, having Teari at the beach house these past few days had soothed the memories. He hoped he could do the same for her. If only she'd really tell him what was going on.

Chapter 12

The humidity was next level rainforest by the time Chel rolled into town, the motorcycle rumbling beneath him like a warning growl. He'd seen heat, but the moisture in the air was drinkable.

Teari had still been asleep when he left. She was curled on the couch with a half-finished book on her chest, a line of light slipping in through the curtains and settling across her cheek. He'd paused in the doorway, unsure if he should wake her. He didn't, even though her face flexed in dreaming.

They'd said too much last night. Or maybe not enough. He still wasn't sure. If he'd learned one thing, Teari was hard to read when she was keeping something from him.

Now, the wind carried heat and sea salt and the roads were quiet for midmorning. He'd noticed Florida didn't wake up until approximately two p.m., which he was fine with.

He parked outside the grocery store, in the same spot with the same rusted parking stripe. The door chimed as he walked in.

Anna, the clerk, glanced up and smiled. "Morning, honeymooner."

Chel cleared his throat. "Yeah. Uh—morning."

She was busy reorganizing gum packets. "You here for another romantic lunch run? Maybe more oat milk?"

"Something like that," he muttered.

He wandered the aisles, pretending to browse. But really, he was watching. Listening.

He'd come here for something else, something that had been nagging at him since the other night. He found the community bulletin board inside the shop—smaller than the town hall one—with handwritten notes, business cards, and under those two MISSING posters.

Both women.

One of them was named Sienna Waller.

Anna was watching him, he could feel her eyes on his back. He moved away from the board and went to the chip aisle. He grabbed a bag of spicy mustard pretzels then found the lemon soda Teari had gotten the other day. And yes, he got more oat milk. It didn't upset his stomach like the other stuff did.

As he went to ring out Anna glanced up at him, but the mood had turned awkward.

"Thank you, Anna," Chel said, remembering his manners.

She simply nodded. He wondered if she didn't like the idea of him looking at the missing persons posters. Maybe she knew the women. Maybe she didn't want him involved in small town politics.

He stepped outside and crossed the street to the diner where a group of servers and cooks were gathered near the entrance, smoking and ribbing each other about weekend plans.

They went still as Chel approached.

Chel nodded and waved. "Got a weird question."

The men chuckled, but the one who had been speaking tilted his head. "Let's hear it."

"Do you all know Sienna Waller?"

"Waller? Yeah," the guy said. "She was sweet. Pregnant and glowing. Until she wasn't."

"Until?" Chel asked.

The man blew smoke out the side of his mouth. "She came into work here one morning crying. Said she lost the baby. No explanation. No funeral. Just... gone. She moved out two days later."

Chel's spine prickled. "Gone how?"

"They never said." A pause. "But she left her sandals at the shoreline that night. Like she went to the water to forget. I saw her waiting on the beach during low tide."

He said it like a local ghost story but Chel knew better.

Chel's voice dropped. "Did anyone see her afterward?"

The man frowned. "There was a rumor she went to live with her sister upstate. Near some mental hospital. But... there was another girl in town not long after. Looked a lot like her. Same boyfriend. Same situation."

"Did anyone ever see them together?" Chel asked.

The man hesitated. "No," he admitted.

Chel turned away, heart hammering.

Same creature. Two pregnancies that ended in disaster. He rubbed his face.

"Hey!" footsteps echoed behind him.

Chel turned to find one of the cooks following.

"It's not just the two." The guy said. He wasn't much more than a kid. "My parents were talking about the situation. There were girls my mother went to high school with and similar situations happened to them." He tipped his head down the road. "There's more. It's the curse of Perdido Key. Every time a lone man comes visiting, girls end up pregnant, their babies die, and then they disappear." The kid was scowling. "Is that what you're doing here?"

The crew of workers stood and focused on him.

"No, man." Chel half-smiled. "I'm here on my honeymoon. We've got an old family house down on Parasol Place."

The kid squinted like he didn't believe Chel. "Where's your wife now?"

Chel thumbed behind him. "Back at the beach

house, reading. If you don't believe me, you can ask Anna down at the grocery store."

CHEL RETURNED TO THE BEACH HOUSE, HIS boots scuffed with sand and his head full of conversations that wouldn't stop replaying.

As he stepped inside, he found Teari curled in one of the mismatched armchairs, barefoot, reading the same dog-eared paperback. She looked up the moment the door clicked shut.

"You were gone for hours," she said, marking her page. "Where were you?"

Chel ran a hand through his wind-tangled hair and set the keys down on the counter. "I was in town. Investigating."

She arched a brow.

He hesitated, his thumb brushing against the ring of his belt absently. "I spoke with a few locals. Kitchen staff. People who don't know they're being watched."

Teari's posture stiffened, but she didn't interrupt.

"They're wary," Chel continued. "I can tell they don't trust single men from out of town."

She folded her arms. "And?"

"I told them you were at the beach house. Reading." He gave her a faint smirk. "Wasn't even a lie."

Teari tilted her head. "You're stalling."

Chel exhaled, the humor draining from his face. "I overheard something about two women. Both lost their babies. No signs of trauma. One of them, Sienna, left her sandals on the beach and disappeared. A few guys think she moved up north but others aren't so sure."

Teari went very still.

"I think it's connected," he said, "to the Angel I saw crawling out of the gulf. One of the cooks said the new girlfriend looked just like the old one. Same guy. Same MO."

Her voice was low. "Why are you getting involved in this, Chel?"

"The White Horse asked me to."

She set the book down slowly. "You think you can learn more from the locals about these women?"

"They talk when they think you're one of them."

"You want to keep up the act. How can you even be sure that was an Angel coming out of the gulf?"

Chel shifted his weight, uneasy. "I don't want to disappoint the White Horse. She trusted me with this. If I screw it up... Meg might force me into retirement for real. I think she's testing me with this."

There was something bitter in the way he said it. Like being forced to rest was worse than death.

Teari's expression softened. "So what's the plan, Hellion?"

He cleared his throat. "I think we should go out to dinner and lean into this newlywed bit. At least until they learn to trust us."

She blinked. "So a date."

"There's a small Italian place in town. I've spoken to half the kitchen staff. If we go there together, acting like newlyweds, hopefully they'll trust me enough to give me more information."

"You're asking me to put on a show." She sighed dramatically. "Chel, you ask so much of me, but I did agree to this."

"I'm asking you to help me help the White Horse. Help Meg."

Teari watched him for a long moment.

Then, to his surprise, she smiled with a nod. "Alright. A date it is."

Chel's heart kicked a little too fast in his chest, trying not to stare too hard as she crossed the room. "Dress code?"

"This isn't a Spring ball in Hell, but we should probably clean up a little bit. Sharp enough to pass for newlyweds. I need to go shopping," she called over her shoulder. "And if you try anything, I *will* stab you with a breadstick."

Chel grinned as the bedroom door shut behind her.

He was going to be murdered by an Angel.

And he wasn't even sure he'd mind.

CHAPTER 13

The boutique in Perdido Key was small and smelled like linen-scented dryer sheets and old ocean wood, but the owner was kind, and the dresses weren't terrible. This wasn't a shop in Babylon, nothing here even remotely resembled the styles in the Seven Kingdoms of Heaven.

Teari tried on six dresses before she found one she liked. She tried on a short white one that looked more like lingerie. She also put on a long black dress with a slit up to her hip that just screamed trouble. And she found a red one that she immediately took off; she couldn't stand the color red.

She finally settled on gauzy number that hit at the knee, the color was deep blue linen and it reminded her of the ocean. It was fitted at the waist, flowing just enough to move when she walked. The sleeves hit below the elbow and hid her scars. It made her feel like a woman, not a weapon. Not a daughter. Not a healer. Not an Angel.

Just her. Maybe even... a little bit human.

The store owner was watching her and smiled. She took a few items off the shelves and walked closer. "A belt would complement your waist." She passed Teari a wide, leather woven belt. "A bit of gold will bring out the color in your eyes." The woman was looking up at her. "You're quite tall and stunning. Are you one of those influencer models from Miami?"

"No." Teari shook her head as she put the belt on and turned to look in the mirror. The shop owner was right, the belt made her waist look defined. "I'm here on my honeymoon."

The lady clucked her tongue. "Oh yes, the couple out on Parasol Place. I've heard of you."

"You have?" Teari pretended to be distracted by the shoes nearby.

"Heard your husband is a giant. Here, you don't need heels with those legs. You'll look like a beanstalk." She pulled out a pair of strappy sandals. "Try these. They match the belt."

"Thank you." Teari took the sandals. "My husband is quite tall. He makes me feel small when I'm around him."

The shop owner was nodding. "Is he a good man?"

Teari paused. She didn't know a lot about Chel, but he'd been pursuing her for years. She'd never seen him do a thing that wasn't noble. He'd cared for Meg's children when they were small. He'd helped them as they grew and turned adults. He was attached to Rue's kitten Lucipurr as though it were his grandchild or something. Teari smiled to herself. He'd held her on the beach when she was *thisclose* to a mental breakdown.

"He's a good man then," the shop keeper was smiling.

"I didn't reply."

"Oh, you did, you should have seen your face." The woman turned. "Let's get you a nice bag and some bracelets."

Teari took whatever to woman put in her hands. She'd done well with the belt and the shoes so Teari trusted her. And she didn't trust herself to figure out the local style without looking completely out of place.

When Teari set the dress and other items on the counter, the lady began scanning tags and said, "I'll give you an extra ten percent off for the wedding."

"That's very kind of you, thank you."

"Will you start trying for children soon?"

Teari froze. She'd never thought about children. She'd been too traumatized by her father to even consider bringing another life into her world.

"Don't answer that," the lady said as she tucked Teari's items into a bag. "I shouldn't have asked. It was rude of me."

"One day, maybe," Teari said quietly as she paid.

Teari didn't realize until she was halfway back to the beach house that she'd never thought that far into her future. Her phone vibrated and a sickening feeling dropped in her stomach. She didn't answer it.

Back at the beach house, she avoided Chel's gaze completely as she locked herself in the bathroom.

"We're going to be late," he called through the door, voice lighter than usual.

"I've got plenty of time," she said, rolling on mascara.

"Barely."

She took her time, thankful for her short, cropped hair; there wasn't much to do with it besides smooth down the flyaway baby hairs at her temple. Eyes lined in black, lipstick stained just dark enough to feel dangerous–she stared at herself in the mirror for a long moment when she was done.

She didn't recognize this human version of herself. But she didn't hate her either. This wouldn't pass at one of Gabriel's balls or dining in Babylon, but it would work just right for Perdido Key.

She stepped out of the bathroom.

Chel was leaning against the kitchen counter in a black button-up shirt and dark jeans. His boots were polished and for once, his dark hair wasn't tied back. He'd gotten it cut. It was trimmed up on the sides and the back, just long enough on the top for someone to run their fingers through.

He looked up and froze.

Teari raised an eyebrow. "Is it that bad?"

Chel said nothing.

His eyes scanned her head to toe.

"Well?" she asked, adjusting the strap of her dress.

"You look..." He shook his head once. "Stunning."

Teari frowned slightly. "That's... very convincing."

"I'm not acting," Chel said, voice lower now. "I wasn't ready for that."

She blinked. Her heart did something strange in her chest, like it had skipped over something sharp.

"It's a dress," she muttered, grabbing her small purse from the table.

Chel didn't move, just watched her like he still wasn't sure if she was real.

Teari crossed the room and brushed past him, leaving just enough space to feel the heat of his body and the slow exhale he released after she passed.

"We should go," she said without turning. "Wouldn't want the locals thinking the honeymoon's already over."

His footsteps followed a beat later, along with a muttering in Hellspeak.

THE LITTLE ITALIAN RESTAURANT SAT TUCKED off the main road wedged between a surfboard rental shop and a used bookstore. From the outside it didn't look like much, just a cracked brick facade and a flickering neon. There were tiny lights strung in the Live Oaks that led to the front door, lending a fairy tale feel.

The hostess smiled wide when Teari and Chel stepped in together. "You must be the honeymooners from Parasol Place. Right on time for your reservation."

Chel tensed slightly beside her. Teari reached for his hand and laced their fingers together without looking.

"Table for two," she said sweetly.

They were seated near a window, white string lights twinkling along the glass and soft instrumental music playing overhead.

A waitress came with water and a grin. "You two celebrating something special?"

Chel looked at Teari, still visibly off-balance from earlier.

She smiled. "Just dinner."

The waitress cooed and asked if they wanted wine. Teari nodded. Chel just cleared his throat and muttered, "Whatever she's having."

When the waitress disappeared, Teari leaned back slightly in her chair, surveying him.

"You're jumpy," she said.

"You ambushed me with that dress."

"That's not why you're jumpy. People wear dresses all the time."

Chel didn't respond.

The wine came and they each took a sip. Chel barely touched his. Teari's fingers lingered on the stem of her glass.

"Relax," she murmured. "We're being watched."

Chel's eyes flicked up. Sure enough, a group of cooks sat two tables over, pretending not to stare. One of them nodded at Chel with what might've been wary recognition.

Teari reached across the table, resting her hand lightly on his.

He blinked down at it.

"Act like you're married," she said under her breath. "Or I'll start talking about our honeymoon night."

Chel's mouth twitched. "You wouldn't."

Her brows rose. "I absolutely would."

She could feel the heat in his hand now, his fingers tightening just slightly beneath hers. Something passed through his eyes. Amusement. Hunger. Restraint. She wasn't sure.

"Careful," he said. "You're good at pretending."

"I'm not pretending," she replied, voice low. "I'm performing."

The food arrived. Beef tagliata and a creamy potato side-dish. There was salad and fried cheese. The wine loosened the edges of her thoughts just enough to let the heat between them creep closer.

Halfway through the meal, she shifted her leg and

felt Chel's knee brush hers under the table. She didn't move it away.

Neither did he.

She cut a piece of bread, dipped it in oil, and chewed slowly while watching him watch her.

"If we keep this up," she said lightly, "you might start believing it."

Chel didn't answer immediately. He was too busy watching her lips, like he was memorizing the shape of every word.

"I think I already do," he said quietly.

Her breath caught. It was hard to swallow the bread. But she didn't pull away, didn't break eye contact.

Teari just sat there in the flickering candlelight, heart pounding harder than it had in years and wondering what the hell they were doing. She was a pureblooded Angel with a horrific secret and he was a Hellion. There were no two creatures between the realms who did not belong together more than them.

She searched his eyes, so dark they were nearly black. In the sun she could see a hint of brown and gold, but not now. She couldn't stop thinking about the other night when he'd held her close and let her cry. It was the first time she'd ever told a soul those thoughts, and she doubted she ever would again. If she started talking about it, her tongue would become loose and she'd spill secrets she'd never recover from. Some that he'd hate her for. She was beginning to understand the kind of man Chel was, the kind of Hellion; he was one she didn't deserve. He'd most likely kill her when he discovered what she never told him that night on the beach.

"What's wrong?" Chel asked, leaning forward.

She plastered a smile on her face and picked up the wine glass. "Nothing. Everything's fine."

THE WALK HOME WAS QUIET. THERE WAS weight to the silence. It was like Perdido Key was holding its breath and the humans were waiting to see what they would do next.

The town had emptied after dinner. They'd stayed late, drinking and eating until nearly everyone in the sleepy gulf town had seen them together. Lights in windows dimmed, the breeze curling off the gulf just strong enough to kiss her skin and raise goosebumps on Teari's arms. Chel walked beside her with one hand in his jeans pocket, the other brushing hers every few steps.

They didn't speak.

Not at first.

The silence between them wasn't awkward. It was as loaded as a Hellion headed into battle, like every step they took toward the beach house was pulling at some invisible thread wound too tight between them. Teari felt it in her chest. She wondered if he felt it too or if she was living in some twisted delusion.

"That was convincing," Chel finally said, his voice low.

Teari smirked. "I aim to please."

"You do that."

Teari slowed as they hit the edge of the beach path. The sand was soft beneath her sandals, the moonlight casting long silver shadows across the dunes.

"Do you think they believed it?" she asked.

"Yeah. I think they did. I recognized a lot of faces. The cooks even came out to watch us."

She turned to look at him.

He was already watching her.

The wind picked up, brushing sand across her cheek. Teari shivered.

"I should have brought a jacket for you." His fingers skimmed her shoulder.

Teari's breath caught.

Neither of them moved.

His hand hovered near her face.

She could feel the heat of it. She looked up and noticed the beach house was a few yards away. She didn't realize they'd walked so quickly.

"I should go inside," she said quietly, even though her feet didn't move.

"You should," he said, voice rougher than before.

She still didn't move. He stepped closer, so close now that she could smell the salt on his skin, the ghost of wine on his breath. She looked up at him, and he looked at her like she was the only thing he'd ever wanted but didn't know how to keep. That scared the shit out of her.

"Teari..." he began.

But she turned away just fast enough to make it clear she couldn't handle hearing what he was about to say.

Not tonight.

He grabbed her arm and tugged her back until her spine hit his chest. His thick arm wrapped around her middle and anchored her. Chel stood behind her, quiet. Waiting.

"Don't," he whispered in her ear.

She swallowed hard and tried to ignore the feeling of him surrounding her and how much she liked it.

"Please stay," he whispered.

"You like this act?" she asked. "Let's make a pact."

Chel tilted his head, lips to her ear again. His breath fanned her face smelling like wine. "A pact?" He sounded interested.

She turned her head and looked up to meet his eyes. "Once a month. Here on this beach. That's it. Just keep showing up. No pretending, no theatrics, no games. Just..." Her voice dropped. "Real. Messy. Honest."

He nodded once. It took less than a heartbeat for him to decide. "Deal."

The word lingered in the air between them like smoke.

She stared up at him, her heart thudding a little too hard now. "But you need to understand something."

"I'm listening."

"Heed this warning, Hellion. You might just be stepping in a steaming pile of shit. You don't want me. You may think I'm fun or something but... I haven't been right since my hands were chopped off and they gave me all that human blood." Teari held her arms up and her sleeves fell away, showing the faint silvery scars below her elbows. "I felt myself slipping away back then. It was like all that blood filled me with too much humanity. Even after Meg fixed me, it lingers. Sometimes it's too much to take. You don't want to be with me, Chel. I'm a fucking mess."

His fingers touched her jaw and smoothed over her neck. He leaned in. She took his hand and held it up to the moonlight. Her fingers drifted over his own silvery scar. "What happened here?"

"Cut my hand off. Me and Meg were handcuffed together by Alastor. We needed to escape and I found a hatchet." He turned his arm in the moonlight and flexed his fingers. "Jed did a pretty good job reattaching it a few minutes later."

"I'm not whole," she said.

He frowned.

Teari shook her head. "After the war. After my hands were removed from my body." She swallowed. "I feel everything now. Too much. My emotions are out of control. I snap. I shut down. I... cry. I distance myself. I'm *not right*."

Chel stared at the scars.

At her.

Then he said, very softly, "You're more right than anyone I've ever known."

Her breath stilled.

He cupped her cheek with one hand.

"I've watched you bleed for people who would never bleed for you," he murmured. "You think I don't want that kind of heart?"

Teari's lips parted, but no sound came out.

Then Chel leaned down and kissed her. His free arm tightened around her middle, his hand splaying across her belly, holding her tight.

She gripped his forearm. Her body leaned back into his. And for one second, for the span of a flicker between the realms, she let herself believe it was safe to want him back.

When they broke apart, he pressed his forehead to hers, his fingertips ghosted over her neck.

She whispered, "You don't want me, Chel."

He smiled. "That's the worst lie I've ever heard you tell. I thought Angels couldn't lie."

She started walking again, sand crunching beneath her steps.

Chel followed a breath behind.

When they reached the porch, she turned toward him but didn't meet his eyes. "Thanks for dinner."

He nodded.

She reached for the door handle.

"Teari."

She paused.

His voice was soft now. "You don't always have to run."

Chapter 14

Chel lifted his hand to the moonlight and traced the silver scar. Sometimes it ached, but nothing had felt like the moment he'd slammed the hatchet down to free Meg.

A History

Then

Chel stumbled and fell to his knees inside the rune circle on the floor, stuck. Blood dripped from his right wrist. His hand was missing and there was no bandage to stop the bleeding.

Shay gasped, rushing to Chel's side, "What happened?"

Chel's face was pale, pain and fear etched into every line. "Alastor chained us together. He made us rebuild the portals. It was the only way to free Meg." He glanced at the door. "She should have been right behind me."

Jed broke the rune circle on the floor, releasing Chel. The Hellion tipped over on his side and rolled to his back with a groan.

"Um," Shay picked up the giant hand that had fallen out of his pocket. "Is this your hand?" she asked with a gulp.

"Oh yeah," Chel chuckled faintly. "I used a hatchet to cut it off. You should've seen Meg's face."

"Alastor didn't do this to you?" Jed asked.

Chel made a noise of exasperation. "Hell no. I did it." He was staring at the door, expectantly. "She was supposed to be directly behind me. She made me go first." He closed his eyes.

"There's blood everywhere," Shay said.

"The castle is overrun. There's no one left," Chel said, blinking slowly.

Jed kneeled next to Chel, he took the severed hand and lined it up with Chel's wrist, then he chanted words that sounded like beach sand sifting between rocks and shells on a cold night. Tendrils of healing magic sprung from his fingertips and began mending Chel's severed limb. It staunched the bleeding and began knitting the blood vessels, muscle, and bone back together.

Chel winced in pain.

"Sorry," Jed muttered between words.

Shay took Chel's free hand, her touch gentle but firm. "You're safe here, for now," she assured him. "We'll figure out the next move together."

Jed looked at Shay, their eyes meeting in silent understanding. This wasn't just about Chel or Meg, the war in Hell was spilling over into the Earthen plane, and they couldn't ignore it any longer. They had precious cargo to keep safe. More creatures were on the Earthen plane than ever before now that word had spread about the double auras. And now there was a Hellion, battered and broken. Shay glanced at his tattered leathery wings. They shouldn't be visible on the Earthen plane, but Shay was looking right at them which meant the Veil was thinning considerably.

"Can you get the med kit?" Jed asked Shay.

She nodded and got up to retrieve it, her mind racing.

Chel closed his eyes, finally allowing himself a moment of respite. He took deep breaths, opening his eyes again when Shay settled next to him and passed Jed items from the med kit. Jed wrapped Chel's wrist and hand then splinted it. Chel gave him a questioning look.

"The magic is good, but I've never done that before." He folded Chel's arm against the Hellion's chest. "Just to be safe. You'll be sore."

Chel wiggled his fingers. "Seems to have worked."

Light footsteps shuffled from behind a bookshelf.

"Who's there?" Shay asked, squinting in the darkness.

The girl walked out; Rue with her dark hair mussed and pajamas wrinkled. "I heard voices."

Chel's eyes went wide and he struggled to sit up. "Are they both here?"

Jed pressed a hand on Chel's shoulder, preventing him from getting up. "Easy."

"You shouldn't be out here," Shay warned. "What if it was a Demon, one of the bad ones?"

Rue stared at Chel. "But I know him. He's not bad."

Tears glistened in the old Hellion's eyes as he reached toward Rue. "Your momma hid you well. Is your brother here also?"

Rue nodded. "He's asleep. He'll sleep through anything."

Jed made a face. "The only problem is, now you're stuck here too."

"No," Chel argued. "I have to get back out there and find Meg."

Jed shook his head. "No, you're not leaving until we have some more answers. Meg didn't want a soul to know about this place. Now you're here."

"She sent me here. She said I'd find friends." Chel rubbed his face with his good hand.

"Can't risk it," Jed said, magic crackling from his fingertips. "We don't have the resources to fight Hell's war here. We'll find another way to get Meg."

Chel nodded, understanding.

Jed placed a reassuring hand on Chel's shoulder. "Rest. Recover."

CHAPTER 15

More History

Then: The Fast-Zombie War

MEG

Teari runs, leaps and—something grabs her. Gray arms tug at her. She screams and struggles until she finds her weapon and frees herself by hacking wildly, then launches herself into the air again.

I dash for the tree. Sparrow follows. So do the dead. They move faster than I remember. Their speed is like a bad dream. Maybe it's the drugs from the party?

"Help me reach," I say, motioning to Sparrow. He lifts me and tosses me up like I weigh nothing. I grab a branch and swing my leg over the side, straddling it. "Come up." I motion for Sparrow to follow. He assesses the brick wall and backs up. The dead are getting closer. Too close. Sparrow runs a few steps and leaps to the top of the wall but one of the dead grab his leg, then another, and another. He groans as they tug, jaws snapping.

"No!" I scream. This isn't supposed to happen. How could this happen? "Teari!" I shout.

I glance back. Teari is on her way, flying at warp speed. She's going to slam into us.

"Slow down!" I shout.

She's gripping her injured arm, her blade glowing in her opposite hand. She lands shakily on the top of the wall next to Sparrow. She grabs his arm and pulls him up the wall. Sparrow kicks off the dead and stands, gripping a branch above his head to steady himself.

"What the fuck just happened?" I ask.

Teari holds up her hand and I notice the rotting teeth marks. Blood drips out of the wound and down to her elbow in dark red rivulets.

"Oh no," I say.

Blackness starts going up her arm, following the outline of her veins.

"Can you heal yourself?" I ask.

Teari's a healer, that's what she's always done; used her Angel magic to heal me and others.

"I've never tried on something like this," Teari says as she closes her eyes and holds her uninjured hand over the wound. She shakes her head, defeated. "I can't."

"You have to," I urge.

"It won't work on this," she says, giving up. "Do you have an extra shirt?"

"Yeah." I move to standing on the giant branch and wobble to my bag that's stuck in the vee of the tree. I never thought to bring a med kit. I unzip the bag and pull out my spare T-shirt.

Teari moves closer to me. "Are you ready?" Sweat is dripping down her perfect face.

"For what?"

In a quick movement she holds out her injured arm and slices it off above the elbow with her blade.

"What in the hell?" I scream.

"Wrap it!" Teari shouts back. "Don't let me bleed out! Hurry up!"

Blood is spurting out, drawing the dead closer to us. They collect along the brick wall. I look to Sparrow. His eyes are on the blood. I've seen that look before.

"Can't you stop it?" I ask.

"You know how you can't poof when you're injured? Similar thing here. Too much energy being used. Forget about my healing powers, we're running on pure science and bog witchcraft until this heals."

"Well this sucks." My fingers fumble with wrapping her stump. My stomach growls. I pause to focus and control the bloodlust.

"Wrap it tighter!" Teari shouts. "You must stop the bleeding. You have to squeeze the arteries."

I wrap my T-shirt around the remaining half of her

arm and stretch it, tying the sleeves. Blood soaks through and drips down the wall.

The dead scramble, licking the bricks and rubbing their faces on it.

"Umm..." a strange thought crosses my mind, probably from too many horror movies and supernatural TV shows. "Teari, what is your blood going to do to them?"

"Huh?" she asks. She's looking really pale.

"Your Angel blood," I specify. "What does Angel blood do to walking corpses on the Earthen plane?"

"Never had the pleasure of coming across that problem," she mutters, her voice weak. "Do you think you could fly us out of here?" Teari asks.

"I can't fly," I say.

Teari makes a face.

We both look at Sparrow. He's watching the dead corpses lick the bricks. I scan the trickles of blood and notice one coming from under his boot.

Shit. Shit. Shit.

I move across the wall, steadying myself by gripping a tree branch overhead.

I bend down and pull up Sparrow's pant leg. There's a large chunk of flesh missing and blood streaming down his leg.

I want to puke. I want to poof the fuck back to Hell so I can be safe in my little castle with my group of Hellions to protect me.

"What's wrong?" Teari asks.

We've been in some whacked out situations, but this is by far the worst.

"He's bit," I say.

"Cut it off," Teari says. "Cut off the bitten limb."

"It's his leg!" I shout. "You want me to cut his leg off?"

"Yes!" Teari screams back at me. "Get us the hell out of here or cut his leg off!" She leans into the tree, breathing heavy.

Sparrow growls. "You will not cut off my leg," he says.

"What did he say?" Teari asks.

"He said I can't cut off his fucking leg," I reply. "So what would you like me to do now?"

"Get us out of here, Meg!" Teari says.

Then: The End of the Fast-Zombie War

Still Meg.

The hospital is still open, the barricades and military thinned to a single crew. The parking lot has a few more cars in it than last time. I walk to the emergency room doors and go inside.

"There is only one inpatient," the lady at the desk says and gives me directions to the room.

The elevator works. I take it to the second floor and pass empty rooms until I get to the big corner one.

I knock on the door before pushing it open.

Teari is sitting in a chair eating hospital food.

"You left me in Scranton, Pennsylvania," Teari scowls. "Of all places."

"What's wrong with Scranton?" I ask, looking out the window.

"It's cold." Teari throws her blankets off her legs and walks toward a cupboard on the wall. Using the nubs of her arms, she opens the cupboard with a rope that's tied around the handle and pulls out her clothes. "Help me get out of this disgusting gown."

I pat my pack. "I brought you clean clothes."

"I hope they're not hand me downs from you. You're much shorter than I am. I like my pants to cover my ankles."

"Beggars can't be choosers." I unzip my bag and pull out the clothes. "I actually stopped at Wal-Mart before coming here. They didn't have a women's big and tall section, but the men's had some good choices."

"Ugh," Teari scoffs.

I'm sure she's not thrilled to slum it in cheap clothes. She's always been dressed to the nines or in expensive combat gear. T-shirts and sweats don't quite compare.

Teari tries to take the bag from my hand. Since she's got no fingers, I drop the bag on the bed and sort through it, laying out all the items I bought for her. She motions to a few pieces. "I'm going to need some help," she says holding up her arms.

I untie the hospital gown and leave it loose.

"I thought you'd love these grannie panties," I joke as I hold out the underwear for her to step into. "And these big white socks are straight out of 1986. It's all they had. I promise." I kneel and hold the socks open for her to put her feet into. She picked out a pair of loose sweatpants. I hold them open for her to step into.

"Don't tie them," Teari warns. "I can't do the ties."

I nod and gather the T-shirt, putting it over her head before pulling the hospital gown away. The nurses in Gouverneur taught me how to get dressed like that. After, I help her into a zip-up hoodie.

"You want me to roll the sleeves?" I ask. The sleeve fabric just sways loose, unfilled because of her missing hands.

She shakes her head. "I'm just going to the bathroom before we go," Teari says.

I sit in a chair by the window and wait for her. I can't imagine going to the bathroom without hands. I wonder if she's drip-drying. My questions are answered when I hear her sniff and hiccup, doing her best to cry softly.

I shift in my chair, uncomfortable with the crying Angel. Comforting someone is not my strong suit. Heck, I don't think I've ever comforted a person in my life, at least nothing more than a few pats on the back from an arm's length away.

Teari finally leaves the bathroom. I avoid looking at

her face. I don't want her to feel like she has to explain the puffy eyes or redness.

"Get me the heck out of here," Teari says.

I hold up a finger. "Shoes. We almost forgot shoes."

"The hospital slippers are tempting," Teari says. "I can't really tie any laces."

"But I've got these." I open another bag and hold up a pair of slides. "Easy." I drop them on the floor in front of her.

I show her the way out and find a car in the parking lot with the keys still in it. It was too easy, but I guess someone on the Earthen plane wants me to win today. I'll take a win after all that's happened.

I open the door for Teari, close it, then go to the driver's side. It's an old Camry with plenty of legroom. Never thought I'd see myself driving an import. I close her door and survey the parking lot. I'm not sure what God looks like. Not sure this was left by him. I was told he's been gone for a long time... seems someone is offering guidance here. Probably eager to get me to leave.

After turning the ignition, I pull away from the hospital and head for the highway.

"What happened to your magical healing powers?" I ask.

"Too many blood transfusions. It will come back after a while." She holds up her hands. "I hope. The bones aren't done healing. Can't do much until I'm in tip top shape."

I guess that's what seems so different about her. She's lost some of her grace in the blood loss.

I fill her in on the shit show she missed while I abandoned her on the Earthen plane. I leave out a few details: Thrush, Nightingale's death, and my father being imprisoned. There will be time for that later.

"Sparrow's still a zombie," I say.

"Did he drink my blood?" Teari asks.

"He bit you. I'm not sure about the blood drinking part."

"My blood could heal him."

"Or not..." I warn.

"I can't give any now," she says. "What I have now is mostly donor. Billy-Bob Jenkins and Laura Doone don't have much in the way of angelic healing powers."

Teari sat on the edge of her bed. There was no balcony in her room. No extra furnishings. There were plenty of clothes and a variety of prosthetic limbs Noah had brought her to try. She stared at her arms; the nub at the wrist, the nub at the elbow. Nothing had prepared her for this. Not the decades of training with the Legion or the decades of being King Gabriel's personal healer. It was rare for an Angel to lose a limb for good. They always grew back. Teari had some practice with that magic. But now, human blood pumped through her veins. It had altered her, stopped her powers. She'd told Meg they would come back but to be completely honest, Teari wasn't sure. And the

thought of being limbless for the rest of her time was too much to handle.

Teari was trapped within a desolate chamber of despair. Surrounding her were frigid walls that echoed with the silence of abandonment. The air hung heavy with oppressive darkness, suffocating any flicker of hope that dared to linger. Teari had once soared among the Seven Kingdoms of Heaven, a radiant beacon of grace, her purpose to heal and protect. Now, her wings weighed heavy with the burden of her own suffering, rendered powerless by the loss of her hands. Tears streaked down her ashen cheeks, the remnants of a shattered spirit. Every breath was a struggle as if the very air had turned against her. Her wounds throbbed, a constant reminder of the Fast-Zombie War. Although, from her hospital bed on the Earthen plane, she hadn't seen the worst of it.

Teari glanced at the four walls of her room. There was no window. And she was sure she knew why Meg hadn't given her a window. The urge to jump out it and plunge to the rocks below was strong. Or... maybe it was glamour. Teari stood and walked toward the exterior wall. She rubbed her arms across the green plaster searching for something, anything. Perhaps something hidden that she couldn't see with the naked eye. She'd take any way out she could find. Teari stood on her toes, crouched on the ground, pressed her cheek to the walls, and inspected every inch of the room. She shoved the bed away from the wall with her shoulder and kept going.

"Let me out," Teari whispered. Something was surging

in her chest, a feeling of panic she'd never felt before. She tore through the room, looking for an escape. She shoved and kicked, she tipped over the nightstand, shoved the small bed aside. The scabbed scars on her arms opened and oozed blood and serous fluid.

Is this how Meg and Nightingale felt all those times they'd been locked up? Empty and cold? Sad and lonely? Pissed off and hating the world?

Maybe Nightingale could help her. Night frequented the Astral plane but the only way for Teari to get there was to sleep. She lay on the floor, in the far corner, hidden by the disheveled room, and closed her eyes.

THEN: AFTER THE FAST-ZOMBIE WAR

FORCING ONESELF TO DREAM IS NEVER EASY. Teari wasn't sure how long she lay on the floor; there wasn't sunlight drifting across a window to give her an estimate of the passing time, there were no clocks, she heard no footsteps in the hallway outside her door. Her eyes felt gritty and her eyelids restless. Her body didn't want to sleep, and her mind was a flurry of coercive thoughts as she tried her best to convince herself that she was tired. When she finally drifted off to sleep, her dreams were nightmares–they had been since she lost her hands. The fast-zombies forever chased her. Their snapping jaws and gnarled teeth threatened to bite the few limbs she had left. Sparrow was there and he was nothing she remembered. He bit her over and over again. He didn't hold back; he didn't recognize her as the healer and Legion guard who had fought by his side, who had once desired him. Nightingale didn't save her. She didn't show up and interrupt the nightmares like she used to. There was only radio silence from the Astral.

Teari woke a few hours later. Her shoulders ached, her wings ached, and her wounds had scabbed over again leaving a crust over the incision scars where the doctors on the Earthen plane had done their best to stitch her back together. It wasn't their fault that her arms looked like Frankenstein. They were doing the best they could. She didn't forget that if the group of them hadn't encountered the National Guard in Pennsylvania, she'd surely be dead, and her soul lost. Teari forced herself to thank her lucky stars every day, but it felt like a lie. She didn't feel lucky and most days, she'd wished she'd just died on the Earthen plane instead of living like this.

A single tear slid down her cheek. If Nightingale wasn't in the Astral, where was she? Teari knew she'd been gone from the Seven Kingdoms of Heaven for weeks. Without a word and unable to reach Gabriel or anyone else, she was certain Nightingale would come looking for answers in her dreams. But she didn't. And Teari wasn't sure what that meant.

Meg was keeping something from her. They all were.

"Teari?" a familiar voice asked.

She didn't hear a door open so it could only be Noah. He was a thing of the Astral but tethered to Meg's soul by lifelong friendship and sacrifice. It was hard to remember with his boyish good looks and habit for pranks and dirty jokes.

"What?" Teari asked from the cover she currently occupied, unmoving; not giving Noah an idea of where she was.

"I need your help." Furniture scraped across the tile floor as he followed her voice. "What the heck happened in here? It's a mess."

"Nothing." Teari rolled onto her back and stared at the ceiling. She blew a small white feather off her face. "Can you just go away?"

"Nope." Noah appeared over Teari. "We got a problem downstairs. The biggest of problems."

"Meg ordered me not to leave this room," Teari reminded him. "So I'm going to stay here." Teari rested her forearm on her head but moved immediately. It was hard to get comfortable in any position.

"Yeah, about that," he reached down and grabbed Teari's upper arms, tugging her to stand. "You want one of the prosthetics?"

"I'm not going anywhere," Teari said as she stood. Her body was limp, lacking muscle tone like a doll.

Noah was already opening her door.

"I don't like the prosthetics." She waved her arms. "They're uncomfortable."

THEN: AFTER THE FAST-ZOMBIE WAR

MEG

I open the door to the chapel and find Teari sitting in a chair and staring at the wall.

"How's it going?" I ask, closing the door and sitting next to her.

"What do you want, Meg?" Teari seems suspicious.

I lean back and pull the snowy owl feather out of my pocket. "I have something for you. Something that I think will help."

Teari holds up her nubbed arms. She clicks the hooks of the prostheses. "These puppies help me more and more every day."

"Then why are you sitting in here alone?"

She makes a face. "It's hard seeing Nightingale like she is."

"At least we get more time."

"True," Teari says. She notices the feather in my hand. "What's that?"

I grab her arm, pull it straight, and stab the quill into her soft skin.

"Meg!" Teari screams. "What are you doing?"

The quill empties of Raphael's blood and I set the

feather on her lap. Teari's face turns red. She knocks off the prostheses, leans back on the couch, and holds up her nubs crossed on her chest. Slowly, her arms start growing. There's a commotion in the room as Jed and Shay and a few Hellions shove open the door.

"I knew we couldn't trust you in here. What did you do?" Jed asks me.

"Oh, just performing a miracle," I say. "But I'm hurt, really. Why must you always assume the worst of me?"

Jed walks over to Teari as her arms elongate into hands and fingers.

"I always assume you're up to some shit," Jed says. "But this is better than I was anticipating." He jabs me in the shoulder, playfully.

I fake a yawn and rub my arm, holding in a wince.

Teari's fingers have grown back. She waves her hands in front of her face, disbelieving.

"Oh my God," Teari exclaims as she stands. "This is the best." She runs toward me, throwing her arms around my neck and hugging me too tightly. "Thank you, Meg."

"It was nothing." I pat her back awkwardly.

THEN: JUST BEFORE THE WAR WITH LUCIFER

"Healer," the Deacon called.

Teari turned.

"Why did you leave the Legion?" he asked. "You were a warrior once."

Teari glanced at the wall and collected her thoughts. "The true battle is not in taking lives, but in saving them. I seek redemption in healing rather than bloodshed."

The Deacon nodded in approval. "That's what I thought," he whispered.

CHAPTER 16

Now

THE KISS STILL LINGERED ON CHEL'S LIPS. A hint of wine, salt, warmth, the ache of something he never thought he'd have. For years he'd dreamed of having Teari at his side and now she was finally there, even if it was for pretend. But, they'd made a promise to meet. At least he had that. Hope.

Teari was inside the beach house and damn if he didn't want to follow her. He closed his eyes and thought of her taking off that blue dress. It was the color of the sky before a storm.

A prickle flittered across the back of his neck. He turned his head slowly toward the dunes. Movement. Not wind. Not animal. A figure. Watching. And gone in the next blink. Chel's entire body shifted. The Hellion coiled tight, pulling away from the softness he'd allowed for one fragile moment.

"I see you," he murmured.

Chel sprinted up the slope of the dune, boots kicking up sand, blood pounding in his ears. The moon cut sharp shadows across the ridgeline, and for a second he saw the figure again. Long-limbed, graceful.

Angel.

Chel's hands curled into fists, knuckles creaking.

Our cover's blown.

He didn't care what happened to him. But if the Angel had seen Teari, if it knew who she really was, this could all unravel before they were ready.

He crested the dune in a blur and caught another glimpse of the figure disappearing between two beach houses near the old boardwalk.

Chel gave chase. His breath stayed steady, his footsteps light. He didn't draw a weapon but he was already calculating how many ribs he'd break if it came to that.

The figure darted down the narrow alley between buildings, silent and fast. Chel followed without hesitation, rounding the corner. Empty. Nothing but shadow and silence.

Chel swore under his breath and scanned the space again. There were no broken footprints in the sand, no rustling cloth, no divine shimmer left behind. But the presence lingered. There was a pressure in the air, the same sickening weight he'd felt that night at the restaurant. He turned slowly, pulse sharp.

"You come near her," he said aloud, "I will salt the Earthen plane with your bones."

There was no response, just the hiss of the tide. Chel stood in that silence for a long time then turned and walked back toward the beach house, eyes still scanning, hands still clenched. Tonight something had changed.

Chapter 17

After the date, the beach house felt too small and cramped. Teari needed space. And goddammit, she needed her phone to stop ringing. So she went to see her father.

Transversing the realm between the Earthen Plane and the Seven Kingdoms of Heaven was always the same. Her lungs shrank and her heartbeat dulled like the realm itself was trying to scrub her down to the bone and make her pure again. Good luck with that. Teari might be an Angel but her purity had been destroyed a long time ago.

She stepped out of the shimmer and onto polished marble, the air sharp with sanctified cold. And it was bright. Everything in her father's kingdom was too white, too clean, too quiet. Deception. The halls gleamed like polished bone, the ceilings arched high and hollow. Her footsteps echoed as she moved down the corridor.

His people saw her. The sentinels. The attendants.

The lesser Angels. The servants. But none of them said a word to her. No one dared. She was the black sheep, the runaway. She wasn't welcome here by some. She never had been because they saw the act of her leaving her father's kingdom to join the Archangel Gabriel as traitorous. Another title to add to the tally.

Two massive gold-inlaid doors stood at the end of the corridor. They opened without her touching them.

Her father's chambers were as she remembered; light pouring through stained glass windows, velvet furniture, and dark walls. In the center of the room, seated on a high-backed chair carved from something that looked like ivory, was the Archangel himself. Tall. Impossibly still. A wolf in white wings.

"Daughter," he said without rising. "I've been calling."

She stepped forward, spine straight. "You're becoming desperate." She held up her phone and the screen showed eighty-four missed calls.

"You took your time."

"I am on leave." She reminded him.

He rose, robes trailing soundlessly across the floor. "You are never on leave from this bloodline."

Teari's jaw tightened. "You don't own me."

He stood and stepped close enough for her to see the fine lines around his eyes. It did make him look handsome, as though he spent a lot of time smiling. If only everyone else knew.

"You walk through my doors reeking of the Earthen plane and... Hellion." His voice was low. Dangerous. "You think I haven't heard the rumors? You think I haven't seen?"

Teari didn't blink. "What I do is none of your business."

He laughed. "You will not soil this bloodline."

"Father. You have no say."

"The judges of Babylon will. They'll have a lot to say about what you've been up to. I have proof."

"Cut to the chase. You did not call me here about this. I'm guessing you are dragging me into another shit storm. Is that why you've called me? You want me to clean up another mess that you've created?"

He smiled, cold and triumphant. "A soldier of mine overstepped. I need it... erased. Quietly."

"In Perdido Key?" she asked. Her tone was even, but her heart pounded. The moment Chel mentioned what he'd discovered, she knew.

His eyes sharpened. "I saw you with that creature. Disgusting."

She said nothing but realized that it wasn't a soldier. It was him. Again.

"Gabriel sent me on leave," she said carefully. "Where I spend my free time is none of your concern."

"You're not *his*." His voice cracked like thunder. "You are mine."

Teari's stomach curled.

"I gave you life," he said, stepping closer. "I gave you

power. And yet you run off with Hellion trash, pretending to be mortal. You ignore me for that beast."

Her breath caught. He knew. Of course he knew. She said nothing. He circled her now, his wings dragging like a net across the floor.

"You will go back to Perdido Key and erase what's left of my mistake. Quietly. Completely. Do it, and I won't tell Babylon about all the innocent, young souls you've sent away. I have decades of proof. Enough to have you banished forever."

"No," she said, throat dry. She hated him. Hated everything about this place and her bloodline.

"You will not refuse." He smiled and she wanted to puke.

She turned slowly, face calm. But inside, her soul was already screaming. Screaming and panicking like a caged animal. There was no way out.

CHAPTER 18

———

The beach house was quiet when she stepped through the door, the scent of sea salt and old wood welcoming. She'd missed it. Chel wasn't in the kitchen or the living room.

Teari dropped her bag by the couch. Her heart still ached from her father's demands. Again. She wanted to scrub every inch of her body in a boiling shower. Even if she were to bathe in bleach, nothing was strong enough to erase the hate flooding through her body.

She didn't notice Chel watching her until he spoke.

"I thought you left." A deep voice broke through the silence.

She paused in the hallway.

"I mean really left," he continued. "Like maybe the other night scared you off."

Teari turned slowly. "I just needed space."

Chel didn't look angry. Just... uncertain. And that

was somehow worse in her mind. He'd seemed very certain the other night. And strong and... what was wrong with her? She knew this was more than pretend. And she was going to break his heart, if he didn't break hers. This wouldn't work out, not even a little bit.

"You didn't leave a note," he added. "You didn't answer my text." A weak smile quirked his lips. "Going back to your old ways of avoiding me? I'm hurt, Angel." He patted a large hand over the center of his chest.

"I didn't think I had to." Her voice came out sharper than intended. She sighed and softened. "Sorry. I wasn't running. I just needed to think. I needed space."

His gaze searched her. "Did you figure it out?"

"No," she admitted. "Not even close."

Chel raised an eyebrow. "Where did you go?"

"To see my father." She shrugged.

"Did it work?"

She arched a brow. "He stopped calling." She held up her phone and the screen had no notifications–for today at least.

Chel pushed off the doorway where he was leaning and crossed the room slowly. "You're back. So... maybe."

Teari shifted her weight. Her shoulders felt tight under her shirt. Her mind wouldn't stop racing. Her secrets were tangled with his mission. There was no way out of this without someone getting hurt.

He stopped just in front of her. "You're allowed to be scared."

She blinked at him. "I'm not scared."

"I know I'm intense. I know the other night got heated." He scratched the back of his neck. "Look, I just... I didn't want to end it on that note."

"It didn't end," she said softly. "It paused."

His eyes lit just a little. "Can I un-pause it?"

Teari smirked. "That depends."

He took a breath. "On whether you'll go on another date with me?"

She blinked. "Another?" What was wrong with this guy? He had a death wish and it started with her.

"Full throttle this time. Not just undercover work." He gave a slight smile. "You pick the dress. I'll pick the place. No lies, no cover story. Just us."

Her heart thudded once, hard. "Do you think you can handle that?"

Teari hesitated, then nodded slowly. "Alright. One more date." She'd put an end to it. She'd let him down easy so he could go on and live his life and so she didn't drag him down with her.

Chel grinned like she'd agreed to so much more.

Yes. She was going to break his heart and she hated herself for it. Maybe if things were different this could work. Maybe if she wasn't her father's daughter or wasn't even an Angel. Maybe if she'd never absorbed an excess of emotion and humanity from all that blood the hospital had given her. One more date, then she'd tell him.

CHAPTER 19

Planning battles? Easy.

Navigating ambushes? Child's play.

Setting up a romantic date for an Angel who made your heart ache and your bones hum?

Impossible. Nearly impossible. He'd done this once before and it went smoothly. He could do it again. No big deal.

Chel stood barefoot in the kitchen, elbows braced on the counter, phone in one hand, frustration brewing like a storm behind his eyes. There were too many tabs open, literal ones on the screen and metaphorical ones in his mind.

"Top 10 date ideas for Florida coast."

"Best romantic restaurants near Perdido Key."

"Do Angels like seafood?"

He scrubbed a hand down his face. This was not his domain. If it involved blood, steel, or training new

Hellion recruits, sure. But flowers and ambiance? Maybe he should call Remington or Rue. They'd know what to do.

He tapped his phone again and opened the menu of the first restaurant that had candles in the photos. Too many negative reviews. Next. Too loud. Next. Too many humans in polo shirts. Next.

He glanced toward the hallway and Teari's closed bedroom door. She hadn't said anything else since she agreed to the date, just disappeared again with a book under her arm and a strange look in her eyes.

Chel sighed and returned to scrolling.

What would she want?

Quiet. Warm. Not too crowded. Maybe something close to the water, something soft. Something new.

He made a note to bring the blanket from the beach house. Worst case, they could picnic on the sand. He'd bring dessert and that wine she liked from the Italian restaurant.

A simple backup plan. He could stash it in the dunes for their walk home.

Finally, he settled on a place called *Mariner's Key*, an older restaurant with good reviews and string lights over the patio. It had seafood and pasta and wouldn't make Meg's credit card twitch. Casual dress. Ocean view. Quiet corner booths. Perfect. Or close enough.

He tapped to reserve a table, hesitated, then deleted the name he entered. Instead of putting it under *Chel*, he wrote: *C & T, Table for Two*.

"Hell's bells," he muttered. "I'm becoming sentimental."

From the other room, the faint sound of a page turning echoed.

He took that as a good omen.

The restaurant sat at the edge of the sand, tucked under a canopy of string lights and ivy-covered latticework. The murmur of the gulf drifted up from the shoreline, just loud enough to veil conversations from surrounding tables. The tablecloth was linen. The water glasses sparkled. And Chel looked wildly out of place. He was too big, too darkly dressed. He didn't realize the restaurant was so small from the pictures. The double booth was barely wide enough to contain his shoulders. He'd knocked over an umbrella stand as soon as they entered. The tight dining made him so uncomfortable he couldn't relax.

Teari appeared to be biting back a smile as she watched him study the menu like it was a battlefield map. He hadn't touched the complimentary bread. He was too uncomfortable to eat.

She leaned over and whispered, "You know you're allowed to relax, right?"

Chel blinked up at her. "I'm relaxed."

"You're holding your knife like it insulted your mother."

He looked down. "Force of habit. Knives sometimes do that."

She laughed, and that sound eased something tight in his chest.

Dinner came and went slowly, one small plate after another, shared between quiet glances and brief touches. Her foot brushed his once under the table. The second time, he didn't move away. He offered her a bite of his grilled snapper, and when she licked lemon from her finger afterward, he had to grip his wine glass to ground himself.

Teari looked breathtaking. Her hair caught the light just enough to glow around the edges. The pale blue dress she wore was modest but soft in a way that made Chel's mouth go dry. She had never looked more mortal, and he had never wanted anything more in his life than to continue looking at her like this.

He leaned forward. "You've been quiet." He said gently, "Since you came back from your father's."

She blinked at him, fork halfway to her mouth. A shadow passed behind her eyes.

"If something happened—"

"It was nothing," she interrupted quickly, too quickly. She set her fork down with a little too much care. "He's just... predictable."

Chel didn't push. Not yet. But he tilted his head, his eyes steady. "Nothing important?"

She offered him a brittle smile, the kind that tried too hard to seem easy. "Exactly. Just the usual snake pit of chaos. You know how Archangels can be. Everything is an emergency."

Chel leaned back in his seat and studied her; the tension in her shoulders, the way she twisted the stem of her glass. She was hiding something. But he'd learned with Teari that pressing too hard only made her retreat further.

So instead, he smiled and said, "Well, if it becomes important, you can tell me."

Teari glanced up sharply, surprised by the gentleness in his voice. Then she looked down, shoulders softening.

"Okay," she said, quiet. "Thank you."

And just like that, the moment passed.

Chel reached across the table and let his fingers brush hers.

"You don't need to run again," he said softly.

Teari looked up, lips parting.

She didn't say anything.

But she didn't pull away either.

They'd been walking out, Teari's arm draped across his inner elbow, the tension between them finally gone. Chel could breathe easily outside of the cramped restaurant. Also, the four glasses of wine helped.

"Wait a second," a waitress called from behind the podium. "I know you!"

Teari froze. Chel felt her arm go limp.

The woman trotted forward, her apron smudged with marinara. "You were a nurse. My sister delivered the other day. It was awful, the baby was stillborn..." Her smile faltered but then lit again. "But you were there. I remember you. You held my sister's hand while the doctors tried to revive the baby. You told her she wasn't alone."

Teari's head was shaking before the woman even finished. "No," she said, voice tight. "I think you have me confused with someone else."

The waitress frowned. "No, I remember. Hang on. Wait right here, I have a photo from the hospital." She started digging for her phone.

Teari's breath hitched. Chel felt her tremble.

"I have to go," Teari muttered, voice thin.

Chel turned to her, unease spreading through his chest.

"Don't—" she whispered, yanking her arm free as he reached for her. She bolted, dress fluttering in the breeze as she darted into the night.

Chel stared after her. He wasn't sure what was happening–this was a different kind of battlefield.

Behind him, the hostess whistled under her breath. "Lover's quarrel?"

He didn't respond, just turned slowly as the waitress returned, phone extended.

"See?" she said, holding it up.

Chel leaned in.

The image was grainy, taken from across the hospital room, but unmistakable. Teari stood near the bed in scrubs, her hand on the shoulder of a sobbing woman. Her expression was anguished, haunted, and matched the look she wore the other night when she'd cried on the beach.

He swallowed hard.

"What was she doing there?" he murmured.

The waitress looked confused. "Working, I think."

Chel didn't reply. He ran out the door. The wind had picked up outside. The moonlight glinted off the waves as he spotted her, barefoot, sprinting toward the surf, dress gathered in her fists. She didn't look back.

"Teari!" he shouted.

She didn't stop.

The water crashed around her ankles, then her knees. She went deeper.

"Wait! stop!" he shouted.

She didn't.

And then she was gone, swallowed by the gulf.

Chel stumbled after her, chest heaving. He kicked off his shoes and ran in after her. Wherever she was going, the portal she activated would take him too. He wasn't going to let her run from this. He wasn't sure why she was in that hospital room or how she was connected to whatever was going on here, but he was going to make her face it. And he'd be by her side. No more secrets.

The waves hissed as if mocking. Chel swam hard, wishing he had his wings in this realm so he could fly over the ocean until he found her and pluck her from the water. But he didn't have wings, just his strength. He swam harder, sure that he saw her head bobbing in the distance. If she'd activated a portal, it should have pulled them away by now. It didn't.

He paused, treading water, frozen, breathless, staring into the dark water. No. The sea had taken her somewhere else. He dove underwater, salt burning his eyes. He couldn't see a thing with just the moonlight. There was nothing. He was too late.

Chapter 20

Water was a conduit. A portal between realms. The gulf was the largest portal on the Earthen plane. But now? Now it was just cold. Salt burned Teari's eyes as she dove, kicking hard, deeper into the black beneath the moonlight. The surface dimmed and blurred above her.

Take me home. Please. Please. She was a coward, such a coward, and she hated herself for it. She hated this life and everything about her existence. She was an Angel and she wasn't even decent.

She opened her mouth, whispering the ancient words she'd once used to open the rift between realms and make stone portals shimmer to life. Nothing happened. No shimmer. No pull. No heat of Babylon. Just water. And pressure. And the sudden, terrifying certainty that the gulf wasn't listening. This conduit was broken, or rejecting her.

She kicked harder, the dress tangling around her legs. Her lungs began to burn. She heard Chel's voice as he shouted to her. She swam harder, trying to get farther from him. She had to put distance between them or she'd run right back to him. She was hanging on by a thread.

Teari reached out, blindly groping for the slipstream, for the signature warmth that signaled a celestial gateway. All she felt was salt. Cold. Silence. A jolt of panic seized her.

She thought of Chel, his hand reaching for her, his voice behind her, calling her name. That confused, hurt look in his eyes. He didn't know what he'd done wrong. He never did. He had offered her kindness and hope. A future. He'd done nothing wrong. It was all her.

She had run from it. She couldn't face him. She swam harder until her muscles ached and burned and the moon slipped behind the clouds. Something rubbed against her foot. Her lungs spasmed. A wave crashed over her head, dragging her under.

She held her breath and tried again, clawing at the water, begging it to open. Another chant, older this time, one that scraped her throat and echoed in her skull. Her mouth filled with sea water. Something tightened on her leg and tugged her down.

It wasn't a passage. It wasn't a portal. No Heaven. No Hell. Only the relentless, crushing pressure. And then her body gave out. She stopped swimming. Her limbs went numb. The last bubbles of air slipped from her mouth. Her vision narrowed to specks of silver.

At least I won't have to keep pretending. For a moment she'd felt warmth and peace in letting go. Her lungs no longer burned. Her shoulders no longer ached from the weight of dastardly duty. She could let go. It was fine. This was fine. No more feelings. No more despair. No more hiding. Darkness folded over her like a funeral shroud.

And then—a snap of force. Not the warmth of Heaven. Not the radiant hum of Gabriel's gates. But *something*. Something colder. Hungrier. Older. The gulf gave way beneath her, not like a door opening but like a floor collapsing.

She plummeted, falling through currents that turned too fast and too sharp, like razors carving through her skin. There was no light. No sound. Just a *pull*. And then, impact. She hit stone. Teari coughed violently, hacking up seawater, splayed on cold obsidian slick with moss. Her dress clung to her, soaked and torn. Her hands trembled as she pushed herself up on shaking elbows.

The air here was thick and difficult to breath.

She looked up. No sky. No stars. Only a domed ceiling of jagged black rock, veined with something pulsing.

But she wasn't in Heaven. She wasn't in Hell. She definitely wasn't on the Earthen Plane. She hadn't been to the Astral but this did not resemble anything she'd read about.

She was somewhere else.

Somewhere she wasn't meant to be.

Or maybe she *was* meant to be. Maybe this was the place she deserved to be after all she'd done.

CHAPTER 21

THE WAVES CHURNED UNDER MOONLIGHT, frothing white against the sand. Chel stood ankle-deep in the surf, chest heaving, clothes dripping with salt water, eyes scanning the horizon for any sign of her. Nothing. Only dark ocean.

He paced back and forth like an animal ready to pounce, fists clenched at his sides. *Teari was gone.* One second she was running and the next, the gulf swallowed her whole.

He'd seen her slip beneath the surface. He thought she was going to open a portal, vanish through the Veil. But minutes passed. Then more. Nothing had opened.

And now? No ripple. No trace.

Chel stepped further into the water until it lapped at his knees. He cupped his hands around his mouth and roared her name again. "TEARI!"

The waves crashed back in reply. Indifferent. Cold.

He spun and marched up the shore, dripping, cursing. At the edge of the dunes, he pulled out his phone.

His thumb hovered. He thought about calling Meg. About calling the White Horse. But what would he say?

Teari ran. I chased her. She dove into a portal that never opened.

He cursed in Hellspeak, a steady stream of derogatory words that would make a Hellion blush, flinging the useless phone into the sand. It was water-logged. It wouldn't work anyway.

The memory of her face clawed at him; tear-streaked, panicked, full of shame she wouldn't explain.

He replayed the dinner in his mind. The waitress. The photo. The way Teari's face crumbled like paper before she bolted. Whatever she'd been hiding, it wasn't just about her father. It wasn't just about Heaven. It was about the stillborn. About the women. Was she connected to the darkness infecting Perdido Key? She knew something.

Chel ran both hands through his soaked hair. "Dammit, Teari," he muttered.

He turned back to the water, scanning again. Waiting. Hoping.

Nothing.

The wind whipped around him. The moon drifted higher, casting silver light over the endless ocean.

She was gone, and Chel had no idea where to start. But he would find her and make her tell him what exactly was going on. He wouldn't lose her, even if he had to burn down Heaven to do it.

By dawn the bad feeling had rooted behind Chel's sternum. The memory replayed; that long-limbed shape in the dunes watching as he and Teari kissed, grace too smooth for human bones. Angel. If it saw them, it knew. If it knew, it might have intervened when she tried to jump planes.

Did it block the portal? Drag her somewhere else?

He strode back to the beach house, grabbing his phone off the counter where he'd left it to dry and hit Meg's contact.

She answered on the second ring. "Tell me you're not calling before coffee unless something's on fire."

"It might be," Chel said. "Teari's gone."

There was a pause. "Define gone."

"She ran into the ocean. She didn't come back. I waited." His voice roughened. "Hours. The portal never activated from what I could tell."

Meg exhaled, not yet alarmed. "Could've landed off-course. Veil-tides are erratic there."

"No. Something is wrong." Chel paced. "There was an Angel here in town."

"Shit." A rustle; she was moving now. "Consult the

White Horse. If the gulf portal was tampered with, she'll know."

Chel swallowed. "You're not worried?"

"Chel." Her tone softened. "If Teari is alive, she'll fight to get back. If she's captured, she'll make someone regret it. Either way, she's not fragile. Go find her."

The line clicked dead.

He stood in the kitchen a moment longer, staring at the empty space where Teari had left her book open face-down. Then he moved. *If Teari is alive.* She must be alive. How could Meg say such a thing?

He locked every door in the beach house, then slung his pack over his shoulder and rolled the bike out into the morning light. He went to the gas station down the road. As the pump clicked full, footsteps crunched behind him.

He turned. It was one of the cooks from the Italian restaurant, the younger one who'd warned him about "the curse." He had dark hair, sleeves rolled, smoking too early for someone with a shift ahead.

"Morning," the kid said. "Where's your wife?"

Chel's jaw tightened. "She took a walk."

The cook made a face. "Hope that *other* guy didn't find her."

Chel straightened. "What other guy?"

"The one I told you about. Tall. Dressed too nice. All charm, no roots. Dates women, bad things happen, he's got a new girl. Like clockwork." The kid flicked ash, eyes narrowing. "Saw him last night. Thought he was passing through. Guess not."

Blood rushed sharp in Chel's ears.

"Where?" he asked.

"Beach row behind the bait shop. He rents the old Kessler house when he's in town. You can't miss it. Ugly porch swing, blue shutters." The kid hesitated. "Look, I don't want trouble. But if your wife's new? And folks are saying you two just showed up? Keep her close."

Chel nodded once. "Yeah."

He slid his helmet on, kicked the bike to life, and pulled out hard enough to spray grit.

White Horse first. Then Hell. Then wherever the trail bled next. He didn't care if he had to crack open the gulf or drag an Angel out by its pretty white wings. He was getting Teari back come Hell or high water. This was his wife. And he'd waited far too long to get her only to lose her like this.

Chapter 22

The road unspooled, miles of cracked asphalt and fading lane lines passing under the motorcycle's tires. Chel did not stop for gas station coffee or for the diners that made his stomach churn with the memory of undercooked eggs, suspicious sauces, and weeks-long sickness.

The only thing keeping him upright was movement and the icy air whipping past his helmet. The wind tore at his coat, but it did nothing to the cold knot inside his chest. By the time the mountains came into view, his joints ached from gripping the throttle too long. The horizon began to soften with light.

Chel pulled into the familiar stretch of land just as the sun broke over the ridgeline, lighting the ranch in golden light. His motorcycle rumbled as he coasted to a stop in front of Jed and Shay's home.

The front porch creaked.

Shay stepped outside, squinting at him with a steaming mug in hand. Her hair was a mess, and she was wrapped in a wool blanket that trailed behind her like a cloak.

"You look like shit," she called out.

Chel killed the engine and slumped forward on the seat for a beat, helmet in hand. "Been on the road for two days."

"That explains the smell." She took a sip.

Chel looked up sharply. "I've got a big problem. Teari is missing."

"No." Shay's jaw dropped and her face went pale.

Chel swung a leg off the bike and stretched with a wince. "I need to see the White Horse."

Shay nodded toward the pasture. "She's out early. Fog's thin this morning. You want breakfast?"

He shook his head. "Can't eat."

Chel turned and headed toward the misty field beyond the barn.

The sun hadn't fully lifted the fog from the valley. He trudged through dew-soaked grass and brittle fence lines until he saw the familiar shimmer in the mist, eyes too ancient to belong to a simple creature of Earth.

The White Horse waited for him to get closer.

"Teari is missing," Chel said, his voice rough.

The horse dipped her head slightly. "The Veil in the gulf was tampered with. She fell through something that wasn't of my making."

Chel stiffened. "Is she alive?"

The horse regarded him for a long time, dark eyes like glass marbled with galaxies. "The place she landed has been cut off for ages."

"Where is it?" Chel's fists clenched. "I'll go."

"You're not ready yet," she said softly. "You need more answers first."

He cursed under his breath and looked away. "She ran because of something she was hiding." He couldn't finish the thought. "Something happened, I can feel it. She didn't go through a portal. She just disappeared into the ocean. That can't be good."

The White Horse stepped closer. "You chase a flame, Hellion."

"What if she's dead?" Chel's jaw tightened. "She doesn't get to die without telling me why. She doesn't get to die without explaining." He ran a hand through is hair. "She cannot be dead."

"She's not dead. Go find her."

That struck like a hammer.

Chel looked up. "How? Where?"

The White Horse turned toward the trees, mist curling around her form.

Chel stood there in the morning light, alone in the field.

"You should go see Meg next. She has something for you." The White Horse shook her head. "Hurry now, Hellion. You don't want to run out of time."

Chel went still. "I thought you wanted me to investigate what was happening to the humans in Perdido Key?"

"Perhaps these events are connected." The White Horse whinnied. "Seems you've ignited a thread of association. Thank you. Now go."

CHAPTER 23

TEARI'S LUNGS BURNED.

The sea had been endless, black and cold and full of nothing. Just her demons chasing her. Chel was going to find out what she'd been keeping from him, and he'd hate her. Her only penance was the sea. And then, without warning, she'd been torn from it.

She awoke choking on fog. The beach was gone. The sky was gone. She lay on rough stone, damp and cold beneath her cheek, her clothes soaked through. The air felt thick.

Wait... that had already happened, but it repeated like a nightmare.

"Where am I?" Her throat ached.

Her voice echoed too far. The question sounded like it had been spoken in a cathedral of petrified bones.

A figure stepped forward from the mist.

There were no footsteps, just a quiet rustling like pages being turned in an empty library.

The woman was draped in fabric that moved as if underwater. Her face was hidden behind a mask of white bone, and silver threads stitched across her arms like veins.

Teari knew this being at once. She'd read descriptions of these creatures plenty of times. This creature had not been seen in ages. They'd filtered into the background when the Deacons took over balancing the realms.

A Fate.

A weaver.

But these creatures had their own realm, long forgotten as it was.

"I don't belong here," Teari said sharply, trying to rise. Her limbs ached. Her skin prickled with fear.

The Fate tilted her head. "And yet, here you are."

"This is a mistake," Teari snapped. "I was..." Where was she again? Oh, yes, swimming in the ocean, trying to escape the truth and trying to run from the one man who she'd disappoint. She was trying to escape it all.

Escape.

Escape.

Escape.

The idea repeated in her head.

"You relinquished your will to the sea." The Fate's voice was like smoke, dry and soft, curling around Teari's ears. "You asked it to take you. And it did. That is enough."

Teari froze. Her shoulders felt lighter than ever. Her wings were gone.

"I didn't." Her voice caught.

But she had in that moment on the beach with Chel calling after her, the weight of everything crashing down. She'd swam far, hoping that the portal would open and take her home.

It never opened though. And she didn't seem to mind. She was relieved. She hadn't fought to live. Only one thought and that was all it took. She gave up.

"I didn't mean to die," Teari whispered.

"No one ever means to slip through the cracks," the Fate said. "That's why the cracks are there." The Fate was studying her. "You were an Angel. The rules are different for you. One thought is a million. You were given something special, one thought of nonexistence was enough to disappoint what made you."

Teari had wanted something different. A change she'd cried about in Chel's arms. But she never thought... wait.

Did her father do this? Was he in her mind as much as he controlled her life? Sickness swelled in her middle.

"So what is this place?" Teari asked. "Limbo? Hell?"

The Fate didn't answer.

Teari stood on shaking legs. "Am I truly dead?"

"You are *between*." The mask tilted again. "You have not been judged for death. You linger. But you cannot leave without penance. Leaving costs a hefty price."

Purgatory. Teari squared her shoulders. She was in

Purgatory and she needed to get out. "Tell me what I need to do."

The Fate drifted back into the mist.

"There is a child," the Fate said, voice sounding far away. "A soul lost in this place. You have healed the bodies he dirtied, wiped the memories he ruined. Now you will help someone you care about. Someone close to you lost a piece of his heart ages ago."

Teari's heart thudded.

"Who?"

"You worry about the sins of your father. The sins you have committed. Regain your soul. Return what was stolen."

A faint light flickered far in the distance. A direction. A single thread. A beacon.

The Fate was vanishing. Its voice sounded farther and farther away.

"How do I know what to do?" Teari called after her.

"You will know."

Then she was alone. This place was dark, like midnight with a sliver of moon. The fog began to move like an ocean. Waves and all swallowed the Fate as it had swallowed Teari and tugged her down to this place. Teari shivered and looked around. She glanced down her body, realizing she'd lost her shoes in the gulf. Her dress was damp. She walked into the fog, barefoot, and cold seeping to her bones, guided by nothing but the fading pulse of light ahead.

Purgatory was not made of fire or brimstone. It was worse. It was made of silence.

There were no screams, no weeping, only the thoughts in her mind blaring with no distraction. Every breath scraped her lungs like broken glass. The sky above looked like a ceiling of ash. She couldn't tell if it was night or day or if time actually existed here. There was simply a moon and shadow.

She paused near a crumbling stone wall that seemed to have once marked a path or border.

"Hello?" she called softly.

The fog swallowed the word whole.

Teari pressed a palm to her sternum, where her healing magic usually pulsed with warmth. It was faint now, diminished, like she'd left part of it behind in the gulf. Like she'd come here without it. She looked down at her arms and the scars near her elbows seemed to glow. She looked like Frankenstein's monster.

Maybe it didn't work here in the in-between of realms. She'd lost her wings, she surely lost more.

She noticed the thread of light flicker again and pressed on, clutching to the single task the Fate had given her: *Find the child.* Maybe if she did this one thing, she could forgive herself for all the sins she'd created at the will of her father. She'd never speak to him again. Teari thought of Meg, and how everyone thought she was a simple human. The Queen of Hell fought tooth and nail for what was right, even though everyone thought she was wrong. Everyone blamed her. Everyone cursed her. Everyone hurt her. Why were they like this?

Teari climbed over the wall and into an orchard. Leafless trees stood over her, their branches twisted skyward in silent agony. Each trunk bore old claw marks and scratches wept sap.

On the other side of the orchard there was movement. The light blinked.

Teari dropped low, heart hammering.

Return what was stolen, echoed in her mind.

Her skin prickled like static in the air before a storm. The figure ahead was crouched low on the ground. It was a child, small and thin, dressed in a tattered yellow dress. She sat hunched beneath one of the trees.

Teari approached slowly. "Hello."

The child didn't flinch, didn't lift her head.

Teari knelt a few feet away. "My name is Teari. I think I'm here to help you."

Silence.

Closer now, Teari could see the girl's skin was pale, like all the color had been drained from her body. When she finally looked up, her eyes were silver and hollow.

"They told me I died," the girl whispered.

Teari's throat tightened. "Who did?"

The child looked down at her dress and rubbed it between her fingers. "I don't remember dying, I only remember running and trying to escape." The girl looked away. "I didn't want to die. I was trying to escape the demons. They were going to hurt me. Steal me. They would have taken me away from my family."

Teari moved closer and slowly dipped to her knees, easy not to startle the girl. "I believe you."

"You do?" she sounded surprised.

Teari nodded as she moved to sit cross-legged next to the girl. "How long have you been trapped here?"

"I can't remember. Forever maybe," the little girl whispered. "I miss my mother." She started to cry quietly.

Teari wasn't sure what to do so she sat there and offered silence and thought about all of the mothers who her father had left missing without their children. It seemed a vicious cycle.

An orchard of broken trees, of broken girls.

Chapter 24

BRIMSTONE AND PINE AND THE SCENT OF BLOOD wrapped around Chel like an old, familiar cloak.

It had been weeks since he'd set foot in Hell. He'd gotten used to the smell of sea salt spray and rain gliding across the gulf.

Shadows curled around his boots as he stepped into the castle in the burning caves, a welcome home from the prince no doubt. Remington must be learning to control his shadows. Chel had missed the boy. Well, he wasn't really a boy any longer–he was a young man–growing into his place beside the throne.

Hellions greeted him with nods and concerned glances. Chel realized he probably looked like shit after driving from Florida to Montana like a bat out of hell, then running straight back into Hell.

Meg was waiting for him.

She sat sideways in the throne, one leg slung over the

armrest. She was reading nearly upside-down with the way she was stretched, arms in the air holding a stack of papers.

Chel didn't bow. He didn't have time to.

"You look like horse shit," Meg said, voice dry as desert bone.

"Hello to you too."

She threw her legs over the chair until she was sitting and leaned forward, the grin fading. "What happened?" She set the papers on her desk.

Chel frowned. "Teari is gone. The gulf swallowed her and won't spit her back out. I think her father pulled her into something... darker. And there's an Angel down there dating the women and killing their babies. I think he's been doing it for decades."

Meg's smile twisted. "I know."

Chel blinked. "You knew?"

"I suspected," she said. "But we didn't have real proof. Not until now. We've seen the pattern. Women disappearing. Babies born and then not. Souls disappearing. Shadowed portals cut through the Veil like rot. The White Horse warned me something was fucked."

"You both knew?" Anger was flaring through Chel's body.

Meg rose from the throne and crossed the room, each step like a warning bell. She was close to him, hands on her hips, tattoos and scars on display.

"We couldn't exactly tell you what to look for. You would have killed and asked questions later."

Chel shook his head.

"No?" Meg asked.

"I think Teari is involved."

Meg's lips pressed into a straight line before she said, "No."

Chel nodded. "Yes. Her father has been controlling her."

"That fuck," Meg grumbled.

"I took Teari to dinner and one of the humans recognized her. She had a picture of Teari at a birth. The baby didn't survive. And the father..." Chel shook his head. "The father was someone who came out of the gulf. I've seen him. I followed him."

Meg spun and paced away. "One of those bastards can't keep their angelic dick in their pants." There was a beat of silence.

"This has been going on for a long time. A few of the locals warmed up to me and talked to me about it," Chel said. "We know that there have been Angels and Archangels mingling on the Earthen plane. We have proof. Jed. And..."

"Nightjar." Meg turned to face Chel. "Yes we have the Nightjar to remind us of the Archangel's transgressions. Despicable."

"Whatever Raphael dragged Teari into, she didn't want to do it. She was crying. She let her guard down. He has a crushing control over her."

Meg nodded. "There is a reason why she left her

father's kingdom to serve Gabriel. She never told me, but I'm guessing this is it."

Meg focused on Chel. "Do you still love her? Now that you know what she's been involved in?"

Chel's jaw dropped and his body went still, leathery wings sagging.

"Oh come on, Hellion." Meg smirked. "Anyone with eyeballs can see it. Heck a worm could see it."

He swallowed hard and it was audible.

Meg's eyes flashed wider as she urged him to speak.

"I love her. Always." The confession burned throughout his body like a lit fuse leading to his heart.

"You forgive her for this?"

Chel's hands curled into fists. "She was forced."

Meg nodded. "Good. I'll notify the White Horse."

"Of what?"

"That you'll dispose of the Archangel Raphael and free Teari from his sins."

"I will?"

Meg made a face. "Chel. You are a Hellion–a monster–and a piece of shit Archangel has dragged the woman you love into a fuck storm littered with innocent death. Tell me you don't want to kill him."

"I will kill him."

Meg nodded with a smile. "Good. Because that motherfucker has had his talons in the Black Mansion," Meg said, eyes blazing. "His monsters stole our girls. Now I'm taking his."

Chel didn't hesitate, turning from the room and stomping to the Hellion lair.

He took a dagger, feeling the hum of rage embedded in the steel. Then he took bags of blood and gulped them down.

When he was ready, he made his way to the door of the castle. Meg was there, Sparrow too.

"What if I fail?" he asked, voice low.

"You won't." Meg stepped closer, palm against his chest. "You're not just a Hellion, Chel. You're something more. A monster with a heart. You've always protected the innocent. Shay, my babies, your sister." She passed him an empty vial. "Collect some of his blood. Always good to keep a little bit around in case of an emergency."

Chel squeezed his eyes closed and nodded.

Sparrow plucked the dagger from Chel's chest strap. He held up something different. "This will put an end to an Archangel."

Chel took the blade, recognizing it as one of the weapons Sparrow had carved from the Basilisk bone and tipped with a poisoned tooth.

Chel nodded and secured the weapon in his chest strap. He had an Archangel to kill.

CHAPTER 25

———

Teari and the girl moved between the brittle trees, their skeletal limbs rattling like bones. The ground beneath her feet was soft, not with soil, but something... else. Ash, maybe. Or powdered memory. Or the thousands of souls who'd perished in Purgatory. Or maybe it was lost shipments of cocaine that had filtered down from the gulf. That would explain this dream state. Teari rubbed her face, her thoughts turning asinine. This wasn't good. Time didn't pass here; it coiled like smoke, thick and choking.

The girl's voice was flat. "They're coming."

"Who?" Teari asked.

"I don't know," the girl said, standing abruptly. "But he's coming."

"He?"

She didn't answer. She just took off running,

vanishing into the trees like Nero jumping between the Veil.

Teari chased after her. "Wait! Please!"

The fog thickened. The trees grew closer. The world twisted. Teari ran blindly into the mist, lungs burning.

Teari ran until the orchard thinned and the earth cracked open beneath her bare feet. The silver fog faded into the sting of smoke. She stumbled down a slope of black stone, twisted and glassy, the air hot and acrid like burnt sugar.

And then she heard a cry. The girl!

The air pulsed with the sound of the girl screaming-overlapping, echoing off the rocks. It got louder and louder and louder.

Teari clapped her hands over her ears.

Stop. Please stop.

She dropped to her knees. The sound didn't fade, it grew shriller, deeper. It sounded like a nightmare.

"Where are you?" she whispered. "Where are you?" She shouted into the smoke.

A voice cut through the cries like a knife.

"You were not there. No one was," the girl's voice said.

She gasped and looked around. All she saw was the dark. Then something moved in the smoke ahead; a figure, tall and cloaked in darkness. Menacing.

She turned and ran.

But the landscape changed with every step. The slope became a maze of charred roots and red-veined stones.

The cries warped into whispers–accusing, wailing, pleading. She tripped, hands tearing open on rough stone. Blood welled up, black instead of red.

A thought rang out above the noise, steady and sharp. *Save the girl and save yourself.* The instructions of the Fate echoed.

She pushed herself to her feet. "I don't know what to do." Tears stung Teari's eyes. She was stronger than this. She'd trained as a Legion warrior, she was a skilled healer. She couldn't fall apart now; she had hope, an escape, a Hail Mary pass. If she could save the girl she could save herself. Things could be different.

The whisper came again, softer now, beneath her skin. *Find what was lost.*

Teari stumbled forward, chest heaving. "I don't know what that means!"

But she knew.

Somewhere in this place the girl was still running. Still screaming. She was alone and scared and she did not belong here.

Teari had to find her.

THE ORCHARD WAS GONE NOW.

Teari pressed on, one shaky step after another through a scorched expanse where the trees had once stood. Their remains curled into skeletal ash, trunks stripped bare, limbs gnarled like hands reaching skyward in prayer or surrender–she wasn't sure. Beneath her feet, the ground crunched with char and brittle bone.

She didn't know how long she'd been walking. The light that had led her to the girl was gone and time stretched strangely here, suspended like breath underwater. The cries had faded.

Shadows twitched at the edge of her vision. She passed remnants of what might have once been homes with burned out doors, rocking chairs half-swallowed by vines of thorns, and cradles long turned to stone. She stopped at one, the exterior all blackened wood. Inside, a doll with no face sat on a tiny chair. Her throat closed. Memories flashed behind her eyes. She swallowed down the tears–she deserved this.

Teari forced herself to keep moving past the houses, into the charred prairie. She noticed a demon hovel tucked into the hill and heard the trickle of water in the distance.

And then she saw the girl again.

A flicker of dark hair in the distance and a pale yellow dress darted between stone pillars that jutted from the ground like ribs from a buried god.

"Wait!" Teari called out, voice hoarse.

The girl didn't stop.

Teari ran after.

The land grew more twisted the deeper she went. The geography itself had been shaped by guilt and grief. One moment she was scrambling over slick rock, the next trudging through a dry riverbed full of broken toys and waterlogged shoes.

Memories weren't real here, but they clung to the air like fog.

Teari... clean this up... Her father's voice was in her head again. She gritted her teeth and pushed forward.

Teari... clean this up...

Teari... clean this up...

Teari... clean this up...

Teari... clean this up...

Teari... clean this up...

Teari... clean this up...

"SHUT UP!" Teari screamed, covering her ears.

Ahead, the girl slowed. Teari caught a clearer glimpse of her: no older than nine or ten, her hair a mess of pitch black. She paused beside a crooked statue, half-swallowed by moss.

"Who are you?" Teari called softly. "Please. I'm not here to hurt you."

The girl turned her head slightly. Her eyes were shadowed, unreadable.

"You've never met me," she said.

"What?"

But the girl was gone again, swallowed by the labyrinth of stone and fog.

Teari leaned against the statue to catch her breath. Beneath her hand, she felt something carved into the stone.

Words.

She squinted through the grime.

The ones we fail never leave us.

A shiver crept up her spine.

Chel. It wasn't just about the girl.

This was about all of them; the children, the lives her father had discarded, the ones Teari had tried to save... but couldn't. She'd erased them out of existence.

And the only way out was through.

She straightened, brushing ash from her hands, and stepped deeper into the dark.

Her phone rang. Odd.

Teari went still before digging the phone from the pocket of her dress.

Raphael (89 missed calls).

Raphael (97 missed calls).

Raphael (113 missed calls).

Raphael (666 missed calls).

How could he reach her here? There was no way.

She answered the call.

His voice, "Come now. I need you. You owe me."

"I... I can't," Teari replied, unsure if the phone call was real. His voice sounded real.

She hung up and dialed Meg.

Silence.

She stared at the phone. It was just another facade of this land. It wasn't working. Just another nightmare. Just another torment.

She threw the phone into the mist.

Chapter 26

The portal to Babylon shimmered with hesitation.

Hellion.

It hissed the word without a voice, like Heaven itself exhaled judgment. Hellions didn't step freely into the Seven Kingdoms of Heaven. They snuck in. But Chel was not sneaking. He wanted that bastard Raphael to know that he was coming.

Chel rolled his shoulders and stepped closer. "You're not going to like this," he muttered.

The blade Sparrow had given him pulsed against his side, as if sensing the divine border ahead.

He shoved his hand into the light and forced through. He was a Hellion, one of the last of Meg's originals. He was fury and wrath and death in this moment. He only saw black and red and hate. He embraced his vile roots and wrapped them around his steadily beating heart because nothing would stop him from taking vengeance for the one woman he loved. Nothing.

Heaven screamed.

Chel stepped into Babylon and out of the giant fountain like a gargoyle, wings spread, water dripping, sharp teeth bared. The sound of gasps echoed, wings rustling in panic, and dozens of Angels drawing back in horror. The white-and-gold sidewalks gleamed underfoot, but his boots scuffed them with Hell's dust.

"Who let *that* in?"

"Is he lost?"

"Is that blood—on his shirt? On his face?"

Chel looked down. Yep. He drank that blood quickly in the Hellion Lair. He waved once. "Hi." He bared fangs.

Angels screamed. One fainted. Many ran.

Legion Angels took formation in the balconies above, spears ready.

Chel ignored them. "Which way to Raphael's kingdom?" He squinted against the too bright sun.

No one answered. Then, one of the Angels pointed as if eager to get the Hellion out of Babylon.

He sighed and spread his wings, dark black, wide, and scattered with battle scars. He took off into the golden sky, cutting through clouds.

Heaven was too clean. Too quiet. The air tasted too pure. Every corner sparkled with sanctimony. No one here knew real truth. Real sacrifice. Not like Meg's court.

Not like him. Heaven was deception. That was all. No lies. Pure deception.

When he landed, it was at the edge of Raphael's kingdom. An ivory palace was nested in the forest, spires and stone glowing. Chel stayed low, creeping along the walkways, dodging guards and servants.

It was too easy. Chel wondered if the Archangel was waiting for him.

Or, Raphael had spent so much time on other endeavors his kingdom had trickled in power. Chel looked around the grounds. There weren't a lot of people, unlike Meg's kingdom where the royal grounds were littered with guards and trainees, creatures, families, and progress. This place was stagnant. It occurred to him that Raphael held little power if his kingdom was this bare. Chel straightened his shoulders. This would be easy.

He made his way into the castle through an open servant door. Empty. The kitchen was even empty. He crept through the gleaming hallways until he found a room with a throne.

And there he was.

Teari's father.

Raphael.

He stood tall in a robe spun from glittering silk, wings the color of fresh snow, eyes like empty sunrises. Perfect. Untouchable. Hollow.

"You piece of trash," Chel growled.

Raphael turned, not startled. Just... bored. "Ah. The mongrel."

Chel didn't blink. "Where is she?"

"Which one? You'll have to be specific. I've made a mess of so many." He held up his hand and began counting on his fingers. "Jessica. Melanie. Greta... I could keep going but why bother?"

"Your daughter." Chel stepped closer, fists clenched. "Teari."

The Archangel's mouth twisted. "She was always soft. Fragile. Cracked with bits of humanity. She let her feelings get in the way. She sinned the moment she left this place."

Chel's vision blurred red.

"She cleaned up your chaos," he growled.

"She *was* the chaos. Weakness like that should've been snuffed out at birth. I should have killed her a long time ago."

Chel surged forward, black wings spread, blade ready, rage filled features. "Do *not* speak that way about *my wife*."

Silence.

The word echoed through the hall like a bell tolling the end of days.

My wife.

My wife.

My wife.

My wife.

It was a ploy but Chel felt it was more real than

anything. She was his, she always had been even if she didn't know it. He'd been utterly obsessed since the moment he'd laid eyes on her when Meg first took the throne. And he would do anything for her.

Then Raphael laughed. "Oh, this is even better than I imagined. You've been playing house with her. You don't even know what she is."

Chel's eyes narrowed. "I know what she *isn't*. She's not yours. She will never suffer under your palm again."

Raphael smirked. "And what makes you think I care?"

Chel grinned. "Because I saw you on the beach pretending to be human. I followed you."

That smirk cracked.

Chel stepped closer, dagger gleaming at his side. "That is the White Horse's realm. And now she knows what a piece of shit you are." Chel sneered. "Pathetic. You looked like a washed-up conman. If Lucifer were still around he'd laugh at how pathetic you are. He'd tell all of Babylon until you disappeared in humiliation. It's all becoming clearer the more we learn about you Archangels. Lucifer must've left in disgust."

Raphael's wings twitched.

Chel bared his teeth. "I'm taking her back. And then I'm taking *you* down. Where is she?"

The Archangel glanced down his perfect nose at Chel before replying, "Purgatory. Good luck finding her. She's dead. I waited long enough dealing with her weakness."

Chel charged—

He moved like a weapon unsheathed. The dagger from the Hellion lair was forged by the Raven King from Basilisk bone, tipped with poison. It sang in his hand, eager for battle.

Raphael's wings spread in fury. "You dare draw a weapon in my kingdom? You filth."

"You desecrated the Earthen plane," Chel snarled. "You murdered daughters, corrupted lives. You made Teari clean your mess. You hurt too many to count. You killed *children*. Innocents. You took their souls!"

"She was *mine* to command. God gave us divine–"

"There is no God!" Chel screamed. "And she was never yours."

Raphel's face twisted at the insult; the blasphemy of denying God was sacrilegious, a sin if there ever was one. And now it had been spoken freely within the Seven Kingdoms of Heaven.

Chel knew how to get under Raphael's skin. And it worked.

The Archangel lunged forward.

They collided like titans. It sounded like thunder echoing throughout all of the realm.

Chel swung first, aiming for Raphael's chest. The Archangel deflected the strike with a burst of light, searing against Chel's leather armor. Chel pivoted, slammed a punch into Raphael's ribs, and felt the crack of bone. Raphael screamed, white fire flaring from his palms. Chel staggered back as light scorched his shoulder.

But he didn't stop. He gripped the Basilisk bone blade.

He rushed forward, ducking under Raphael's blade of flame, and drove the dagger into the Archangel's side.

Raphael howled. Wings beat against the marble walls, knocking pillars loose. Blood spilled down his white robes and across the stone floor. It ran and ran and ran like a river.

"You think this makes you a hero?" Raphael gasped, blood like sunlight pouring from the wound.

Chel didn't answer. He drove the dagger deeper, twisting. "This is for Teari. And every innocent soul you erased."

Color drained from Raphael's face.

"You are nothing," he hissed, trembling. "Just a guard dog. A rat. Scourge of the realms." He spit on Chel's face.

Chel leaned close. "And you're just another monster pretending to be divine."

With a final push, the dagger reached the Archangel's heart. Raphael's scream echoed through every corner of Heaven.

And then he was gone.

Ashes.

The room fell silent. Only Chel's ragged breath filled the void.

Then Chel remembered. The blood. He dug the vial out of his pocket and began scooping up Raphael's blood until the vial was full. He capped it and tucked it away.

A moment later, alarms shrieked through the kingdom.

Chel turned, wings flaring, just as Legion soldiers descended. There were too many to fight alone.

CHEL WAS SHACKLED WITH THE BLOOD OF AN Archangel still drying on his clothes. He sat beneath the stained-glass arch of Babylon's judgment hall. Angelic guards ringed the chamber, spears angled at his back. He didn't flinch.

The remaining Archangels sat behind a long table: Gabriel, Michael, Uriel, Raguel, and Saraquel.

Chel smiled internally–their numbers were dwindling.

Saraquel spoke first. "You killed a reigning Archangel. That is a capital crime."

Chel tilted his chin up. "He was a butcher."

Whispers echoed through the chamber.

Then, a string of curse words echoed and the marble doors opened. Meg swept in like a storm wrapped in black leather. Her blue eyes blazed with fury.

"Finally," she said, striding into the circle. "Someone killed that sanctimonious bastard."

"Meg," Uriel said, voice cold. "This is not your court."

"Well, I'm not so sure about that. I am the Queen of

Hell and the Queen of the Raven King's lands. So I think you can listen to me. I'm not exactly out of place here." She nodded to the Archangel Gabriel. "Hello, father."

Gabriel smiled, blue eyes glinting with mischief. Chel got the feeling this was planned.

Meg stood beside Chel, resting a hand on his shoulder. "The Hellion acted on my command. I gave him the dagger. I told him the truth."

"What truth?" Michael asked.

Meg snapped her fingers. A scroll unraveled midair.

"Raphael kept records of the mortals he defiled and the infants he erased. You think I came unarmed? This is your evidence." Meg's face twisted in disgust. "The sinner kept *records*."

She pointed toward the table. "He had dozens; illegitimate daughters and sons hidden in mortal bloodlines. Nearly all are dead. And Teari? He made her scrub every trace clean until it broke her. He threatened her. He colluded and dragged her into this."

Gasps turned to roars. Angels stood, arguing and shouting.

Gabriel raised a hand. "This will need to be investigated."

"Do it," Meg said. "But Raphael is dead. And his only legitimate heir is Teari."

Chel looked up, eyes burning.

"Unless you want to speak to the Nightjar."

The room went silent.

CHAPTER 27

Teari wandered the dreamlike twilight with her nerves frayed to threads. She had nearly lost track of how long she'd been here. Time bent in this realm. Minutes stretched like hours, and memories slipped in and out of the air like vapor. The orchard had long since given way to a dense, dark forest.

The girl was always just ahead, laughing and vanishing before Teari could catch up. Until today.

Teari emerged into a clearing, breath catching in her throat. The girl stood at the edge of the woods, framed in a veil of pale light. She was younger than Teari had first thought, maybe six or seven. Her dress looked like something out of another time, and her little hands clutched a broken wooden sword.

She was watching a memory play out in the open air.

Teari stepped closer.

The scene shimmered.

A boy, shirtless and with sweat on his brow, chopped wood in a clearing. His hair was tied back with worn leather and his muscles, already too defined for someone so young, bunched and strained with each swing of the axe. A girl, the same one Teari had been following, tugged on his sleeve.

"Come play with me," she pleaded. "Please? I've been good all day."

The boy set the axe down with a sigh. "I will after chores, I promise. But if I stop now, we won't have enough wood for the fire and he'll be angry. And you know what happens when he comes home angry."

The girl pouted. "He's always angry."

"I know." The boy knelt and took her hand gently. "But you're my girl, right? And I'll always come find you."

"Promise?"

"Promise."

He kissed her forehead, then turned back to the woodpile.

Teari watched the memory ripple and fade.

She could barely breathe.

That was Chel, younger than she'd ever known him but that was him. She'd never seen him like this before, never seen him not as a Hellion.

The girl was Chel's sister. Yelena. The one who'd disappeared. The one Chel said had gone to the river and never returned.

A snarl cracked through the trees behind her.

The girl turned toward the sound, her eyes wide. Something was slithering through the underbrush.

Teari's heart clenched. "Run," she whispered. "Run now!"

But the girl had already taken off.

She sprinted through the clearing, feet bare, and dark hair bouncing behind her as the demon gave chase. Teari followed, dodging branches. The forest blurred around her.

The trees opened to reveal a narrow bridge, a sturdy arch of rough wood suspended over a rushing river.

The girl hesitated at the foot of the bridge.

Another demon emerged from the other side, grinning and blocking her escape.

She was trapped. There was no way out.

"No, no, no, no!" Teari surged forward, desperate to intervene. But they didn't notice her.

The girl backed up one step, then two. Her little hands gripped the side rail. The river below screamed. She was deciding.

One last look. She was terrified.

"Come here, little girl," the demon laughed. He had a length of rope coiled in his fist.

"We won't hurt you, pretty one," the other demon soothed. "Come with us."

"I want my mother," the girl whimpered.

"She doesn't want you. Come with us."

"No." Yelena shook her head. "You'll hurt me."

"No more than the others," the demon on the far side of the bridge sneered.

Yelena gripped the side of the bridge rail, then she jumped.

"No!" Teari screamed and dove after her. She swam as hard as she could, reaching for the girl. Her arms grew tired the river water was rushing like rapids. She saw Yelena's dark hair dip under the frothing water.

Teari plunged into the river's wrath.

The last thing she saw before going under was the girl's pale face breaking the surface for one brief gasp.

And then nothing but darkness.

Chapter 28

"She's gone," Chel admitted. "She... disappeared into the gulf."

Gabriel's jaw tightened. "Then she's dead."

"No," Chel said. "She's in Purgatory, according to her father."

Uriel stood. "That is not a place mortals—"

"I'm not mortal." Chel's voice was low. "And neither is she."

Suddenly, the door to the courtroom swung open. The Raven King had arrived dressed in black leather, the tips of his black wings dragging behind him like a cape. He first glanced at Meg, nodding. Then Chel. Then the table of Archangels. He moved to the empty seat. "Thanks for inviting me," he said as he sat.

The Raven King was not one of the original Archangels, but the son of Raguel. He took the throne when Raguel was killed by Meg. It was one of those uncomfortable I-killed-your-father-but-we-are-all-better-off-without-him type of situations.

Gabriel lifted two fingers in a small wave. Meg's father seemed to approve of all the changes. He didn't appear distressed over the death of Raphael in the slightest.

The Archangels conferred silently for a moment before Gabriel turned back toward him. "We have a bargain for you, Hellion."

Chel crossed his arms, chains rattling, and waited.

"You bring Teari back alive. She must take the throne."

Chel pressed his lips together.

"If you don't bring her back, you will rot in this chamber until your bones turn to dust," Uriel said plainly. "You broke a sacred balance. You killed an Archangel."

Chel didn't flinch. "You let Raphael destroy souls. Destroy people. You let him use his daughter to cover his sins. Vile sins."

Uriel's eyes darkened. "And now you have the chance to set it right."

Chel stared at them. Seven beings with more power than most could dream of, yet none of them had the spine to kill the monster among them. That had been left to him. Chel's gaze stopped on the Raven King. No, that wasn't true. There was more to this. They didn't need to tell Chel to go find her, he'd planned on it all along.

"I'll find her," Chel said finally.

Michael gave the faintest nod. "Then we'll grant you temporary release until you bring her back."

The chains clattered to the floor. Chel rubbed his wrists.

"Just remember," Michael said as he turned away, "if she doesn't return, neither do you."

Meg reached for Chel and looped her arm through his.

It was a sight; the Queen of Hell with her scarred back and much smaller frame walking through the courtroom of Babylon with a giant Hellion, his black leathery wings tucked tight against his back. Their darkness blotted out the brightness of Heaven with each step.

"I knew you could do it," Meg whispered.

Chel glanced down as she patted his hand.

"You are the only one who would never stop looking for her."

He nodded once and an angst flooded his body. He needed to get out of here. He'd never been to Purgatory, wasn't even sure how to get there or get back out. But he had to go and he had to go now.

Meg and Chel exited the portal, stepping into the courtyard of Hell only to be greeted by the Prince of Hell, Remington, and his soon to be bride, Evelyn.

Evelyn was holding a scroll of tattered cloth. "I did some digging in the library." She held the cloth out to Chel. "There is not a lot written about Purgatory in this realm. A lot of the books had the pages ripped out. But we went to the mountain shoppes and found an old demon with this."

Remington stepped closer to Evelyn as she passed the scroll to Chel.

He uncurled the cloth and stared, then turned it to the side.

Meg leaned over to get a look. "Oh, a map. Wonderful."

"Now, it might not be absolutely correct." Evelyn was using her hands as she spoke. "The mountain demon said that the Deacons had a lot of this information destroyed. But this is the oldest piece of evidence in this area that Purgatory is a real place." She glanced at Remington. "We didn't have time to search far." She stepped closer to Chel and moved the map. "Okay, so Purgatory is separated into three lands. Each of the Fates controls a land–it is theirs, their kingdom. From what I can find they had been without power for a long time. Souls didn't go to Purgatory because the Deacons trapped every soul here in Hell and then distributed them as they saw fit. Usually to the Seven Kingdoms of Heaven so the Archangels had all of the power."

Meg grumbled. "They were meddling fucks all along. Corrupt."

Evelyn waited for Meg to finish, eager not to interrupt. When Meg motioned at the map, Evelyn said, "Now the Fates are getting power again. Before they'd have to steal souls but now that the Deacons are gone, souls go where they belong. The Fates are growing stronger." Evelyn pointed to a section of the map with what looked like skeletal trees. "Remember; three kingdoms, three Fates. One weaves a lifeline, one determines the length of a life, one cuts the thread of life."

"Which one will have Teari?" Chel asked.

Evelyn's eyes widened and she shook her head. "I don't know."

Remington stepped forward. "You can't reach Purgatory from these portals."

"I'll leave you all to it," Meg said as she walked toward the castle in the burning caves with a wave.

Remington scowled as he watched his mother go.

"Don't," Chel warned. "Don't judge her. She isn't sticking around because she knows something."

Remington cleared his throat. "I've always worried about my mother. She's been a bit flippant lately. Holing up in her office or running off with father."

Evelyn touched Remington's arm. "I think Chel's right. I have a feeling about her."

Remington went still as he watched the castle door close behind his mother's shadow. "She knows things?"

"Your grandmother, Clea, could see parts of the future. Rue can also." Chel was studying the map and committing it to memory. "Do you think that power skipped a generation?"

Remington's head tipped to the side–a birdlike mannerism-like his father the Raven King. He considered the Hellion's words.

"Meg doesn't trust a soul. She learned that the hard way." Chel pointed at the castle. "I'd bet my life that she knows more and she's not telling anyone." Chel shifted on his feet. "Now, tell me how to pass into Purgatory."

It was a subsidiary of the Black River, of all places. The darkest waters in all of Hell branched off into the mountains and past demon hovels. Chel recognized the landscape as they drove closer. He swallowed hard.

This was his childhood home.

His father lived in a hovel not far from the road, Chel assumed, but he wouldn't know if the old man was there because he hadn't visited since he was a new recruit. And if the branch of the Black River flowed through these lands that would mean Chel and his sister had played near the portal to Purgatory on a daily basis.

Remington parked the Jeep Grand Cherokee near a bridge in an alcove cut away from the trees as though it were a frequent stopping point. Chel considered demons stopping here to fish in the dark waters. He got out of the SUV and waited for Remington to round the vehicle.

It was just the two of them. Remington didn't want

Evelyn harmed or pulled into Purgatory. The dark prince was untrusting of anything new when it came to his female being nearby. Not so long ago she'd nearly been killed watching the Hellions train. A blast of uncontrolled magic from Thrush came dangerously close to her. Since then, Remington was eager to keep her very close or secured in the castle.

"How far?" Chel asked.

"There's a cave by the water's edge. I scouted it out a few days ago." Remington began making his way along the bank of the river. "Thrush came and marked the cave opening with protective runes, so others wouldn't wander too close. When Evelyn said the Fates had succumbed to stealing souls..." He slid down an embankment of mud with a grunt. "Damn it." Remington regained his footing. "Let's just say we took precautions to keep the balance."

They walked along the shoreline.

Dread began slinking through Chel's body. He recognized this riverbank more and more with each step; the tall pines, the smell of sap and dark water, the feel of the mud under his feet, and the destroyed bridge in the distance that spanned a narrowing. His childhood hovel wasn't far.

"Right here." Remington stopped him.

Chel didn't see a cave.

Remington bent and pushed against a giant rock. It slid across the riverbank, revealing a small opening.

"That's the portal?" Chel could barely believe it. If he

were lucky, he could crawl into the space. If he were unlucky, he'd get stuck and meet an early death being crushed by the riverbank. "I won't fit in there." He crouched and studied the opening. "There's no way."

Remington slapped Chel's shoulder, just like the Hellion had done to him so many times throughout his life. "You gotta, big guy. It's the only way."

CHAPTER 29

Yelena screamed. Water splashed. Demons growled.

No matter how many times Teari ran, how many times she clawed through the underbrush or called out warnings it always ended the same.

Each time the memory loop reset, it stuck deeper, like a thorn in her chest. It latched under her ribs and tugged. One moment she was jumping into the river with Yelena and the next she was wandering the orchard again.

The girl's laughter echoed through the orchard. Her braid bounced behind her as she skipped ahead. Teari ran faster, breath burning in her throat, legs churning through the warped time of Purgatory. She *knew* what came next.

The growl.

The demons.

The fear.

The drowning.

Bare feet kicked up dirt as she ran. Teari's dress was perpetually damp. In the distance she could hear the ringing of the cell phone she'd thrown into the mist.

Yelena's scream split the trees. She shoved herself forward, heart pounding, the pain in her ribs sharpening. Her feet hit the wooden planks of the bridge, the demon's claws reaching out as she passed. The other laughed. Teari was trapped on the bridge, Yelena having already jumped.

"NO!"

Dark hair bobbed in the rapids of the river then went under. Teari jumped, water rushing into her mouth and filling her ears until she couldn't hear. She reached and dug at the water. Nothing.

Too late.

Always too late.

A splash shattered the silence. The little body vanished into the current.

The loop collapsed.

The voice returned.

"You failed," the Fate whispered, its voice curling like smoke in her skull. "Again."

Teari collapsed to her knees as the world stitched itself back together; trees bending unnaturally, the river reversing, the laughter beginning again like a music box wound too tight.

She tried to steady her breathing, but her hands trembled.

She wasn't just failing the girl.

She was reliving the failure of *every* soul she couldn't save, every child born still, and everyone she'd been ordered to eliminate.

How many times had she chased the same fading footprints in the mud? Ten, fifty, a hundred?

How many times had her fingers just brushed the girl's wrist before the current swept her away?

Too many.

And it was wearing her down.

The Fate didn't yell. It didn't chastise or warn like her father had. It didn't *have* to. The shame of failure was enough.

Teari dragged herself up. The wind in the trees whispered her guilt, her memories, her sins. The scent of the orchard twisted into rotting fruit.

Teari took off in a sprint toward Yelena's voice.

She ran.

She chased.

She failed.

"Why can't I save her?" she whispered into the wind as the world reset once more.

The Fate didn't answer this time.

But the bridge waited.

And the river screamed.

Teari got as far as the hovel and went still.

The scene shimmered as it replayed. How many times had she watched the young Chel with his sister?

His hair was tied back with worn leather, and his

muscles bunched and strained with each swing of the axe. Yelena tugged on his pants.

"Come play with me," she pleaded. "Please? I've been good all day."

Young Chel set the axe down with a sigh. "I will after chores, I promise. But if I stop now, we won't have enough wood for the fire. And you know what happens when he comes home angry."

Yelena pouted. "He's always angry."

"I know." Chel took her hand gently. "But you're my girl, right? And I'll always come find you."

"Promise?"

"Promise."

Chel kissed her forehead, then turned back to the woodpile and began chopping again.

Teari went still.

I'll always come find you.
I'll always come find you.
I'll always come find you.
I'll always come find you.
I'll always come find you.
I'll always come find you.
I'll always come find you.
I'll always come find you.

It echoed in her mind. A tear slipped from the corner of her eye. She missed him. She'd ruined it. And she wondered if they'd met at a different time if things would have worked out. If he had found her before her father's corruption, before the sins he'd forced her to hold, maybe they could be together. She could never face him again now that he knew the truth.

Teari stood in the clearing beside the hovel and watched Chel. Yelena's screams echoed in the distance. Her cell phone rang from the mist.

She walked toward young Chel and studied him. Yes he was a demon; he'd killed as a Hellion, but he lived by his own rules, and he had gentle side. Teari swallowed hard. Demons didn't used to be like this–only since Meg took the throne of Hell and everything changed. But Chel, it seemed Chel was always like this.

She watched him stack the wood, wave to his mother as she hung laundry on the drying line, and as he sipped water from a nearby cup.

A crunching sound echoed.

Young Chel went still before slowly turning. He wiped the back of his hand across his lips.

A tall shadow emerged from the path near the hovel. His coat was tattered, soaked with something dark at the hem, and his boots left streaks of soot behind.

Teari felt it before she understood it, felt the fear knotting inside the boy's chest. It stabbed in her own ribs like a thorn. Young Chel stepped back, chin tilting downward, shoulders curling in instinctively.

"Finished stacking already?" the demon rasped. Its voice was too loud for the stillness of the orchard.

Chel nodded. "Yes, sir."

The demon circled the pile like a predator sizing up its kill. "Crooked," he muttered. "Sloppy." He kicked the pile, sending logs tumbling across the dirt. "Do it again."

Chel bent immediately to gather the wood.

The demon's gaze flicked to the laundry swaying on the line. Chel's mother. She flinched at the noise but didn't move. Teari saw her hands tremble.

"You got something to say?" the demon barked at her. The woman shook her head and disappeared behind the sheets like a ghost into fog.

Chel's hands shook as he restacked the logs.

Then came the snap.

Not of a log.

Of bone.

The demon grabbed him by the shoulder and yanked him upright.

"I said *straight*," he growled, shaking him. "What are you? Useless? Dumb? You look dumb."

Chel didn't cry out. He didn't beg.

He bit his tongue until blood ran down his chin.

Teari's hand flew to her mouth.

This was not a mere memory. This was a wound echoing. It had settled into Purgatory like rot beneath the skin. Why would the Fate show this to her?

The demon shoved the boy to the ground. Dust and woodchips rose in a choking cloud.

"Clean it up before I get back," he snarled, already turning for the house.

The silence afterward rang louder than the violence.

Chel didn't move at first.

Then he sat up, slowly. He rubbed his sleeve across his mouth, smearing blood and dirt. He stacked the wood again, neater this time, hands red and raw.

Teari wanted to rush forward and stop it.

But she knew this was not *him* now. This was a memory replaying in Purgatory like all sins and griefs and haunts.

Still, the ache in her chest was real.

Still, the tears burned in her eyes.

Young Chel sat beside the pile once it was done, holding his broken arm close to his chest.

Teari pressed a hand to her sternum, heart aching.

Chapter 30

Chel crawled forward, the opening to the portal tighter than he'd imagined and he could feel the pull ahead. He dragged his body through the tunnel by his arms without enough distance for him to bend his knees. He hissed as his wings scraped against the rock and hard-packed soil surrounding him.

The air changed, pulsed. And then the solid ground went out from underneath him.

It was not a fall.

It was a dissolution.

Chel landed on damp moss. His big body didn't even make a sound. What met him instead was silence, thick and endless. It was the kind that pressed into the ears like a hollow hum.

His breath left his lungs. His leather armor peeled itself from his body as if the place rejected it. His boots crumbled into ash the moment he touched the ground.

If this could be called ground.

It was mud and mist, a plain of boggy land beneath him, stretching forever. Above, the sky was a bruised gray; no sun, no stars. It seemed there was a moon of some kind.

Chel took a step forward and something tugged-a weight.

Purgatory knew him. Greeted him. Expected him. Stripped him to damp clothes and bare feet to get a better look at its guest.

"Fuck," Chel whispered, his voice devoured before it could echo.

He pushed forward, barefoot, the mist rising around him. It was sensing him, testing him. A sudden weight was removed from his shoulders. One giant hand flew to his upper back and Chel felt his wings were gone.

His Hellion strength remained, but it felt dulled.

"I'm here for her," he said aloud. It felt important to say it. "I'm not leaving without her."

The mist didn't answer.

He walked. He walked until the sod gave way to sand, and the sand gave way to scorched root systems, tangled like veins. Then he saw the first sign he wasn't alone.

"Teari," Chel said.

The creature's face was still, and only after a few moments did Chel realize it wore a mask of bone.

That wasn't Teari.

"You didn't even bring me flowers," it said with a female voice.

He let out a breath with nothing to say.

"I know why you are here." She moved, her long shroud brushing the stone floor.

She pointed.

A scrap of blue cloth, pale and frayed, was caught on a branch of a rootless tree. It fluttered like breath. He reached for it.

Teari.

His heart twisted so hard he nearly doubled over.

She'd been here, was here still.

Chel straightened. His fingers clenched into fists.

No one had ever accused him of being clever. But he was determined. And stubborn. And loyal to a fault.

He would find her, even if it meant pulling Purgatory apart one memory at a time.

The creature was gone, disappearing into the mist.

Chel walked through the veil-thin groves of dead trees. With every step, the world seemed to shift and react to him—not like it was trying to help, either.

Like it was trying to confuse him.

He didn't know how long he walked. Minutes, hours, centuries. Time didn't work here. His body ached in strange places.

He rounded a bend where the roots glistened like sinew and found himself in front of a door.

It stood alone, upright, no frame, no house, just floating in the mist. Familiar.

The metal was scorched black. Common demon markings scratched deep into its surface. Chel's breath caught.

He knew this door.

He opened it and stepped into his childhood.

The interior was exact; his mother's kitchen, made of warped wood and soot-streaked glass, the stew bubbling. His father's boots were by the door and his sister's laughter echoing.

"Chel," a voice said behind him.

He turned and froze.

It was his sister. Exactly as she'd been the last day he saw her. Windblown. Grinning. Barefoot. Yellow dress.

"I asked you to play," she whispered. "You said no."

His throat closed. "I had chores. You know that."

"You said later," she said, taking a step forward. "You said you'd come find me."

"I tried." His voice cracked. "I searched for you until I couldn't anymore."

"You let me go," she said. "You forgot the sound of my voice."

Chel sank to his knees. "I did."

"You let him hit me." Her voice grew colder. Older. "You let him take me. You let him hurt me. You let him sell me to the skin trades."

"I couldn't stop him."

"You didn't try hard enough."

Sharpness yanked tight around his ribs. The thorns of the family burned and ached and it bit into his skin.

His sister's face flickered, shifting, and became the bruised face of Shay. A panicked Evelyn. Then the girl from Perdido Key. Then Teari.

"No," Chel growled. "*No.* You're not her."

The illusion cracked and screamed. The door slammed shut with a metallic shriek. Chel staggered back, gasping.

"I couldn't save them all," he said aloud.

He pushed forward past the door and through the mist. Every now and then another memory rose; a burning battlefield, a boy he trained who bled out in his arms, Meg, Sparrow, Rue and Remington on the beach as children... Chel, the protector, never quite enough. All the voices screamed in his ears.

But one thread anchored him. *Teari*. He had to find her.

He followed the sound of Yelena's laughter. He came to a riverbank. Dark water rushed. He glanced down and noticed a footprint in the silt, small, wet and fresh. Chel's pulse jumped. She was close. But the moment he stepped forward, the river surged and something in it screamed. It was Yelena's voice. He saw the demons at the bridge. He saw her jump. No. He'd been told she was kidnapped and had died. But that was untrue. She'd jumped to escape.

Chel squared his shoulders. That wasn't just any demon. That was their father blocking her path.

He ran.

Chapter 31

This is what made him, Teari thought. This is what carved him and molded him into the shape she knew.

She'd seen cruelty in Heaven. She'd seen it dressed in gold and good intentions. But this was different. Raw. Personal. A wound that had never closed, seared with salt. It festered. But it hadn't broken him.

Teari stepped back, hand pressed over her lips. Her father's voice echoed somewhere in her mind,

"He's unstable. He's a weapon. He's a beast."

She swallowed hard.

He wasn't a beast. He was strong. He was good.

He'd learned how to choke on his pain in silence, smile with blood on his tongue, and to carry the fire without letting it burn others.

But sometimes it did burn; when he was pushed too far or when someone threatened what little softness he had left. She'd seen him burn on the battlefield when they'd fought against Lucifer. He chose a side: Meg's.

She thought of the night on the beach and the way he'd held her like she mattered. The way he'd danced with her under the moon was like her world wasn't torn, like she was more than a clean-up crew, and more than a graveyard.

Teari's fingers trembled at her sides.

This wasn't just Chel's Purgatory. It was hers too. The Fates had mixed them together but still, it felt like more of a home than Heaven. Maybe because he was there.

They'd both been drowning long before the gulf ever swallowed them. And she'd pushed him away while he'd held her up.

She took a shaky breath, trying to ground herself. The orchard, the dirt, the river, the bridge, the sunless sky, it was all a dream twisted in punishment. But the emotions were real. They stuck in her throat like thorns.

No one taught him how to be gentle. No one taught him how to receive gentleness. Just like no one had taught Meg how to love in those early days.

He'd carved that kindness out for himself despite everything.

Teari's eyes closed. *You deserved better than this, Chel.*

The memory began to dissolve, grain by grain.

And Teari whispered into the vanishing air, "I miss you."

Creaking wood echoed. Teari was on the bridge. Yelena was close. Teari reached out.

Yelena turned and looked at her. "My father did it." She pointed to the demon blocking their exit on the opposite side of the bridge. "He was going to sell me to the skin trades." She pointed to the demon opposite her father. "That one was going to take me away. I was trying to escape."

Escape.

Teari was trying to escape as well. Escape the truth, escape judgement, escape fate.

CHAPTER 32

Chel slowed as the river's cries faded into eerie silence.

A presence unfurled from the fog.

The Fate.

She stepped from the smoke and bone-strewn path with no sound at all, barefoot in a black robe like smoke that trailed too long behind her, stitched from the threads of the memories. Then Chel remembered what Evelyn told him—this must be the weaver.

"Hellion," she said softly. "You walk where you do not belong."

Chel squared his shoulders. "I'm not leaving without her."

The Fate tilted her head, her eyes like a bottomless sea beneath the bone mask. "This realm is not meant for Hellions. Or warriors. Or creatures who think they can fix what was never theirs to mend. Or creatures who take and destroy and bury us. This is my realm. Mine and my sisters'. Enough was taken from us. Decades. We were starving." She flashed sharp teeth.

"I'm not here to fix anything," he said. "I'm here to help her. You took her."

"She gave up."

"I do not believe that."

The Fate's head tipped to the side. The creature exhaled a breath. "Her father sold her to me. She is mine."

"No." Chel gripped his fists.

"No," the Fate echoed, as if tasting the word. "Do you mean to carry her burden? Rip the thread from the loom before it's woven?"

Chel clenched his fists. "I mean to keep her from drowning."

"She is not the one drowning," the Fate whispered. "There are rules here."

Chel's jaw tightened. "Then tell me what I can do."

The Fate stepped closer. Her voice dropped low. "You may not save the girl. You may not fight her battles. You may not rewrite what Teari has been sent to learn. But—"

She raised one pale hand, and a thread of light shimmered between her fingers.

"—I never said you couldn't help Teari."

Chel's heart thudded in his chest. "What does that mean?"

"It means your presence has weight," she said. "You

cannot reach the child but you can reach her. Anchor her. Remind her of who she is. And, perhaps, remind her of why she must live." The Fate looked up. "I never liked the Archangels. Bigots, the whole bunch."

"Her father is dead."

"Oh?" the Fate sounded interested.

"I killed him."

"Good, good. I can't wait for my sisters to find him."

Chel took a breath. "I'll find her," he said.

The Fate nodded. "Be warned," the Fate said. "Every step you take now is a gamble. She will walk toward her pain. And you must let her."

Chel looked past the Fate to the river again, then to the other side.

He said, "I won't let her be alone."

Chel stood in the reeds, hidden, breath locked in his chest. He'd seen this before. He'd stood in this exact spot for more than a handful of loops of the scene.

He'd watched her jump.

He'd watched her die.

And he'd watched Teari dive in after her, again and again, dragged under, ripped away by the current. He'd lost count how many times he'd watched them get ripped away back to where he'd started. All the while the Fate's words repeated in his head.

I never said you couldn't help Teari.

This time, he was ready. He'd figured it out. The plan solidified, and his muscle memory prepared to act.

Teari appeared on the opposite bank, emerging from the mist, hair slick against her cheeks, her blue dress torn. Her eyes locked on Yelena. She ran just as she had before.

The girl turned toward the bridge. Teari shouted. Yelena stepped onto the slick wood. The demons closed in. Teari moved faster, arm outstretched, fingers nearly grazing the child's sleeve...

The girl leapt, hair and yellow dress whipping as she fell.

Chel's whole body tensed.

Teari didn't hesitate.

She dove.

And Chel ran.

He ran into the water through the surge. He let it slam into him, churn him under. But his eyes were open, and he didn't take them off her. He couldn't.

He saw them. Teari's hand was gripping Yelena's wrist, spinning in the current, Teari's other hand reaching—searching—

Chel stretched toward her. His giant hand slapped against her arm and grabbed on for dear life. He wouldn't lose her again. Never again. His fingers circled around her arm, felt her scars under his calloused fingertips.

"Teari!" he shouted, water crashing over his face. "Don't let go!" His feet slid over the slippery river rocks.

She turned, eyes wide and terrified as Chel grasped her forearm tighter. Water slid under his fingertips, threatening to break the contact.

She nearly slipped, but he gritted his teeth and pulled.

His muscles screamed and the current tore at him. Yelena thrashed in Teari's grasp, but Chel kept dragging them backward, step by brutal step until his feet found rock and mud and then shore.

They collapsed in a heap of coughing, shivering limbs. Chel curled protectively around them both.

Yelena spat up water, blinking. Then, with a soft gasp, she looked at Teari and Chel and whispered, "I didn't die this time."

Teari broke—not in a dramatic sob, but a quiet unraveling. Her head bowed, tears falling freely as she gripped the girl tighter. "You're safe. You're safe," Teari whispered over and over again. "He won't hurt you."

Chel tucked them both close, pulled them into his arms, and squeezed.

"Not this time," he murmured. "Not ever again."

The current stilled.

The demons disappeared into the mist.

CHAPTER 33

"I NEED TO GET YOU BOTH OUT OF HERE," CHEL shifted, preparing to stand, although he didn't want to release Teari or Yelena. He wanted to hold onto them forever, but he knew Purgatory wouldn't allow that.

Yelena watched Chel with wide, thoughtful eyes.

"You're real," she finally said.

Chel glanced up from his thoughts. "Yeah," he said, unsure how to respond.

"You were my brother," she whispered, as if testing the words against the reality in front of her. "You had that scar on your left thumb. From the fishhook."

Chel stilled.

Yelena's gaze sharpened, her voice a little louder now. "And you told me stories about monsters that could be chased off with salt. You let me sleep in your bed when Father got too loud. Too mean."

He said nothing, his throat too tight to speak.

Teari shifted beside her, wrapping an arm gently around the girl's shoulders.

Yelena continued, quieter now, like her soul had cracked open and the pieces were drifting out one at a time. "You were supposed to protect me. But I left without you that day."

"You did," Chel said hoarsely. "I looked for you. Every day. They said you were kidnapped."

"Almost." Her tone was eerie. "But I got away."

Silence fell, deep and uncomfortable. Chel stared into the mist.

Yelena turned and scooted closer. Her small fingers reached out to touch his scarred hand.

"But you came for me anyway," she said.

"Every day I searched for you until I had to leave," Chel's voice was thick.

Teari watched them, knowing this wound would never fully close, but she hoped maybe it could stop bleeding.

THE WIND WHISPERED THROUGH THE TWISTED reeds at the river's edge. The sky above Purgatory was a dull bruise, shifting black and gray.

Chel stood at the edge of the tunnel that led to the portal, its center now glowing faintly as if welcoming them back—a shimmer of escape carved open by Fate's reluctant permission. The price had not yet been named, but they all felt it hovering.

Teari held Yelena close, brushing leaves from the river out of the girl's damp hair. "Let's get out of here," she murmured.

Yelena looked up at Chel, hesitant. "You'll be right behind us?"

He nodded and crouched to her level, cupping her cheek. "You'll see my friends on the other side." His voice cracked. "You're going to be safe."

Her small hand gripped his tightly, unwilling to let go.

"I promise," he whispered, giving it a squeeze. "Ladies first."

Yelena turned toward the tunnel, blinking against the silver-blue light. Teari gave Chel one last glance and then she followed Yelena in, crawling behind the girl.

The portal pulsed. A wind whipped through the grass.

Remington's voice echoed from the other side as Yelena went through. "I've got her! Pulling the girl through—Teari, I see you—!"

Then silence.

Chel crawled forward, back scraping the tunnel as he reached and dragged his body through.

The light trembled.

His hand hovered over the edge.

He hesitated.

Something in the pull of the veil shivered unnaturally, like a string about to snap. The portal rippled.

Chel breathed in long and steady. Something wasn't right.

From the other side, Teari turned in the flickering shimmer of the gate. "Chel?"

But it was too late.

The portal sealed shut.

CHAPTER 34

THE TUNNEL SHUDDERED AROUND THEM LIKE IT was going to collapse. Shadows peeled away as Remington's grip locked on Teari's arm, hauling her and Yelena upward. The taste of Purgatory clung to her, ash and stale air.

Remington gripped her hand and yanked her free of the darkness. She collapsed against the muddy riverbank on the other side. Teari scrambled toward the mouth of the tunnel.

"Chel!" Her voice cracked. She reached a hand into the swirling dark, waiting for his broad figure to break through, waiting for his hand so she could pull him out just as he'd pulled her out of the river rapids.

But he didn't come.

The tunnel trembled, shadows writhing, and the only thing pressing forward was silence. Behind her, Yelena gave a sharp gasp. Teari spun, heart jolting. The girl clutched her stomach, her form flickering like a candle in the wind.

"Oh no. Something is happening." Yelena's eyes widened, panicked. She lifted her trembling hands, staring as her fingers blurred at the edges. "I don't feel so good."

"No!" Teari clambered to her knees, reaching for Yelena, but her hands passed through Yelena's shoulders as though she were smoke.

"I can't—" Yelena's words broke off, her face full of fear. And then she was gone. One final shimmer of light, like glass breaking underwater, then... she disappeared.

Teari's chest hollowed out. "No! no, no, no!" Her fists slammed against the ground. "Where did she go?"

Remington's face had gone pale watching the scene play out. The dark prince moved closer to Teari, afraid that she might disappear too.

Remington's phone buzzed. He cursed under his breath, pulling it from his pocket, his dark eyes narrowing at the name flashing across the screen.

Teari couldn't breathe. Her panic surged hotter, louder than her pulse. Chel hadn't come through. Yelena was gone. And whatever thin thread of hope she had been clinging to unraveled all at once. Everything and everyone was lost.

Teari sat frozen, her palms pressed to the cold stone where the girl had just been, heart pounding in uneven bursts.

"What?" Remington looked at the phone screen, one

brow lifting, and then held it out toward her. His voice was dry. "It's for you."

Teari blinked, disoriented. She took the phone with shaking hands, clutching it so hard her knuckles whitened. "Hello?"

"She's here now," an unfamiliar voice said.

Her brows knit together. "Who is this?"

"I was instructed to call you when she arrived."

"Okay, but who is this?" Her chest rose and fell quickly, the panic mixing with confusion.

On the other end of the line, the man cleared his throat. "It's Jasper. From the Peabody Library." A pause stretched between them.

She had no idea what was happening. "Wait... I trained an Angel-medic named Jasper many years ago, just before he was sent on a mission."

"Yes." His voice was steady. "That's me. She's here. I've been waiting for her to arrive."

The words landed like a blow, and for a moment she forgot how to breathe. *She's here.* But Yelena had just slipped through her fingers. She had just faded before her eyes.

Her gaze lifted to Remington. He was watching her carefully, jaw set as though bracing for whatever came next.

Teari wondered if fate had stolen Yelena only to deliver her somewhere else entirely.

CHAPTER 35

Chel backed out of the tunnel, covered in mud. The river roared behind him, its silty churn fading into a whisper. He gripped the slick edge of a rock with one hand, then something snapped.

Chel's back arched, his lungs seizing as invisible talons hooked into his spine and yanked. The wet ground turned to sludge beneath him. He clawed at the mud, fingers scraping stone, but the force dragging him backward was unrelenting.

He slammed into something cold and unmovable. The world tilted. A gust of wind howled through the space, and when Chel blinked, the riverbank was gone.

So was the tunnel that led to the portal.

He knelt on a floor of smooth rock, slick with mist and starlight. The darkness was not empty. There were eyes.

Three forms emerged from the gloom, cloaked in

layers of shadow and cloth, their eyes glowing with memories too ancient for language. Each wore a mask of bone.

Three.

The Fates.

Chel had seen a lot of monstrous things in his time: bloodlords, soul devourers, Angels twisted by pride. But nothing had ever unsettled him quite like the sight of these creatures.

The one on the left was tall. Her eyes were milky and unmoving. When she spoke, it was with a voice like shattering glass, "You were warned."

The one in the center moved more fluid, her robes flowing like ink in water. Her gaze fixed on him. "You did not seek permission to leave."

The third smiled as if she knew every secret he'd ever tried to bury. Her voice was warm, almost kind. He knew better. "You were always going to save her."

Chel tried to rise, every joint aching from the strain of being pulled through Purgatory and swimming through the river.

"I did what you asked," he said, focusing on the Fate that had first met him when he arrived. "Teari has done her part."

The middle Fate tilted her head. "Yes. But *you*... are not finished."

He clenched his fists. "I did not die. I did not come here to stay."

The first Fate moved forward, her steps silent. "She was ours."

Chel's jaw tightened. "I kept her from drowning."

A long pause.

Then the third Fate laughed softly, like water tumbling over stones. "You are not here to argue technicalities, warrior."

Chel finally stood. The mist curled around his ankles, alive and restless. "Then why am I here?" This conversation was confusing. It was missing parts.

All three answered at once, their voices layering in harmony and horror, "Because you are not done."

The middle Fate stepped closer. Her expression was unreadable. "You carry wrath in your bones. You were forged in fire. Tempered in war."

The one on the left added, "You wear your father's shadow like armor. Even now, it drips off you like old blood."

Chel flinched. "That's not who I am."

"Isn't it?" the third Fate asked. She raised a single finger and pointed toward his chest. "You killed the Archangel. You bathed Heaven in vengeance."

Chel's breath hitched. "He deserved it."

"Maybe," they said. "But so did others who wore the same mask."

Another pause.

"You seek to protect the Angel. The healer. But you cannot do so while you are chained to your legacy."

"You must choose, Hellion. You cannot carry her out unless you leave something behind. You owe us now."

"What?" he rasped. "What do you want me to give?"

The mist writhed. Something distant echoed like war drums underwater.

The third Fate whispered, "Your certainty. Your rage. Your armor. Your name."

Chel's voice cracked. "If I say no?"

The mist stilled. The shadows folded inward. "Then you remain. Here. Always."

Silence followed.

No wind. No sound. Just the question ringing in his mind.

Was she worth it?

He thought of the way she smiled when she thought no one was looking and the feel of her skin rubbing against his. The fire in her voice when she told him, *"Don't bite me,"* echoed in his head.

"Yes," Chel said quietly. "She's worth it." He lowered his head, his body shuddering in the dark. "I'll stay. If that's the cost."

The Fates smiled.

But none of them moved.

The Fates waited.

"You said I still owe," he rasped. "So tell me what it is."

The center Fate raised her pale eyes to his. "You are the last of your kind."

Chel's body tensed.

"The last Hellion forged in the fires before the great betrayal," said the second, her mouth drawn thin with judgment. "The others burned protecting your queen."

Their names echoed inside him like war drums.

Skeele.

Tukka.

Klaus.

All dead. All slaughtered in the Hellion Lair when Alastor stormed the castle. His brothers. His blood.

Chel had escaped with the last of Meg's Basilisks, smoke choking the night as they ran through the corridor connecting the castle to the Hellion barracks. He had run like a coward. He should have stayed. He should have died with them. He had sworn to remember each of them, and he had. Every scream. Every moment they stood between Meg and death.

"You lived," the third Fate said softly. "And you hate yourself for it."

Chel squeezed his eyes closed. Did he hate himself? He couldn't forget the moment Alastor entered the Hellion Lair and took them all down.

THEN...

Alastor chanted in Hellspeak and the floor opened up. Lesser Demons and strange creatures began crawling out.

Cockroaches and spiders and black beetles swarmed the group, biting and scratching, bringing chaos and destruction.

Skeele stepped closer to Meg. Klaus followed. Tukka was too far away to get closer without making a scene.

A knowing look passed between Tukka and Skeele.

The creatures scrambled toward them, bugs skittering and snakes slithering. Skeele, Klaus, Meg, Tukka, and the remaining Hellion recruit begin slicing at the creatures and stomping them.

Alastor waited, letting his creatures do the hard work. Slowly picking up the nail-bat, he gripped it and shook away the voice in his head.

The fighters' blades were dripping with ichor, their boots slimy with bug guts. Lesser Demons are thrown against the wall, slapped across the room. They bite. One hung from Klaus's arm, teeth sinking deep as the Hellion roared and tore the creature off, ripping out a good chunk of skin. Klaus gripped the little Demon with two hands and tore it in half, throwing the pieces in defense as more came crawling out of the hole.

The silence that followed was deafening, a stillness that belied the imminent threat. They stood ready, weapons in hand, eyes locked on the gaping hole in the floor that seemed to breathe malevolence.

Meg glanced at Skeele, his eyes gleaming with predatory focus. Klaus stood tall, his stance disciplined, his blade glinting in the dim light. Tukka, ever the wild card had a *manic grin on his face, twirling a chain with restless energy.*

The ground trembled, a low rumble sending a shiver down Meg's spine.

Tiny Demons and creatures of chaos clawed their way out of the darkness, their eyes glowing with unholy light. They moved with primal ferocity, their growls and roars filling the air, a cacophony of madness and rage.

"Here more come," Klaus muttered, his voice steady but laced with tension.

The first lesser Demon lunged at Klaus, who was closest, a twisted mass of muscle and teeth. Klaus moved instinctively, his blade slicing through the air with a satisfying thwack as it connected with the creature's head, sending it crashing to the ground.

"Stay focused," Skeele said, swinging his blade to keep the next one at bay. "We can't let them overwhelm us!"

Skeele was a blur of motion, blades slashing through the Demons with brutal efficiency. He fought with a focused intensity, each strike fueled by a deep-seated rage. "Just keep them coming," he growled at Alastor, his voice a guttural snarl.

Tukka laughed manically, his chain spinning faster and faster as he waded into the fray. "This is what I've been waiting for!" he shouted, his eyes alight with a wild excitement. "Let's show these bastards what we're made of!"

Klaus was a pillar of strength, his movements precise and controlled. He fought with a calm efficiency, his sword cutting through the chaos with deadly accuracy. "Watch your flanks," he called out, his voice carrying over the din of battle. "Don't let them surround you!"

Meg could feel adrenaline coursing through her veins, sharpening her senses and dulling the pain of each new scratch and bruise. They fought as one, a seamless unit, each covering the other's weaknesses, their movements perfectly synchronized.

The creatures kept coming, a seemingly endless tide of darkness and fury. Tukka lashed out with his chain, feeling the satisfying crunch of bone as it connected with a Demon's skull. "Just keep fighting," he gasped, barely pausing to catch his breath.

Skeele let out a triumphant roar as he tore through a mess of Demons and bugs and snakes. His blade dripped with black blood. Meg glanced to him, just once to make sure he was okay, and his eyes were ablaze with determination.

Meg swung her blade, splitting heads, chopping necks. The scene was all very bloody and gory and disgusting. Alastor was impressed. He didn't know much about Meg, had never seen her in action, but this was a tiny bit impressive. He was slightly disappointed that she was going to die immediately.

"Get back," Skeele warned.

"I'm fine," Meg shouted back, stomping on a giant cockroach. "Everything is fine," she muttered under her breath.

But then it wasn't. Alastor was headed for the duo on

the opposite side of the room. Klaus and the other Hellion didn't see him, too busy with battling the creatures. Alastor swung the nail bat at the other Hellion, piercing his shoulder, then his stomach, then the back of his neck. The last hit took him down.

Tukka noticed and raised his chain.

"What will it be, Queen Meg?" Alastor shouted. "Tell me where the bones are or I kill your Hellion."

"You've already killed enough," Meg shouted back.

"What's one more?" Alastor said as he swung the bat toward Tukka.

The Hellion moved fast, swinging his chain and blocking the nail-bat before it had a chance to crush his skull.

Tukka and Alastor swung weapons, barely missing each other. Metal slammed against wood. Alastor lurched forward, hitting him in the knee. The Hellion roared as nails pierced his leg and his knee gave out.

A sickening squelch echoed in the room as Alastor pulled the nail-bat out of Tukka's leg.

Tukka let out a breathless laugh, his chain finally still. "That was one hell of a fight," he said, a note of satisfaction in his voice.

"Bleed her out. Bleed them out until they confess where my bones are," Lucifer's voice shouted in Alastor's mind.

Alastor swung the nail-bat, circling the air until there was enough momentum, then he whipped it in Klaus's direction.

Klaus didn't see the nail-bat coming, he was too busy

tearing apart lesser Demons and tossing their body parts aside. The nail-bat hit him in the back, embedding in his shoulder blade.

Klaus roared as blood dripped out of his skin. He struggled to bend his arm behind his back and pull it out. When he finally reached the handle, he tugged and the nails tore his skin; blood trickled down his body and pooled at his feet.

Alastor smiled, knowing that the two Hellions would die quickly without blood to heal their injuries. He glanced to the Commander, the one named Skeele. He needed to get that one next. Alastor chanted in Hellspeak. Suddenly the ground beneath Skeele seemed to ripple and a dark, writhing mass of small demons, bugs, and snakes emerged from the cracks in the floor. The deluge ascended upon Skeele with an unholy fervor, their eyes glowing with malevolent intent. Snakes wrapped around his legs, tripping him. Spiders and cockroaches and giant beetles bit him.

Skeele snarled, his claws flashing as he slashed at the oncoming tide. He managed to tear through several of the creatures, but for every one he killed, ten more took its place. The sheer number of them was overwhelming. He felt a sharp pain in his leg as a snake's fangs sank into his flesh, its venom spreading through his veins like wildfire. He stumbled, swatting at the bugs that had crawled up his arms, their bites searing his skin. The small Demons leaped onto him, their claws digging into his flesh, their teeth tearing at him with relentless ferocity.

The creatures swarmed until Skeele was a writhing figure on the floor, not an inch of his skin could be seen.

Meg tried to get to Skeele, kicking and chopping at the creatures. She'd never killed so many spiders or beetles in her life. Still, she could barely see him under the creatures.

Alastor called upon his Basilisk next; the giant creature slithered into the lair and it started toward Tukka.

"No," Meg shouted as she tried to clear Skeele of the deluge of creatures that were consuming him. "Leave them alone." Meg was glaring at Alastor. "Leave them. You want me, take me."

"I want the bones," Alastor said.

"I already told you," Meg was out of breath, panting as she fought and bartered, "I don't know where Lucifer's bones are."

"She's lying," Lucifer roared in Alastor's mind.

The Basilisk darted forward and gobbled Tukka in one bite.

"No!" Meg shouted.

A dark smile quirked Alastor's lip. "You've only got two Hellions, Queen." He shrugged. "Well, what's left of them."

"Stop!" Meg shouted, pleaded. Panic pricked through her limbs as she took in the shit show erupting around her.

Alastor chanted and his creatures receded to the hole in the floor, the Basilisk slithered to a corner and waited.

Meg inhaled a sharp breath as the creatures scattered away from Skeele. His right leg had no skin, chunks of flesh were missing from his body, a hole had been bit in his cheek. Dark eyes flashed open and focused on her. She'd spent enough time with him she could read his face, or what was left of it. He was in agony, nearly eaten alive.

"Commander," Klaus started to say as he dashed across the room to offer help.

The Basilisk darted from the ceiling, consuming Klaus in one bite.

Skeele tried to turn his head, a gasping breath echoed.

"No," Meg whispered, grief flooding her body like a tidal wave, cold and unrelenting. Every piece of her threatened to crack, as if her bones had become fragile glass, splintering under the weight of the moment. Her knees trembled, wanting to give in, to collapse under the crushing sorrow. She stared ahead, unblinking, as reality set in. This couldn't be real. Not him. Not now. It was too early in the fight.

Meg's heart screamed to shatter, to weep, to let the agony consume her–but she couldn't. Not here. Not now. This was not the time to fall apart. She forced herself to breathe, each inhale shallow and ragged, her chest tightening as if bound by iron chains.

Meg bit her lip, the taste of copper filling her mouth, a feeble attempt to keep the flood of emotion from breaking through. She couldn't afford to fall apart–not when danger was watching her from across the room, not when others still relied on her.

Chel ran full bore down the dark passageways, boots slipping on blood and gore. He was following the Basilisk, the creature slithering fast through the hallways, eating the dead and offering him safety out of the castle in the burning caves.

They turned left, then right before coming to the Hellion barracks. They were on the edge of Meg's lands here, past the sparring grounds and the stables. The Basilisk cleared the room of the dead. No one had survived. The Fast-Zombies were too fast. No Hellions remained here.

"Wait," Chel warned the Basilisk. They watched out the windows to be sure no one was nearby. All bodies were on the ground or re-animated and headed toward the castle. "Okay," Chel nodded, motioning to the door.

The Basilisk nosed the door open and the duo slithered into the nearby forest like shadows.

Chel stuck to the cover of the tree canopy while the Basilisk hovered above the nearby road. They ran as fast as they could toward the portal closest to the castle. It was a good thirty miles away; easy to reach by Jeep, but the trek was another story on foot.

They slowed, coming upon a horde of the dead ambling through the forest. Chel breathed a sigh of relief when he realized they were not fast, but the typical stumbling slow. Still, there were so many of them.

The view of the dead Deacons came to mind. Chel was connecting the dots, the rumors of the past few years, and the intel. If there were this many souls trapped and roaming Hell then the Safe Houses were gone.

Chel ran faster, glancing to the Basilisk as it kept pace. He swerved around the dead, felt dread tickling his shoulders when he realized they'd follow and expose him. He cleared the canopy of Hellforest, ducked under the Basilisk as he crossed the road and made it to the cover of the forest again. They were making good time, but Chel was thinking of the scene he'd left behind; he hoped to Hell everyone was still alive. It was the only way. With all these souls collecting, Babylon would come looking for answers. Chel didn't want to serve another throne, he didn't want to go back to the days of Lucifer.

The sun peaked in Hellsky as the duo kept moving. The portal wasn't far and Chel was sure he could get there alone. He made his way to the road and motioned to the Basilisk.

"Go back to the castle," he told the creature.

CHAPTER 36

The shadows curled around Teari and Remington like smoke as Remington led her through the familiar stone halls of the Castle in the Burning Caves. Her feet moved on instinct, eyes glazed and vacant.

She was cold, still dripping from the water, head echoing with the river's pull, and still aching from the way Chel's hand had vanished through the portal and never returned.

They reached the doors to Meg's chamber. Remington gave her a look. "She's waiting," he said quietly.

Teari swallowed and nodded, then opened the door.

Meg stood behind her desk, backlit by firelight and tall windows.

"You made it out." Meg smiled.

Teari's throat closed. "Chel didn't."

Meg's expression flickered. "No. Not yet."

The healer's breath hitched. "Not yet? When is he coming back?"

Silence.

Meg walked around the desk and leaned against its edge. "Try not to focus on time."

Teari blinked. "What?"

Meg clarified. "The Fates kept him."

"Why?" Her voice cracked. "Why would they keep him? He does not belong there."

Meg studied her. "Because he interfered. Because that's who he's always been." Her voice dipped low. "He has always been bound by duty."

Teari's knees buckled. She moved to the nearest chair and sat down, stunned. The room was suddenly too hot. Her heart was too loud.

Meg folded her arms, tone shifting. "He gave you something in return."

Teari looked up, hollow. "What could possibly—"

"Your father is dead. The Archangel Raphael is no more."

The silence that followed was deafening.

The words didn't make sense at first. Teari blinked. "No. He's too powerful to die. There is no way."

"He is dead." Meg's voice was final. "Chel killed him."

Teari couldn't breathe. Her mind reeled. "That's impossible..."

"He infiltrated Raphael's Kingdom when you disappeared into the gulf. Got through the throne room. And ended it."

Teari stared at the cracks in the floor tile.

Meg pushed forward, her voice less sharp now, steadier. "You're free, Teari. Free from his demands. From his control. From everything he forced you to clean up, hide, suffer with. You are free."

Teari went pale and the room seemed to spin. She stood but stumbled before catching herself against the edge of the desk.

"Come on," Meg said as she took Teari's arm. "Sit. This is a lot. It's not the time to take a face dive onto my new tile."

"I don't feel free," she whispered. "I don't think..." She rubbed her face. "Am I still in Purgatory? This doesn't feel right."

Meg crouched, leveling with her. "Freedom doesn't always feel like wings. Sometimes it feels like grief. And how dare you consider my realm Purgatory?" Meg winked.

Teari swallowed hard, vision blurring. "What am I supposed to do now?"

Meg stood again, walking slowly back to her desk. "Now... you decide."

Teari looked up, tears dripping down her cheeks.

"You're his heir. His kingdom is yours, Teari. You can rebuild it. Burn it down. Sanctify it. Whatever you choose."

Teari shook her head, panic flaring. "I can't. I'm not ready. I never wanted—"

"Then the next rightful heir," Meg said carefully, "is the Nightjar."

Silence sliced the air.

Teari's heart skipped. "What?"

Meg turned slowly. "She's your sister."

The world tilted. The heat in the room didn't come from the fire anymore—it came from the truth.

Teari stood. "Her soul is lost. She cannot rule a kingdom the way she is."

"I'm not so sure Raphael's soul was unlost." Meg nodded once. "You're not the only child your father tried to break. But you might be the only one strong enough to heal what's left. He didn't baptize her and her soul has wandered ever since. She is the next rightful heir, even as broken as she is. We could capture her, drag her to Babylon, and baptize her with the hope it would turn her back into an Angel. But we've fought the Nightjar before. I don't have a good feeling about forcing that upon her."

Teari staggered back into the chair, her mind fracturing with a million questions.

Meg poured a drink and placed it silently on the table beside her. "You don't have to decide tonight." She pulled a blanket off the nearby chair and draped it over Teari's shoulders.

Teari stared out the window, but all she could see was the river. The hand that let go. The one that didn't follow her though the tunnel.

CHAPTER 37

"I LIVED," CHEL GROWLED THE FACT LIKE A curse, knowing deep down that if he'd stayed in the Hellion lair and died with his comrades, Meg would have died too. Lucifer would have risen to take the throne once again and Hell would have never seen the light of day. There would only be pain and suffering. The Veil would have split between the realms and the Earthen plane would be nothing. Dust, lava, destroyed.

"Yes but you hate part of yourself for it," the Fate said.

Chel's fists clenched. He felt the burn of disgust and the shame, rage, and grief so sharp it hollowed him out. For so long, he believed the pain was purpose and that carrying it meant honoring them. He was sure that was one of the reasons Meg sent him on vacation and even urged him to retire and recover from it. But Hellions don't retire. They die.

"Why am I here?" he asked. He'd asked the same question so many times.

"To choose," said the first.

The ground cracked beneath him.

He fell and fell and fell; through time, through memory, through years, storms, battles, births, and death. Back to the battlefield. The Hellion Lair burning. The clash of blades and the wails of the wounded echoing. His Hellion brothers falling again, over and over, always in front of him. He screamed at them to move. And when the smoke cleared, only he remained. He dropped to his knees.

"I can't change it," he whispered. "I should have died beside them."

"No you should not have," the Fates' voices said in unison. "Because you were not made to die in that Lair. You did not die in Hellforest as you ran with the Basilisk. You did not die when you were captured and went back to find Meg in the dungeons. Your end lies elsewhere. You must see and embrace it."

The battlefield faded. When Chel rose again, the Fates stood before him in the mist.

"You must see it," the second said. "You must free yourself from it."

The third extended her hand. "You could become something different. A guardian. Not a weapon."

"A guardian of what?" he asked hoarsely. "I have only known being a Hellion, a demon. That is all I am."

"The Veil. The balance. The threshold between

realms," said the first. "You could serve the greater quiet between chaos and collapse."

Chel stared at the mist, considering.

He looked down at his hands, eyes tracing the thin scar around his wrist. Born for war and sacrifice. Bred for blood. And yet Teari had touched them like they were worthy of more. An Angel had touched him freely and she let him touch her back in the most intimate ways. And the sound of her voice as she called his name after returning to Hell, the echo of her words coming through the portal still wrapped around his heart.

"Choose, Hellion," they said once more.

Chapter 38

Heaven was colder when Teari returned to face the aftermath of her father's death. Usually it was hot, but today she did not feel the heat beating down from the suns. She felt absolutely nothing.

But *her* father's realm had always held a different tone than Gabriel's. Old secrets had begun rotting the kingdom to the root. The wind through the giant trees whistled. The high corridors of the castle echoed with silence. The Angels inside didn't know what to do about her.

Teari walked the perimeter of the estate her father ruled with cruelty and precision and desperate secrets. Now it was hers. She was left to clean out the rot that had festered.

She passed rows of servant quarters, many still empty from all of the deaths during the Fast-Zombie War. The

Seven Kingdoms of Heaven had been taken by surprise–the dead had never walked in this realm before–and when they did arrive, they ran. The Seven Kingdoms were decimated.

The head steward trailed behind her with a ledger, reciting names of loyal staff, those who had stayed, and those who had "taken leave" after the fall of their Archangel. She didn't blame them. The halls still smelled faintly of him. It would take time to cleanse.

At the center of it all was the great hall, a sweeping structure of glass and light. Her father's throne stood untouched. She hadn't sat in it. She wasn't sure she ever could. The Archangel Gabriel had moved away from formalities like a throne. He simply sat at the dining room table and did his work after he'd rebuilt. Maybe she'd do the same.

"You're cataloging the empire now?" came a voice from behind her.

Teari turned and found Gabriel in the threshold, wings folded, looking a little more casual than usual. He wore slacks and a button down shirt and... boots.

"I guess I don't get a resignation letter," he said, walking slowly into the hall with a wry smile.

She raised a brow. "You did send your daughter to tell me I was the rightful heir. Kind of feels like that was your version of notice."

Gabriel chuckled, rubbing a hand across his beard. "Fair point."

"I haven't taken the throne," she said, glancing at the ornate seat behind her. "Not officially. I'm just making sure the servants aren't stealing anything. You know how butthurt Angels can behave."

"They wouldn't," he said gently. "Most of them were afraid of him. Not you."

She sighed. "That's the problem, isn't it? No one's afraid of me. No one here wants me. I left. I betrayed my father by choosing to work for you."

"Maybe that's exactly what this place needs." He leaned on the armrest of the throne but didn't sit. He rocked it a little. "Toss this crap out. Burn it. It's ugly."

She crossed her arms. "Don't tell me what to do."

Gabriel shrugged. "You've got the sharpest mind I know. You're one of the most gifted healers we've ever seen, and you've carried your father's sins longer than anyone should have." He lowered his chin. "Why didn't you tell me what he was making you do?"

"I was ashamed. Still am." Teari looked down at her hands. "I don't want to be him. I hate myself."

"You won't be him. Not even close."

They stood in silence for a moment. The afternoon sun filtered through the skylight in fractured beams, catching the dust motes.

"I can help you find a new healer," she offered, glancing at him. "Someone to replace me."

Gabriel's mouth curved slightly. "That's generous. I was hoping you'd offer."

"Consider it a trade," she said. "You sent me into chaos, and I'm handing you back order."

He barked a laugh. "That *does* sound like us."

She smiled, and for a moment it felt almost normal, not like the world was shifting under her feet and not like she was the reluctant ruler of a kingdom built on sins.

"I'll help you settle things," Gabriel added, more softly now. "If you need anything."

Teari looked up at him. "Thank you."

He nodded. "You've already done more than enough for the rest of us. Time someone did something for you." He opened his arms.

Teari stepped into his embrace without another word. Gabriel had been more of a father than her real one.

Gabriel smoothed her hair. "Change something. Change everything. Make it yours, make it nothing like Babylon has ever seen before. This is how we break the old ways. Just like Meg did."

Teari was nodding as Gabriel released her and she suddenly felt too cold.

As he turned to go, she looked once more at the throne and at the jagged crown still resting atop it. It was shaped like a halo but bore thorns around the rim.

"The thorns of the family, these thorns are the sharpest. The ones you're born from. The ones that think they have a right to grow inside you. They hook us, bury inside so deep we'll never really be free."

The great hall echoed with Gabriel's footsteps as he walked away.

Teari remained still at the foot of the throne, her boots quiet against the marble floor. Outside, sunlight streamed through the etched glass windows, spilling across the cracked tiles like golden lace.

She wandered toward the high arched windows, looking down into the courtyard. The place was still in recovery. In the distance, soldiers patrolled in crisp formation, but there was no joy in their movements—only duty. Several low-ranking Angels huddled near the fountain. They didn't look at her. They didn't know how to look at her. She was the daughter of the tyrant, the heir to a haunted house; a haunted heir.

Her fingers rested on the window frame as she exhaled, slow and quiet. She didn't cry, not anymore. There was nothing left to grieve except what she'd already lost.

She should've felt victorious. Free. Her father was gone. The shackles were broken. No more emergency calls, no more cover-ups, no more cleaning his hands of blood with her own. No more deaths.

And yet... the silence was deafening.

There was no Chel.

Her throat tightened at the thought.

She had felt him across the Veil. It was a thrum in the back of her soul, a warmth just beyond reach like the sun behind clouds. But there was no voice. No touch. No confirmation that he still breathed. He had pulled her from Purgatory. He had saved her. And now he was gone.

She pressed her forehead to the cool glass. "You stubborn bastard," she whispered. "You better come back or I'm gonna find you and kill you for real."

But even as she said it, doubt twisted through her. She only knew stories of Purgatory, only knew ancient lore that had been twisted and diluted. She needed to do some hard research because it seemed the old gods were returning and the world she'd once known was crumbling.

Her hands curled into fists.

Chel didn't belong there. He had earned rest, peace, a quiet life in the sun. Not darkness. Not ghosts. Not sacrifice to the demons of the mind.

And yet... wasn't that always who he was? A Hellion made for war. A blade forged in grief.

Teari closed her eyes.

Come back, she thought. *Please.*

A breeze swept through the corridor and it smelled faintly of sulfur and river water. Her eyes snapped open. No one was there. But her heart beat a little louder in her chest.

Something was stirring across the realms. She'd never felt it like this before but now that she'd taken the throne, now she could feel something strange. This must be how the Archangels were always one step ahead.

Teari stared at her reflection in the glass.

Gabriels words echoed, *Change something. Change*

everything. Make it yours, make it nothing like Babylon has ever seen before.

She touched her cropped blonde hair then used her healing magic to grow it to a chin length bob, then darkened the color to a shade lighter than black. That was a good start–respectable even, and at least it wasn't bangs.

Chapter 39

Weeks had passed since Teari had taken up residence in her father's kingdom. Her days were filled with audits, oaths, and angelic disputes, but still her nights were filled with dreams of Chel and Purgatory and everything left unsaid. And then there were the nightmares of the young souls she'd released. She was finally free of her father's demands, but that didn't make the nightmares disappear.

Teari moved her room to an abandoned wing of the castle. She'd be dead before she slept in her father's quarters and considered having it demolished. She didn't want to go back to her childhood room. Too many memories there.

Yes, Teari's days had been filled with duty and tasks, but today she had left the kingdom entirely. She'd scheduled a meeting with someone she hadn't seen in a long time.

The Peabody Library was a cathedral of books and shadows, its vast domed ceiling stretching above. Dust floated in slow spirals. The scent of parchment and ink settled over everything.

Teari took in the runes etched into the doorframes and window frames, the runes drawn on the floors with chalk and charcoal and salt. If she didn't know better, bro was doing some serious work on the Earthen plane if he needed to keep all kinds of creatures away.

She found Jasper waiting in the rare manuscripts room, backlit by a stained-glass panel. The Angel stood tall, calm, unreadable, but his eyes softened when he saw her.

"Teari," he greeted. "It's good to see you."

Jasper looked not much different than he did during healer training. He seemed more relaxed now, like humanity had sunken into his skin. He was dressed for the Earthen plane in jeans and a button down short sleeved shirt with sharks printed on it. The blue color of the shirt made his blue eyes seem lighter.

"You said you had information for me." She crossed the room to greet him. "About Yelena."

"I do." Jasper motioned for her to walk with him as he shrugged on a leather jacket. "But first, you need context. And a little patience. We have to do this just right so we don't upset the balance."

She arched a brow but followed him without complaint. They passed through the marble halls of the library, down a narrow stairwell, and exited out a side door that opened onto a quiet street at the edge of the city.

The sun was warm. Earth felt slower than the other realms. More rooted. More human. Her fingers tingled and the scars on her arms felt tight.

Jasper led her down an alleyway, and she noticed a portal hidden amongst the overgrown vines. He motioned for her to follow and they walked through a courtyard, down another sidewalk, and to a river walk.

"This close to water?" Teari asked.

"It's a risk but worth it. The little girl you rescued," Jasper said as they turned the corner. He slipped on a pair of sunglasses.

Teari's voice was low. "Chel's sister."

"She was reborn when she left Purgatory. That's the rule for children. They are restored but not to where they were." He glanced at her. "Yelena's soul entered the mortal plane years ago. She's not a child anymore."

Teari stopped. "What?"

"She's twenty now. A college student." He handed her sunglasses. "Put these on."

"That's not possible. It's been—what, six weeks?" She slipped the sunglasses on and the world around her darkened.

"Earth doesn't follow the timelines of a freed soul slipping through the Veil," Jasper said. "Souls are placed where they belong. Her spirit was young, but her path required time to grow into herself again."

Teari stood there, stunned. "Where is she now?"

Jasper gave a faint smile. "Come with me."

They crossed the street and slipped into the rhythm of a bustling farmer's market. There were booths lined with hand-poured candles, herbal soaps, and jars of jam. The air was filled with the scent of sage and bread and apple cider. Laughter spilled through the crowd.

"That smells delicious," Teari said as she sniffed the air as they passed a food stand.

"Fried dough," Jasper said. "It's good with cinnamon and granulated sugar. I always choke on the powdered sugar."

Teari glanced at him with concern.

He tried to explain, "You can't inhale as you chew, the powdered sugar goes straight down your windpipe. I never remember."

"Thanks for warning me."

Jasper touched her arm and tipped his chin toward a booth.

And then Teari saw her.

A young woman sat beneath a canvas tent, her long braid streaked with the color of coal. She wore a loose shirt dusted with stains and a pair of patched jeans. Her hands moved quickly as she wrapped delicate clay pendants in cloth, tying them with twine and handing them off with a soft smile.

She was radiant. Whole. Happy.

Yelena.

Teari's breath caught in her chest. "She's... okay?" she whispered.

"She's more than okay," Jasper said. "She's thriving."

They watched from a distance. Yelena laughed at something one of the customers said, brushing her hair behind her ear with a motion Teari remembered from Purgatory.

"She doesn't remember," Jasper said gently. "Only enough to stay away from the water."

Teari's throat burned. She hadn't realized she was crying until Jasper reached into his coat and silently handed her a folded napkin.

"I'm sorry. I didn't think this would make me emotional," she said.

"Your sacrifice meant something," Jasper said softly. "That you did what the Fates couldn't."

"And Chel?" Her voice cracked. "Does she know—?"

"No." Jasper looked out toward the sky. "That story will find its way to her when it's time. That's a world she doesn't quite remember. She likes supernatural books and movies. I've caught her staring into the shadows as though she might see movement. She knows she's different. She's just not sure how or why."

Teari nodded, eyes never leaving the young woman.

Yelena was free.

And somehow, in this quiet afternoon, that mattered more than anything else.

"I wish Chel could see this," Teari muttered into the napkin as she dried her tears.

Jasper hooked her arm in his and led her away. They sat on a bench beneath a maple tree turning to flame. Cool air chilled Teari's cheeks.

Teari didn't speak for a long time. She simply watched Yelena work as she wrapped stones in wire, arranging her displays, laughing with the college couple who bought one of her beaded bracelets. Her movements were confident. Her smile was easy.

"She's never going to remember me, is she?" Teari asked at last, her voice quiet.

Jasper moved closer, keeping his voice low. "Maybe not everything. But something in her soul will remember. You gave her another chance. That kind of gift doesn't go unnoticed by the universe."

Teari clasped her hands together in her lap. The sun touched the top of the market tents, casting long shadows, painting the world in gold and rust.

"I wasn't sure I'd done the right thing," she admitted. "It was all so..." She shook her head. "The whole experience was extreme."

"You did what was right. And more." Jasper looked at her. "You helped a child escape the cycle. You altered fate. You did a good thing."

Teari turned toward him, expression unreadable. "And I lost someone I cared about."

"What makes you think he's lost?" Jasper smiled, and

the light caught his eyes. "Maybe he's exactly where he needs to be right now."

"What does that mean?"

"It means you have more power than you think. It means Heaven, Hell, and everything in between will be watching what you do next."

She gave a humorless little huff. "That's not comforting."

He stood. "Come on. There's a bakery at the corner. We should celebrate the living."

Teari rose slowly. "I don't want her to see me."

"She won't," Jasper promised. "Not yet."

They walked down the sidewalk in silence, the fading day soft on their shoulders.

Behind them, Yelena reached for a new skein of cord. Her braid swung gently over her shoulder. She wore a pendant around her neck, a small swirl of obsidian and bone that caught the light as she laughed.

Jasper led her to a small building not far down the street.

"A bakery?" Teari asked.

"I figured it might be better than organic carrots."

"No powdered sugar?"

"Definitely not." Jasper coughed.

WEEKS LATER

"You're torturing yourself," Meg said, propping her boots on the edge of her desk. "You know that, right?" She wrapped the long laces around her ankle.

Teari didn't answer. She only traced the map on the table with one finger, following the invisible ley lines between realms, then the circle that she and Remington had marked as the old portal to Purgatory.

"He will return," Meg said gently. "He just needs more time."

"That's what you said last time," Teari replied. Her voice was calm, but her hands shook. "And the time before that. And the one before that."

"Because it's still true."

"What if it's not?" Teari looked up. "What if he's just... stuck? What if he never comes back? I need to go help him."

Meg sighed and rubbed her brow. "You cannot interfere here. You must let time play out. We are not going to interrupt omens like the Archangels and Deacons did before."

Teari closed her eyes. "I miss him."

"I know." Meg stood. "But when he comes back, he'll need you to be strong."

Teari opened her eyes, and tipped her head to the side. "Did you just say *omen*?"

Meg closed her mouth and looked away. "I don't believe in omens."

Teari's eyes narrowed and she took a step closer to the Queen of Hell. "What are you not telling me?"

Meg grabbed her leather jacket off a nearby chair and stretched an arm through it with her back to Teari and scars on display. Omens... Yes, trying to interfere with omens had gotten Meg those scars on her back. It had gotten her wings cut off, her birthmark cut out, the runes, the marks from being struck by lightning when she was cast out of the Earthen Plane. Omens had not been kind to Meg.

There was only one person who could see the future, that Teari knew of. Rue, Meg's daughter. But they'd never referred to her visions as an omen before. That was a term from Meg's mother, Clea. And Clea was gone. Teari took a deep breath as Meg turned around, face expressionless.

"Oh," Meg pointed, "I forgot to tell you, I like the new hair."

Teari touched the darker strands, the color a shade lighter than Meg's.

The sound of feathers dragging across stone interrupted them. Sparrow entered the room, tall and handsome and just as dark in presence as his mate. They had a vibe.

Sparrow whistled a light trill that sounded like a blue jay in the morning.

Meg smiled and her cheeks flushed. "There's my old Sparrow man. Where have you been?" She crossed the room.

Teari suddenly felt like she was interrupting something intimate and excused herself.

Weeks later

The sand was warm beneath Teari's feet as she stood at the edge of the gulf, the wind tugging at her coat, the sea lapping at her ankles. She didn't move. She just stared at the horizon as if it might open for her the way it once had. She never thought the beach could feel so cold when the air was seventy-four degrees. She shivered, missing warm arms around her. She didn't understand how she could miss it all so much when she only had him for a few weeks.

This was her ritual now. The first day of every month, no matter her schedule or realmly duties, she returned here just as she promised she would. And waited. Just in case.

But every day was the same. The ocean didn't part. The Veil didn't open. And Chel did not come.

She wanted him to. She wanted to see him tall and strong walking out of that ocean toward her. She wanted his jokes, his incessant requests for dates, his lips on her skin. She wanted him back. She wanted the Fates to let him go.

She crouched at the shoreline, fingers dragging lines

through the wet sand. She didn't cry. She rarely did anymore. Her grief had worn down to something quiet. The humanity she'd absorbed from all that blood thrummed under her skin and swelled behind her ribs, humming like a bruise that wouldn't fade.

Eventually, the tide crept too close. She rose and turned from the sea and walked the familiar path to the beach house. It was silent when she entered. The air was stale, untouched. A few of his things were still here. She hadn't moved them.

A book lay open on the side table—one of the novels he'd been flipping through in his idle moments. His polished boots sat near the door, sand-dusted from their date that ended at the beach. A cracked mug still held the dried remnants of blood she'd poured him during the last day they'd shared together.

She stepped into the bedroom and opened the closet. His clothes still hung there. Black shirts. Faded jeans. A leather jacket with a torn seam on the shoulder.

Teari reached for one of the shirts and rubbed the soft cotton between her fingertips then pressed it to her face. It still smelled like him. Leather and sea spray. Blood and salt. Hellion. Something wild and steady. Safe. Something that had once held her through nightmares and kissed her beneath moonlight and called her his wife when the world wasn't paying attention. He'd killed for her and she couldn't even repay him. She'd been warned to wait and that was it. She'd never felt so useless in her whole life.

She folded the shirt carefully and held it to her chest as she left.

CHAPTER 40

"Again?" Chel asked. He'd fallen through time more cycles than he cared to remember.

"You must," said the Fate.

The ground cracked beneath him.

He fell back to the battlefield. He was out of breath, muscles burning. There was no wind in Purgatory but there were a thousand lost voices wailing through fractured time. For the faintest second he was sure he heard his mother's voice. And then, he was dropped outside his childhood hovel.

Purgatory had a way of making silence feel like it was watching you.

He stood barefoot on a warped wooden floor. Dust motes spun in the thin moonlight leaking through cracked curtains. Home. He recognized the smell of oil and iron, the faint copper tang of blood never scrubbed from the boards.

Chel's chest tightened.

Through the door, voices murmured. They were low and dangerous and laced with threats in Hellspeak. His father's voice was one of them, all grit and thunder. The other voice he didn't quite recognize, though the cadence of it made his stomach clench.

The door to the study was ajar. He pushed it wider.

Inside, his father leaned over a heavy oak desk, one massive hand braced on a set of rolled blueprints.

"...construction will start when the foundations are sanctified," the stranger said, running a leather-gloved finger along the paper. "The wards will keep the Veil thin. Your name will never be tied to it. It will move with each successor. They will never be able to track it down when control changes hands."

There was movement in the closet. Chel remembered the air in that room, thick with smoke from the cigars his father favored when deals were made.

There was a boy hiding in the closet. If found, he'd get the beating of a lifetime.

The stranger tapped the corner of the plans. "The Black Mansion will stand for centuries. With this, they will never stop feeding us. And the creature will never get loose. Everyone benefits from this design."

Chel's father grunted. "We will complete it soon."

The boy Chel had been froze in the closet, not understanding the weight of what he was hearing, only that it was dangerous. His gaze slipped to the plans, to the lines and symbols and runes etched into the layout. He remembered the sharp smell of the ink.

And then his father's head turned.

Those black eyes locked on him. "Out," the demon snarled.

Young Chel ran out of the office and to his room. He leaned against the door to catch his breath. He remembered this, vaguely. He didn't realize how important it could have become. He'd seen the blueprints and the planning.

The memory blurred at the edges, spinning away like ash in the wind.

Chel was back on the black sand, breathing hard.

"You saw it," the Fate with the gold hair murmured. "You were a child, but you saw the birth of the Black Mansion. You knew the shape of it before you knew what it was. You heard what they said. The creature will never get loose."

Chel swallowed hard, the sound too loud in his ears. "Why show me this now?"

"Because you will face it again," the gray-eyed Fate said. "And you will burn it to the ground."

Chel's hands curled into fists. He could still smell the cigar smoke. He dropped to his knees. But then, he heard a familiar voice. Something different.

"Chel! Where are you?"

He knew that voice.

He stood at the edge of the cracked riverbed. It was the place where he'd first seen Teari and Yelena, where he'd watched them drown, and where he had almost escaped with them.

He hadn't seen the sky in weeks.

He hadn't seen anything but the fog that always seemed to coat this realm.

Until the light came.

It shimmered from the corner of the mist, like a blade slicing through the gray and then a voice cut through, just as sharp.

"Chel! You stubborn, bull-headed bastard!"

Chel blinked, head snapping toward the tunnel near the riverbed. There, tethered by a thick rope wrapped around her waist, stood Meg and her eyes full of fire. Behind her, the other end of the rope vanished into the tunnel

"What the hell are you doing here?" he asked, stumbling toward her. "You're not supposed to be here. They'll make you stay," he warned, hands out to shoo her away.

"Spare me," she snapped. "I've been breaking rules since the day I was born. You think Purgatory's going to stop me?" She looked around. "You think some old fucking Fates are going to stop me?" She shouted that line.

Meg looked pissed.

"I need you," she said. "I need you *out* of here. You're lingering. What's the hold up?"

Before Chel could speak, another voice echoed.

The fog parted and a hundred threads blew in the

wind, twisting like snakes, braiding through the air. The Weaver appeared.

"Never thought I'd see the day that the ruler of Hell came to visit," the Weaver whispered.

"He gifted you power when he killed the Archangel," Meg said, chin high. "And what's coming isn't just one war, it's all of them. Again. You're playing games with him. Do not."

The Weaver tilted her head. "Tell me more."

Meg unrolled a parchment, her voice tight. "The Black Mansion is growing. Its influence is twisting into Heaven and Earth. Again. The walls remain anchored by old bargains and *souls*. Chel is the last living Hellion from before Lucifer's betrayal. I need him to help take it down. I need my strongest Hellion. And I have been waiting long enough."

"And why should we care?" the Weaver asked.

"Because," Meg's eyes narrowed, "if the Black Mansion falls, the souls trapped within will be released. Power will flow again. Not just to Hell, not just to Heaven, but to *you*. The Fates. The old gods. The flow of souls will return to the ways before the Archangels were born and started twisting the world to their image. You already know this."

Chel's breath caught as he realized the tangled web he'd been dropped in.

The Weaver turned slowly to Chel. "You can destroy this place?"

"I could," he said quietly. "They took our girls."

He looked at Meg. "We have been trying to put an end to the Black Mansion and it's followers for a long time."

The Weaver moved forward. Her fingers touched his chest. "You were always a weapon. But now, you are also a thread. Thin. Pulled. Barely clinging."

"I'm strong enough," Chel growled.

"Your body is old," she said. "But your soul is strong."

Chel's eyes widened. He was suddenly reminded of racing Nero and his knee giving out.

"I will return your soul," she murmured. "But not your body."

Behind him, Meg cursed under her breath.

Chel stared at the Weaver. "Why?"

"Because this realm requires balance. I let you go, but you leave something behind. And if you promise the Fates power, you better not disappoint."

He hesitated. "Fine," he said.

"There is no better alternative?" Meg asked, voice tight.

"He must destroy it. And the rules stand, to leave something must remain. It will not be the Queen of Hell. It will be your body. And when you defeat the Black Mansion, it will be the souls you release to *us*. The realm of the Fates will have power again. We have been starving."

The Weaver raised her hand.

A golden blade appeared, threaded with runes and

white-hot fire. She sliced it once across the air, and Chel staggered as his body buckled.

He fell to his knees. The pain wasn't sharp, but it was bone deep. He felt pressure behind his eyes, behind his ribs, his back arching as light spilled from his chest. His brothers had been skinned by Alastor and that would have been a relief from the pain of being separated from his body as his soul was cut out.

A shimmer appeared around him.

He let out a wild agonizing scream.

And then he was standing and looking down at his own crumpled body, lying empty on the riverbank floor of Purgatory.

"Chel," Meg whispered. She glared at the Fates.

He looked at his hands. They were whole, but shimmering. He was now a soul woven from thread and grit and stubborn hope.

The Weaver stepped back, threads whirling. "Go now. The path will not stay open long. A body will come to you as you pass through."

Chel turned. He reached for Meg as they made their way to the tunnel that led back to Hell.

"You should not have risked your life for me," Chel warned.

Meg smirked as she lifted the rope that wrapped around her waist. "Sparrow is holding the other end. If they tried anything, he'd fucking slaughter them. Then he'd be a king in three realms."

Chapter 41

Hell smelled different when Chel wasn't in his own skin.

He now wore a body that was taller, leaner. Younger. The hands weren't calloused the same way, the gait was too smooth. It felt like trying on a suit made for someone else. Expensive, efficient, and hollow. Even the reflection he caught in the molten glass walls of the chamber was unrecognizable. He had lighter hair instead of dark brown and eyes that shimmered amber instead of nearly black. But beneath the skin, the fire of an old Hellion soul still burned.

Chel stood silent as Meg paced. Only she knew the truth.

"This is a bad idea," Remington muttered, arms crossed as he studied the newcomer with quiet suspicion. "I don't like bringing strangers into this, especially not when we're planning to destroy the Black Mansion. What if he's a spy?"

"He's not a stranger," Meg said smoothly. "He's exactly what we need. Trust me."

Remington narrowed his eyes. "You're awfully sure of that."

Meg smiled tightly. "That's because I know what he's capable of."

Chel didn't speak and didn't blink. He simply lowered his gaze to the cracked leather map of the realms spread across the table. The Black Mansion pulsed red tendrils reaching into every plane, spreading like rot from a wound.

Meg flicked her gaze to him. "Tell us what you know."

He studied the pins, the routes, the ward lines, then finally pointed to a faint marking at the base of the northern chasm. "There's a door here. Alastor used it to feed human women into the lower halls. If we cut it off, the entire web destabilizes. Everything collapses inward."

Remington arched a brow. "How do you know that?"

Chel didn't look at him. "Because my father helped build it. I saw the original plans." His finger traced a tendril. "And I have a pretty good memory."

Silence.

Meg pressed on. "If anyone can lead this final strike and make sure we don't fail again, it's him. We've been trying to pin this mansion down for years. Every time we get close it moves." Meg started pacing again. "Asmodeus is too weak to move it again."

Chel finally met Remington's gaze. "You don't need to trust me. Just follow the plan."

"How can you be sure Asmodeus survived the Angel's light?" Remington asked.

"I just know." Meg unrolled a scroll. "He'll infiltrate the mansion with the scouting party. The wards won't recognize him, so we have one chance to get inside before the alarms sound."

"And what about afterward?" Remington asked, still not sold.

Meg looked at Chel. "Then we burn it to the ground."

Chel's soul flickered just beneath the borrowed flesh. He thought of how long they'd been gathering intel on the Black Mansion. He thought of the missing women and the stolen children. They'd taken Rue, Evelyn, and Layla. They'd even tried to get Shay. And he thought of Teari. The way she'd looked at him on the beach. She hadn't fallen to the Black Mansion but her father seeded its dirty deeds with souls and human blood. The corruption was deep-seated and Chel began to wonder if they'd even scratched the surface.

He would finish this war not just for Hell, not just for Meg. But for Teari and his sister. He would not let another innocent be blackened by the sins of the Black Mansion. Not another soul would fall into its grip.

"All right," he said. "We'll bring it down. For all of them."

THE BARRACKS WERE ALWAYS TOO LOUD BEFORE battle. Steel scraping, voices barking, flame-cracked walls echoing with anticipation. Chel had never liked this part.

"Suit up," barked the squad leader. A broad-shouldered Hellion leader named Vex tossed a charred armor vest to the newest member of their unit. "We move in one hour."

Chel caught the vest mid-air without looking. The others had started calling him Ash because he didn't give a name and didn't speak unless necessary. He let them assume he was a transfer from the mountain demons. A drifter. A ghost with nothing. As were most of them. They were either bred to be a Hellion or wound up there because they had nothing left to lose.

They weren't wrong.

He strapped the vest over the unfamiliar frame of his borrowed body. It was sleeker than his old one and faster maybe, but not as strong. Not as scarred. The man's skin was too smooth.

"You got experience with fortress infiltration?" one of the younger Hellions asked, a kid barely old enough to drink fire-whiskey.

Chel didn't answer, just checked the edge on the

dagger Meg had given him. It was the Basilisk blade, he'd used it to kill Teari's father. Now he'd kill another piece of shit with it.

"Guess that's a yes," another Hellion muttered. "He gives me the creeps."

"Yeah, but he moves like he knows death," someone else said.

Chel almost laughed. Almost. He'd met death. The Fates, all three. These kids didn't know shit. Oh the stories he could tell them.

He listened while they joked, while they speculated. Vex explained the breaching route again. Three outer towers had a break in the protection ward that only opens once every rotation when the Black Mansion's own security switched out.

Chel had already redrawn the entire layout in his mind, marking weak points and potential fails from the blueprints on his father's desk. He knew every hall and horror inside and he knew exactly where to make it bleed. Find the demon in charge and put an end to him. The Mansion would wait for someone new to take over and move it. But the building would be shuttered by then.

A Hellion named Krick sat beside him on the bench, his warpaint half-done. "You're too quiet," he said.

Chel shrugged. "Talking won't keep you alive."

"No," he agreed. "But it might make dying feel less lonely."

He offered a flask. Chel took it and tipped the

burning liquid past lips that didn't belong to him. It didn't matter. It burned just the same.

"Where you from, Ash?" he asked.

"Doesn't matter," he said.

Krick narrowed his eyes. "You're not here for glory."

"No."

"You here to die?"

Chel looked down at the dagger. "No," he said again, voice low. "I'm here to finish something. Death has knocked on my door too many times."

Krick watched him a moment longer then nodded. "Well, good. Because if we pull this off, Hell won't be the same."

He didn't reply and definitely didn't tell the Hellion what he knew.

The Black Mansion held power it was never supposed to hold. It fed on stolen souls, siphoned blood through forgotten rites.

Chel's task wasn't vengeance.

It was the end of a sickness, an end of the old ways.

He stood when Vex called for final checks. Weapons were counted. Armor was fastened. They filed into formation at the edge of the tunnel that would lead them into the Veil and then straight to the Black Mansion's outer ward.

Chel walked behind them all, silent and focused. Fire was building beneath the skin of a stranger.

They made their way through the forest surrounding the Castle in the burning cave to the nearest portal.

Remington had recommended one further from the castle in case something came through.

Chel stepped through last, the cold breath of the in-between wrapping around his borrowed skin like chains. The moment his boots struck the cragged terrain on the other side, he felt the power of the Black Mansion.

The squad fanned out like they'd trained, silent gestures and split paths. Vex led them across jagged obsidian stone toward the low access tower built into the cliffside.

Chel could feel the hum of the Masion beneath his ribs. The thrum was in his ears as they climbed the ledge in silence.

Krick hissed a warning, "Ward up ahead."

Chel stepped past him before anyone could stop him. His hand lifted and with the twist of his wrist and a word in Hellspeak, the ward fizzled and snapped.

The others stared.

"You weren't supposed to—"

"Move," Chel said, not explaining.

No more questions. He wasn't going to tell them what he'd seen on the blueprints. He'd told Meg and she'd gotten him here. That was all that mattered.

They descended into the mansion's outer halls and slid along twisted corridors lit by unnatural fire, walls lined with bone-carved scripture and the hanging remnants of failed experiments. Chel's jaw clenched.

He remembered these halls.

They moved deeper.

Vex's voice barely carried. "Next room has two guards. Shifts every eight minutes."

"We don't have eight minutes," Krick said. "There's something wrong. It's too quiet."

Chel gripped the dagger Meg had given him. "I'll handle it."

Krick grabbed his arm. "You can't just go in alone."

Krick blinked. "Who are you?"

Chel didn't answer.

Instead, he slipped through the shadows and was gone.

THE BLACK MANSION GUARDS WERE HIGH ON blood.

Chel came from behind. The dagger whispered through flesh. One down. The second turned, mouth opening to scream, but Chel was already there with a hand over the guard's mouth, blade under the ribs. He dragged the body into the dark before it could hit the ground.

When he returned to the group, his chest was splattered with ichor.

Vex stared at him. "You're not a mountain demon," he said quietly.

"No," Chel replied. "Not even close."

"Who the fuck are you?"

Chel's gaze could have lit fire. "Something worse."

THEY REACHED THE HEART OF THE MANSION AN hour later. The hallways were littered with bodies, Demons and Hellion alike. They approached a room that had been marked as a throne room on the blueprints. The Black Mansion should not have a throne—this was Hell and there was only one ruler.

The throne was black and made of what looked like bone. At its center lounged Asmodeus, or what remained of him. Asmodeus was of Lucifer's bloodline; the demon had been itching to take over the Black Mansion since before Alastor had control. The demon had even conspired with the Raven King in an effort to overthrow control before Alastor's death.

One side of Asmodeus's face had been burned to the skull, eye melted to pulp. The holy fire had never fully faded from his bones. His skin crackled with every breath, as if the Angel were still smoldering him. His suit was charred, his nails painted in blood, his grin all cruelty and charm. It was a terrible look for the demon.

"So," Asmodeus said, dragging a finger down the arm of the throne, "the Hellions have arrived."

Chel didn't speak.

The others behind him hadn't followed into the central hall, watching from the edge of the shadows.

"Get the girls out," Chel whispered. "Search every room. Get them gone. Release any souls you find."

"Meg sent you, didn't she? Always sending her wolves to die in my house." Asmodeus rose from the throne.

"You're not supposed to be alive," Chel replied. "After the Angel lit you up like dry brush, you should've burned to ash."

Asmodeus sneered, his ruined face twitching. "I did burn. I burned and I am still burning. And then I crawled back to my throne." He gestured to the room. "You wouldn't know about crawling, would you, Hellion?"

Chel's expression didn't change, but his fists clenched. "You will die today."

"I have died so many times," Asmodeus said, stepping closer. "Lucifer's bloodline does that. But we come back. We always come back. I am nothing put a puppet."

Chel's jaw flexed.

He reached into his jacket and pulled out the dagger Meg had given him. The Basilisk bone gleamed, the tip Basilisk venom.

Asmodeus laughed. "Oh, she really did send you to kill me."

"She told me to make sure your legacy ended in fire."

They collided in the next breath.

The handful of Hellions that remained braced themselves for an onslaught.

Asmodeus moved fast despite his eternal burning. He

was still a prince of the old hells, still twisted with forbidden power. His clawed hand cracked against Chel's ribs and sent him sliding back across the floor, the tiles scorching hot beneath his boots.

Chel caught himself, rolled, and came up swinging. The dagger met flesh. Asmodeus shrieked.

"You piece of—"

Chel surged forward, stabbing again, the bone blade dragging across Asmodeus's midsection, but the demon vanished in a snap of smoke and reappeared behind him, arms already raised for a killing blow.

Chel ducked, spun, and his wing unfurled and struck Asmodeus with a whipcrack. The impact shattered a pillar.

"Oh, I see who you are. A soul switch. Been a long time since I've seen one of those. You were never strong enough," Asmodeus spat, coughing blood. "Not then. Not now. I heard how you watched the other Hellions be torn apart the day Alastor stormed the castle and thrust that whore off the throne."

"Shut your filthy mouth," Chel growled. He drew a second dagger, one he'd hidden in his boot.

Asmodeus hesitated, a flicker of real fear in his burnt eye.

Chel lunged.

They fought in brutal silence now. There was no witty banter, no posturing. There was only raw hate and history bleeding onto the tiles. The daggers screamed with every slice, hungering for the soul of the corrupted demon.

Finally, Chel buried one blade in Asmodeus's neck.

The second, in his stomach.

The demon dropped to his knees, blood pouring down his chest.

"You should've stayed dead," Chel whispered.

Asmodeus smiled through the pain. "You think this ends with me? I am nothing. There are worse creatures to fear here."

"It ends with this mansion."

And with a final twist, Chel ripped the blade across Asmodeus's throat.

The demon collapsed.

The throne groaned, cracked, and the walls began to scream and shudder.

Chel stepped back, panting, the blades heavy in his hands.

Krick and Vex finally moved closer, faces pale, weapons ready.

"It's done," Chel said. "Burn it all."

And he turned his back as the Black Mansion began to crumble.

One Archangel dead and one high demon dead, Chel had quite the checklist going these days.

Chapter 42

The Black Mansion burned until it no longer existed. There was only ash and cinder and Hell-soil. Chel waited until the last smolder went out then he raked through the debris with a stick to ensure no skeletons or magical objects had survived. He didn't want to risk the chance of something surviving and rebuilding.

Meg stood beside him as the final timbers collapsed into fire. "You did it," she said, her voice low enough that only he could hear. "I knew you'd do it."

He didn't answer. His thoughts were a storm behind the mask. He wasn't sure what this victory was supposed to feel like. The souls that had been trapped within the Black Mansion were freed. Some had survived and were returned to their rightful homes and planes. The ones that had passed were sent to the Fates, as promised.

Chel raked the soil, eyes scanning for anything peculiar.

"What was that?" Meg asked.

"Hm?" Chel went still. There was subtle vibration under their feet. Chel closed his eyes and brought up the plans for the mansion. A lot of time had passed, and he could have missed something.

"They altered the plans," Meg said, crouching, fingertips to the soil.

The Raven King was across the way, watching. It was only a second before he began walking toward Meg, giant black wings dragging on the ground.

Meg leaned closer to Chel. "You should approach Teari like that." She nodded in Sparrow's direction and a shiver went through her. "It's very alpha male. Girls like that kinda thing."

"Sure, Meg, I'll get right on that," Chel muttered. "In this skin she'd kill me though. She has no clue who I am like this."

"Might be worth it," Meg said. "It's a tunnel we missed." Meg pointed to a divot in the center of the soil where the Black Mansion once stood.

Chel cursed just as Sparrow approached Meg's side.

"I'm taking you out of here." Sparrow was reaching for Meg. "Something is wrong."

I am nothing but a puppet. Asmodeus's words rang through Chel's head.

"Meg?" Chel's eyes flicked from the forest overhang to the soil. He turned and glanced toward the mountains. "Are you sure Asmodeus was in charge here?"

Meg pressed her lips together in thought. "He had to be. All of our intel said he was."

THE CASTLE IN THE BURNING CAVES BLAZED with light, torches licking the carved walls, Hellions, Angels, and demons from every realm crowded into the hall for the celebration. The victory feast stretched from one end of the grand chamber to the other. Goblets of demon whiskey overflowed. Music from a dozen instruments tangled in the air.

Chel stayed in the shadows where he belonged.

Krick and Vex had taken the front row of the dais near the throne. Rue sat cross-legged on the carved armrest of Dacre's chair, giggling at something Dacre whispered in her ear. Dacre's gaze was half-cynical, half-lost. But he smiled when she smiled. That was enough. He was untrusting of the room with his princess, the bodyguard act hard to drop. Chel knew that was the only way to be.

Lucipurr joined the party. The black cat wound his way through the crowd, tail twitching like a metronome of mischief. He leapt onto Chel's shoulder with no warning, nestling into the crook of his neck like he'd done a thousand times before, and purred.

"Off," Chel muttered, trying to nudge him away.

Lucipurr let out a loud *Mrrrp* and flicked his tail in the face of a passing servant.

Meg raised an eyebrow from the throne but said nothing.

Chel could feel the eyes starting to drift toward him. Rue, Remington, and then Evelyn. He turned, easing deeper into the gloom at the edge of the celebration. The damned cat was going to give him up.

Then she entered.

And Chel froze.

She wore white. The gold thread at her cuffs caught the torchlight like stars, and her wings shimmered pearlescent. There were other Angels in attendance, but none drew the eye like Teari.

Chel stopped breathing.

She scanned the room as if searching for someone.

Don't look this way. Don't see me.

Lucipurr nuzzled Chel's jaw as if to soothe him.

Teari walked past the throne, pausing only to touch Meg's shoulder. The queen said something, then Sparrow, and Teari nodded.

Then she moved into the crowd.

Chel turned away, his heart a hammer against ribs that didn't quite feel like his own. He couldn't speak to her. Not yet. Not like this. But he wanted to.

My wife.

She didn't know what he'd done to return or what price he'd paid or that he no longer wore his own skin.

"Trouble, Ash?" someone whispered behind him.

Krick.

He leaned on the stone pillar beside him, one eye studying the dance floor, the other watching him. The Hellion was too observant for his own good. And it wasn't normal that his eyes went in opposite directions like a fucking frog.

"What's up with the cat?" Krick asked.

"It's Princess Rue's kitten," Chel replied. "You'd have to ask her but her bodyguard would probably kill you before you got close enough to open your mouth."

Krick made a face. "Probably." He followed Chel's gaze. Krick's grin was suddenly all knives. "You watch her like you know her."

He said nothing.

Krick shrugged and walked away, but not before tossing over his shoulder, "A Hellion and an Angel would never work out."

Chel stayed in the shadows long after the music rose again. He'd survived the war. Burned the mansion. Freed the souls.

Meg was serious when she'd said, "The Black Mansion took our girls, now we take his." Now she had another ally within the Seven Kingdoms of Heaven.

But Teari didn't know.

And he wasn't sure when he'd have the strength to tell her. Maybe when the time was right. Maybe when the Fates released him he could show her.

Chapter 43

━━━━━━━

The flames had died down outside and so had the laughter. Chel leaned against the balcony railing. The heat from the rocks below curled upward like the breath of sleeping dragons. Behind him, he heard a soft footfall he would always recognize.

"You saw her?" Meg asked, a goblet of wine in her hand. She leaned beside him, not touching, but near enough to feel the heat radiating off her.

He said quietly, "I'm thinking."

Meg nodded, eyes distant. "It's a good thing Hellions can lie or that might've burned your tongue."

"I was thinking about my sister, Yelena. Where is she? What happened to her after she escaped?"

Meg looked away. "I cannot discuss that. Just know she is safe."

Chel didn't answer right away. He looked out at the tawny horizon. "The Black Mansion is gone. But we missed something. Having a celebration is dangerous."

Meg shrugged. "It might help draw out whatever we've missed."

"I want my body back."

"I know," she said.

"When?"

Meg sipped her wine. "I think it will be soon. Maybe we can go back in the morning. After you've had some rest." She glanced over.

"I am tired, Meg," he said. "You sent me on a *vacation* and it was anything but. I am never going back to my old life, am I?"

"Do you really want that old life?" she asked.

He made a grumbling sound deep in his throat.

That got a small smirk from her. "That's what I thought."

A soft knock on the chamber door interrupted them. Meg turned.

Teari entered. She looked different, solemn. But in that white dress... Chel couldn't keep his eyes off her. She'd changed her hair. Well, Chel had changed his entire body. If she had any idea who he really was then they'd be even.

"I just wanted to say goodbye," Teari said, walking toward Meg. "I'm heading home for a while. There's still a lot of work to do."

Meg grinned and opened her arms. "Don't forget to burn anything that looks remotely corrupt."

Teari laughed softly. "That's always the plan."

As they stepped apart, Meg gestured. "This is Ash. He was with the team that brought the mansion down."

Teari turned toward him.

Chel tensed at the introduction.

She was studying him. Those healer's eyes saw beneath layers of skin and bone, straight to his soul. He wondered if she recognized anything.

Please recognize something, he begged internally.

"Nice to meet you," she said softly, offering her hand.

He took it, sliding his big hand into hers and squeezing. He had to go quickly. The contact stole the air from his lungs. He wanted to tug her into his arms and hold her and kiss her. But he wasn't who she remembered.

Teari's brow furrowed and her head tipped. "Do I know you?" she asked. "Have we met before?"

He shook his head and stepped back. "No. Just another Hellion."

Teari looked at him for a long moment. Her mouth opened like she was going to say something, but then she simply nodded. "Thank you for putting an end to the Black Mansion."

His throat was tight so all he did was nod.

She turned back to Meg, said her last goodbye and left through the corridor, the sound of her shoes echoing off the tile.

Chel leaned on the railing again, his shoulders hunched as he crossed his arms.

"That was close," Meg finally said. "I thought you were going to eat her."

"No." He looked out, vision blurring. "I might eat the Fates though, if they don't give me back my body. I'm done with this game." He looked down at Meg.

She set the goblet down gently. "I only want the best for you, Chel. You're my last one. We've been through so much together. You deserve peace as soon as we are done with this last mission."

He was studying her with these new eyes. Meg, the Queen of Hell who had battled Lucifer and Archangels and her own heart, she was keeping something from him. She was once known as a liar and a disruptor, but she'd grown into something different over these years. She'd become more secretive. She'd started showing her heart. She seemed grateful.

He stepped away from the balcony, closer to her. "Where is Sparrow?" Chel asked.

Meg glanced up and a smile spread across her face. She waved, a nonchalant gesture. "Oh, he'll be here soon, he had to go get something."

"Something?" Chel echoed, realizing that when Sparrow had left, Meg hadn't left Chel's side. Something strange was happening. "Are you in danger?"

She shook her head. "No. I don't think any of these fools in their right mind would come for me."

Chel paused and studied her.

"We have time to get you set straight." She patted his arm. "Don't worry, Hellion."

Chel looked down at her hand and noticed a new rune etched between her fingers. It looked like an eye.

"Have you been to see Jed and Shay?"

Meg smiled. "Don't meddle, Hellion. You're not a Deacon."

Chel walked away feeling as though his Queen was keeping information from him.

CHAPTER 44

Yelena woke to the sound of water dripping, slow and rhythmic; the kind of sound that might drive a person insane. It echoed like a heartbeat through the cavernous room, pulling her consciousness back one fragile thread at a time.

She opened her eyes.

Cold stone. A high ceiling, arched like a cathedral, stretched above her. Shadows gathered in the corners where a light flickered weakly. She tried to move but her arms felt too heavy and her head pounded.

Drip. Drip. Drip.

She blinked. Her wrists were bound by a loop of cord that shimmered with an iridescent sheen. That wasn't normal rope. Panic bloomed throughout her body.

"I wouldn't struggle," said a voice from the dark. "It reacts. Fear tightens the rope."

Yelena froze, feeling the shimmering cord tighten around her wrists.

Footsteps echoed off the stone floor. A figure stepped forward. His boots were polished black. His coat, long and ash-colored, trailed behind him like a shadow. His eyes shimmered gold.

Definitely not human, Yelena thought. She squeezed her eyes closed and searched her mind to try and figure out where she was. Was she dreaming? She had been watching a horror movie before bed. She'd have to stop doing that because this seemed too real.

He smiled.

"You must be confused," he said gently. "The last thing you remember is your little apartment, tucked safely in bed and all the doors locked. Locks only keep out humans. They only keep out the unobservant." He tilted his head. "But you've been watched for a very long time, little phoenix."

Yelena narrowed her eyes. "My name is Yelena."

He crouched beside her. "I know. But that's just what they called you *this time*."

She jerked back, breath catching. "What do you mean, this time?"

The man didn't answer. Instead, he reached for a silver bowl beside her and lifted it to the light. It was filled with glowing sand.

"When a soul escapes Purgatory, it doesn't just reenter the world," he said, swirling the sand slowly. "It drips through the cracks in time. Your soul has worn many faces, Yelena. But the one thing remains constant is that you are a key."

Yelena blinked. This definitely wasn't a dream. "A key to what?"

His smile widened. "To an ending. Or a beginning. Depends who finds you first."

Yelena's breath quickened. "Who are you?"

"Oh, I'm no one important," he said. "Not anymore. I used to wear a nicer face. You'd be surprised how well Heaven tolerated me when I wore white robes and my eyes were blue. But now? I'm simply... the Collector." He stood, brushing dust from his sleeves. "You see, I gather the ones who slip between the cracks. The ones who don't belong anywhere. Lost souls. *Dangerous* ones." He tapped his fingertips together.

Yelena struggled again, panic mounting. "I'm not dangerous!"

The Collector smiled. "Not yet."

He turned and walked toward a heavy iron door. "But you will be. I like to collect shiny souls like yours but someone is breaking into my house again. One moment please."

CHAPTER 45

Meg ended the call with a sharp flick of her hand, setting the sleek black phone down on her desk like it had personally offended her. Her jaw was tight, mouth pressed into a line.

Chel watched her from the far corner of the room, arms crossed over his chest. He didn't speak until she did.

Meg leaned back in her chair and sighed. "Something is happening at the Black Mansion site."

His heart skipped. "What?"

Meg looked up, eyes locking on him like she could see through the borrowed body to the soul still smoldering beneath.

Meg held up a hand in surrender. "Calm down, Hellion." She picked up her phone again and pressed on the screen. "Ev, come to my office. And bring the books."

Chel's brow rose in question.

Meg set her phone down again, sat, and crossed her

arms. "You will remember Layla found a book for Rue on the Earthen plane. We originally thought it had bound her to the Astral in some way."

Chel nodded.

"The girls did some digging and deciphering of the ancient language." Chel was staring straight into Meg's eyes and made sure to soak up every word she was saying. "Rue has been researching our history for a while now. Her undergraduate degree uncovered ancient caves used for sacrifices in the mountains on the Earthen plane. Then the runestones. Then she found the Enochian text at Loyola University's library. The one Layla brought us."

Chel was nodding along, remembering.

"Evelyn obtained another text from a mountain gypsy that is filled with Astral history." She paused and a knock on the door echoed. "Come in."

Evelyn stepped in carrying a giant stack of books.

Chel rushed to her side and took the books. He carried them to the nearby table.

"Thanks," Evelyn said, tucking a strand of long blonde hair behind her ear.

Meg moved closer. "Ev, I need you to tell this Hellion what you've discovered."

Evelyn bit her lip in hesitation. "I think Rue might be able to explain it better." She reached for the massive, silver-edged book. Its cover was dark blue, and a silver spiral twisted into a star shimmering on the front.

"Rue isn't available right now," Meg said.

Evelyn motioned to the book before turning a few pages. "This was a hard read, some of these runes and language we've never come across before."

Chel leaned over the table as Evelyn flipped the pages covered in densely written text and swirling illustrations of the Astral Plane; a chaotic sea of spirits, twisting pathways, and towering shadows. She reached for another book which he recognized as the Enochian text that Layla brought to them.

Eveyln opened the leather cover and turned to a specific page with drawings and a ripped page.

"This is ages old, from before the Seven Kingdoms of Heaven were formed. A time of the old gods, the gypsy demons have said." Eveyln cleared her throat. "We know of the Kingdoms in Heaven, the Earthen Plane, Hell, and the Astral. But before, there were more planes. The Fates had a realm." Evelyn's finger dragged down a page. "And Heaven had more than seven Archangels, more than seven Kings."

"More than seven?" Chel asked.

Meg nodded.

"Where are they?" Chel crossed his arms, taking it all in.

Evelyn pointed to a drawing in the Enochian book. Then she flipped a few pages on the Astral book and pointed to something that looked similar. She looked to Meg, "Do you have the blueprints?"

Meg walked to her desk and grabbed a piece of paper.

When she returned, she opened the paper and laid it across the books in front of them.

"Okay," Evelyn was biting her lip. "I don't know where the missing Archangels went. I read about a battle and some of them were cast out."

"That's the Black Mansion blueprints," Chel pointed out as he pressed his hands to the table and leaned closer.

"Watch this." Evelyn moved the blueprints over the drawings on each book. "They line up." She traced a line. "And it appears the Black Mansion wasn't just a building, it was a moving realm of its own."

"So we burned it and did nothing?" Chel said.

"You definitely damaged it." Evelyn pointed to a drawing of a black and white bird.

"Oh, that's a magpie!" Meg said. "I read about those in one of Sparrow's books. I think it was titled, *Birds of Western North America*."

"And here, under the Magpie image, these runes say Collector." Evelyn moved to the other book and ran her finger under the runes on the page. "Ah, here it is. Collector."

"Magpies do like to collect things," Meg said, tapping her lip with a finger.

"Uh hm." Evelyn slid the books around and moved the blueprints. "So I found a stone with this marking." Evelyn pointed to the half-page. "One of the sacrifice stones." She swallowed hard.

"They called to Lucifer's bloodline," Meg reminded Chel.

Chel was nodding, following along but still pissed that the Black Mansion wasn't done with completely.

Evelyn pressed her eyes closed and took a deep breath as if she were remembering. She pressed a finger to the paper again. "There are all of these tendrils underneath the Mansion."

"We entered through one," Chel said.

"They seem to be ley lines into each realm." Evelyn cleared her throat.

"There's too many tendrils," Chel leaned closer, counting at least ten. But there was a rip in the page. "There could be dozens more."

"You entered through Hell's tendril." Evelyn licked her lips. She moved the blueprints over the books again, flipping pages until she found the drawings that matched. "Here's one that leads to Heaven. The Astral. The Earthen Plane."

"Where do the rest lead to?" Meg prompted.

"Now we know of the realm of the Fates." Evelyn tapped a finger on the page. "Then the rest is missing. We haven't found the other realms. Yet."

Chel exhaled and rubbed his face with both hands, stepped back and turned in a tight circle. "Let me get this straight. The Black Mansion still exists?"

Meg held up a finger. "Only a small piece of it."

"Sure." Chel frowned. "Its lower levels reached into each realm, some we haven't heard of in ages. I've never heard of anything like this."

"Fucking Archangels and their coverups." Meg was shaking her head.

"Your father is an Archangel," Chel reminded her.

"True. I asked him about this. Seems the Deacons and some bad players were highly involved. Gabriel actually gives a fuck about humanity. Which has gotten him imprisoned multiple times. They locked him in a cage for being my father just after the Fast-Zombie War. But he does know who was cast out and imprisoned below the Black Mansion."

Chel continued. "It sounds like you're telling us, Ev, that we've been halfway right but halfway wrong the entire time."

"Rue actually put all of this together but she ran back to her research lab to grab some notes we needed. And there was a book Layla found for us at Loyola University Library that has another map in it." Evelyn was gripping the edge of the table. "I'll present this theory. What if you were banished from heaven, banished to a singular realm, a building of sorts, a private island that thrived on blood and moved from place to place, hard to track... and you spend your time collecting all of the shiny souls you want. Because you have a back door into *every* realm. And no one noticed because you were forgotten about and slowly dug into every realm to get what you wanted. So you could collect and collect and collect under the radar. Magpie. Collector."

"Shay, Rue, Evelyn, Layla..." Meg whispered. "Who else?"

"Binding the child of an Archangel would keep the veil thin enough for possession. We were wrong, it wasn't a forgotten sect. It wasn't possession of a body. It was a banished Archangel. It *is* a banished Archangel. Whoever it is possesses the Veil between worlds."

"It wouldn't really be an Angel any longer." Meg was rubbing her teeth with a finger.

"Binding the child of an Archangel…" Chel whispered then stared at Meg. She was the child of an Archangel and the Raven King was clearly on edge these past few days. Meg hadn't let Chel leave her side since he'd returned in this new skin.

"It's not me." Meg finally told Chel.

"How can you be so sure?" he asked.

She shrugged. "I don't think it's me."

"Who else is there?" Chel asked.

There was a beat of silence.

"Jed," Evelyn said. "There aren't many. Nightingale is in the Astral. Nothing with a spec of survival instinct would touch the Raven King."

"The Nightjar," Meg said.

Chel looked up. "*Teari.*"

Meg was silent.

"Asmodeus said something to me before I killed him. *I am nothing but a puppet.*" Chel was reaching for the book.

"We have been wrong about it," Meg said. "All this time. A Demon sat at the throne of the Black Mansion but it was a charade."

Evelyn stood up straight. "Remington is coming," she announced.

On cue the dark princeling slipped into Meg's office and nodded a greeting. His dark eyes settled on Chel, still untrusting of the new Hellion. He bent to whisper something in Evelyn's ear. She nodded and began collecting the books.

"Son?" Meg greeted.

"Father is on his way." Remington was stacking the large books in his arms. "Rue is here and she asked for Ev and these books back."

Meg nodded. "Thank you, Evelyn. Good work."

As Remington led Evelyn out of the room, Chel heard her whisper, "He called me, Ev. Only my friends call me that."

"Just stay away from him," Remington whispered back.

Chel cleared his throat, hating that this new body had such good hearing. He wanted so badly to tell them who he was.

Meg waited for a beat longer. "Are you ready for the next mission?"

Chel scoffed. "You sent me on vacation and it has turned into a complete shit show."

She nodded. "Sorry about that." She took a deep breath before glancing at the time. "We're going to get your body back in the morning. Then you'll return to the Earthen plane."

"What about the White Horse?" Chel asked.

Meg shrugged. "She knows things are fucked, that's why she's allowed you in her realm. I can't send anyone else."

"Are you sure you're not in danger?"

"Not with me here," the Raven King's voice sounded from the doorway. He crossed the room with a brown paper bag and Chel smelled chicken and French fries.

Purgatory was quieter this time. There was less screaming and no shifting ground–just a low hum that seemed to crawl up Chel's borrowed spine, wrapping around his mind. The thick rope of Meg's tether coiled in her palm, trailing behind her like the tail of some predatory serpent as she led the way.

The Weaver waited in her obsidian loom, her hands resting on silver threads that crisscrossed the space like a web.

"You've returned for what's yours," the Fate said. "And the souls came from the Black Mansion."

"He's done what you asked. The Black Mansion burns, the souls were released. We need his body now."

The Weaver's head tilted, moonlight reflecting off her bone mask, and one of her threads twanged in the silence.

"You'll take it... but you will not leave unchanged."

Chel's borrowed heartbeat stuttered. "Wasn't that part already handled when you ripped me out of it?"

The Weaver's hands moved, pulling a thread taut. A shape emerged from the shadows. It was Chel's body, bound upright in cords of light and shadow. It looked exactly as he remembered; broad shoulders, the half-healed scars, the slight tilt to his stance. But the skin was paler, like it hadn't seen sun or blood in years.

Meg moved closer, inspecting it. "You've kept him well."

"A body is not hard to keep," the Weaver said. "It's the soul that rots without purpose. This one will be hungry when it returns."

Chel stepped forward, every muscle in this unfamiliar form tense. He reached out. The Weaver's threads pulsed, as if warning him that once he stepped back into himself, there would be no undoing.

"If you take it now," the Weaver murmured, "you carry what you've seen here. You'll feel it in your bones, hear it in your dreams. Every thread you touched, every memory I unraveled will be woven back inside you. You will remember everything."

Chel's jaw tightened. He thought of Teari and the way she'd looked right through him in this false skin. He thought of Meg, of the work they'd done, the monsters they'd burned out. He thought of the Black Mansion's tendrils still slithering in hidden realms.

"Good," he said. "I'd rather carry it than forget."

The Fate asked him, "Tell me, Hellion, are you glad

you were the last of your kind to survive? Has that guilt dissipated now that you know? Now that you've seen what you were needed for?"

"I understand now."

The Weaver's hands snapped the bindings, and Chel's body stepped forward as if drawn by gravity. The threads slid from his limbs, and he staggered once before the connection between soul and flesh snapped back into place with a lurch that made him gasp.

The false body behind him collapsed into nothing, dissolving into the Weaver's threads.

Meg stepped to his side. "Welcome back, Hellion."

Chel flexed his hands, feeling the familiar weight, the old strength. "Let's get out of here before she changes her mind."

The Weaver only smiled as the mist shrouded her.

Chapter 46

The ropes fell away from Yelena's wrists with a rough scrape. She flexed her fingers, the pins-and-needles sting fading into dull ache as the Magpie straightened.

"There," he said, almost cheerfully. "I wouldn't want my little guest looking frightened when company arrives. Frightened things tend to make messes."

Yelena hesitated. "You're... letting me go?"

A chuckle slid from him, low and rasping. "Walk around if you like. Stretch those mortal legs. But you're not leaving this place."

He gestured, and the heavy door to the adjoining hall swung open. Yelena followed him and stepped into a narrow corridor that smelled of stone, candle smoke, and something faintly metallic. Cells lined either side, thick bars sunk deep into the floor. Shapes shifted behind them.

A pale, translucent figure sat cross-legged on the floor, its eyes clouded, its hands endlessly braiding its own hair. In another, a man in tattered angelic robes pressed his palm to the wall, lips moving silently. Across from him, something with too many joints and a face hidden by a shroud tilted its head toward her and breathed slowly like a spider ready to pounce.

She froze. "They're... alive?"

"Oh yes," the Magpie said, his voice dripping with pride. "All in excellent condition. I take good care of my collection. Fed. Watered. Kept in a state where they'll last."

Her stomach churned. "Where did you take them from?"

"Everywhere," he purred. "Some from Heaven's shining gates. Some from the bottom-most pits of Hell. A few from those quaint little human cities that think themselves safe from the Veil's reach. I've walked realms your kind has never heard of, plucked the most exquisite pieces, and brought them here."

He stopped before an empty cell, its single chair set in the corner like a waiting sentinel.

"This one's yours," he said.

Yelena's breath caught. "Why? You said you didn't want me hurt."

"I don't," he agreed, smiling with all his teeth. "But the ones who come for you? They'll be easier to deal with if you're contained. At least while I think of what I really want."

The heavy door creaked open, and he waited until she stepped inside. The iron bars shut with a ringing finality, the sound echoing down the hall like the toll of a bell. The Magpie shivered. "Bells," he hissed.

The Magpie stepped back, his gaze sweeping over her one last time. He murmured, "You belong to me now."

The lamplight dimmed as he walked away, leaving her in a haze of shadow and the quiet, restless breathing of the Collector's other prizes.

CHAPTER 47

The Florida sun had dropped lower, painting the sky in streaks of rose and gold. Teari sat barefoot on the sand, her toes buried deep in the warmth, listening to the slow sigh of the tide. This was her ritual, her monthly check-in though there was no one to check in with. There never had been because it all had changed too quickly. They had made a promise to meet each month but so far Teari was the only one who'd followed through. She knew Chel couldn't help it. He'd been delayed in Purgatory and she'd been told to wait. So she waited, for months and months and months. And she came here because she *hoped* that one day he'd be freed.

The ocean was calm, save for the restless glint of light on its surface. She stared at the gentle waves and thought about all of the tasks she had to do this month. The castle drapes needed to be switched out for the coming autumn season, she was demolishing her father's rooms, that would be—

There was movement in the gulf. Far out, close to the shrimp boats. She squinted against the sinking sun. A shadow broke the surface, not the sleek arc of a dolphin or the chop of a wave, but something else. Something was moving closer. Her breath caught. Her heart shuddered against her ribcage.

The figure waded forward, the water sliding off broad shoulders, rippling down familiar lines of muscle. The distance shrank with every step until she could see him clearly. He was soaked to the skin, eyes locked on her like no time had passed at all. He looked desperate, watching her like she was the only thing on the beach, and he was moving fast.

"Chel..." Her voice broke, barely more than a whisper, and then she was on her feet and running.

The sand slipped beneath her toes, wind pulling at her hair, water sloshed against her knees, but she didn't stop until she collided with him. His arms came around her instantly, strong and firm, pulling her against the heat of him despite the cold water clinging to his skin.

She tipped her face up to his, searching, needing to see him, needing to believe he was real. He felt real–she had dreamed this moment so many times.

"My Angel," he whispered and he didn't give her time to doubt. Chel's mouth came down on hers, rough with need, tasting of salt and something that made her ache all the way to the marrow in her bones. The world fell away; there was no beach, no ocean, no months of aching silence, only this, only him. Finally.

He dragged her through the ocean toward the sand. Teari's arms tightened around his shoulders and her middle pressed to his chest, she dragged her legs up and wrapped them around his waist. Large hands gripped her bottom as she leaned into the kiss, deepening it. He tasted like ice and smoke. And while they'd kissed a few times, she never wanted to forget it, she never wanted to stop. She never wanted to let him go.

A sharp whistle echoed across the beach and a male voice shouted, "Get a room!"

Teari pulled away as Chel's hands moved to her waist and set her on her feet.

"Want me to kill that human?" he grumbled.

"No." Teari shook her head. "We don't kill humans."

He grunted and it sounded feral. In the moonlight she noticed the glint of fangs; he looked pale.

"When did you get out?" she asked.

"A few hours ago."

She was looking him over but wished for more light. She took his hand and dragged him toward the beach house. "Come on."

It was just a few hundred yards through the sand but Teari noticed when Chel stumbled and shook off an unsteadiness. She pulled him into the beach house and slammed the door closed. He was right there, one hand pressed flat against the door, the other on her hip, dragging her closer.

"You waited?" Dark eyes searched hers.

"Every month, like we promised." Her fingers drifted down his arm and wrapped around the scar on his wrist. "And remember, you came and rescued me in Purgatory. What kind of an asshole do you think I am to let you get away after that stunt?"

She was searching his eyes; there was so much she wanted to ask him, so much they needed to talk about. But she recognized the signs of hunger. His control was loosening. He'd either eaten and was deep in Bloodlust or he was starving. Or he was injured.

His hand flattened across her back and he buried his face in her neck. She felt his mouth against her skin.

"Chel..." Her voice softened, coaxing, "What happened?"

He looked away, a flicker of tension in his jaw. "It's nothing."

She stepped closer, her hands pressing against his chest, feeling the subtle tremor in his muscles. "Don't lie to me. Not now. You think I don't know the difference between you being hungry and whatever this is?"

A shadow passed over his expression. "I didn't want you to see me like this."

Too late.

She slid her hands to his shoulders, guiding him toward the bedroom. "Sit," she ordered with no room for argument. He obeyed, lowering himself to the edge of the bed with the weary heaviness of someone bone deep tired.

Her fingers worked at the soaked buttons of his shirt, peeling the fabric away. What she saw made her breath stutter. Purple-black bruises bloomed across his ribs and stomach, the mottled color sinking deep beneath the skin. Each inhale was shallow, his body guarded like movement itself hurt.

"Chel..." Her hands hovered, afraid to hurt him.

"I'm fine," he said, his voice low, almost distant, "nothing a little blood can't fix."

She met his eyes, fierce. "You came here like this?"

"I couldn't wait to see you again." For a long moment, he was silent, gaze turned toward the window and the restless sea beyond. Then, quietly, "The Fate removed my soul."

The words landed between them like a stone.

"They took me apart. They unstitched *me*." His breath shuddered out. "Separated my soul from my body. And it hurt like hell."

Her throat tightened, but she kept her touch steady as her fingers ghosted over the worst of the bruises. Old wounds she'd seen before looked fresh.

"Let me see," she whispered, shifting next to him. "Let me see what I can fix."

His eyes closed for a moment and Teari had the sensation of stones sinking in her gut. If he was this hesitant, it wouldn't be good.

"Christ," she muttered, helping get his pants down. It looked like the Fates had pulled his soul through every scar he had on his body.

"I didn't have enough glue," Chel chuckled before wrapping an arm around his ribs.

"Don't move," Teari said. "I'll be right back."

Teari slipped away just long enough to fetch a bowl of ice, a clean cloth, and a glass of water. And she called Meg.

"What happened to Chel?" Teari asked.

"He spent time in Purgatory. I cannot imagine he came out unaffected. I went in to get him and I'm still having… feelings I don't like."

"Can someone bring blood to the beach house?"

"That's probably a good idea. He didn't stop to eat before he left to find you."

Teari rubbed her face and glanced toward the dark hallway. What was she going to do with this Hellion?

When she returned, Chel hadn't moved. His head was bowed, hands resting on his knees, the faint rise and fall of his chest uneven.

"Lay back," she urged, setting the supplies on the nightstand.

He didn't argue. She helped ease him down, working carefully so his weight settled against the pillows without pulling at his ribs. The air between them felt fragile, like the wrong word would make him vanish back into the ocean.

She pressed the cold cloth to the worst of the cuts along his side. He hissed but didn't push her away.

"They did something," he murmured, eyes fixed on the ceiling. "The Fates, when they pulled me out, it was like every thought, every memory, every... *want* I've ever had was dragged through burning coals. I felt them sorting through me. Deciding which parts to keep."

Her hand froze. "They *took* parts of you?"

A shadow passed through his expression. "Not in the way you think. I'm still me. But it's... thinner."

Teari replaced the ice, tracing the cloth lower over his ribs. "You came back," she whispered, like it was a defiance against everything that had tried to break him. "Maybe it's the pain."

He caught her wrist, his grip warm despite the chill in his skin. "I came back for you." His gaze locked on hers, steady now. "Every month like we promised."

Her throat tightened. "Even if it kills you?"

"Especially if it kills me," he said with the ghost of a smile, though the pain in his eyes betrayed him.

She leaned forward, brushing her lips against his temple, her other hand splayed over his chest to feel the stubborn, steady beat of his heart. "Then you're not leaving this bed until you heal," she said.

"I'll be fine by morning," he said softly.

Teari rubbed her hands together and gathered her healing magic. She splayed her hands over his middle and began healing the smallest of wounds first. She left some of the bruises for later, stitching closed the internal bleeding. He lay still as a stone while she worked; this was nothing compared to when she found him collapsed on the floor with sickness. She swallowed hard and closed her eyes, magic flowing deeper into his body. She began to realize he was right-they'd peeled his soul from his bones and there was an ache deep in his body that she'd never come across before. She glanced at him from the corner of her eye. He looked exhausted. She hadn't gotten past his midsection when there was a knock on the door.

"Angel?" Chel whispered. "Did you invite company?"

"That's your dinner, Chel. And no, never in my right mind would I invite anyone to see you like this." She wanted to slap him but she was afraid of hurting him.

"It's not that bad, I'd still fuck 'em up."

"You are delusional."

Teari walked out of the room and went to the door. Just like months ago there was a cooler packed with blood.

She took out her phone and sent Meg a message.

Teari: Is this fresh blood?

Meg: …

TEARI WAITED FIVE MINUTES AS SHE STOCKED the blood into the fridge. Meg had left her message on read and never replied.

She stared at the two bags of blood in her hand. Well,

she wasn't going to let him suffer. She glanced at the couch, remembering Chel high on Bloodlust. She felt her cheeks flush. She took another bag just in case he got bitey.

He was staring at the ceiling when she walked into the bedroom. Teari tossed him a bag of blood and Chel caught it mid-air. Seems he still had decent reflexes.

Chel ripped the top and consumed the blood. Teari tossed him another and set the third bag on the night-stand. Then she went back to work.

She healed the old wounds, or tried to, but the tissue appeared both inflamed and singed as though his soul had been pulled through them. There were some scars that would remain. She focused on the internal injuries, healing bruised ribs and a laceration on his liver. There was a hairline crack in his sternum. The deeper she dug into his body the more disbelief she had that he walked out of the ocean and didn't wash up on shore half-dead. Even his heart was bruised.

Her hand smoothed up his chest and she knitted together fascia that was torn in his shoulder. She noticed the third bag of blood was gone. A hand grabbed her wrist.

Teari sucked in a breath and looked up.

Chel's pupils were blown wide, his eyes half-lidded and Teari knew instantly that Meg had sent fresh blood. What a troublemaker.

Heat flooded through Teari's body. She leaned down, lips close to his ear and whispered, "I've been waiting for this moment. Haven't been able to get the memory of you fucking me on the couch out of my mind." She licked his neck.

Teari wasn't prepared for what a little dirty talk could do to a Hellion high on blood. His hand was around the back of her neck, maneuvering her lips to his. Chel kissed her like he was starved, like he hadn't just downed three bags of fresh blood. He sat up and dragged her body between his spread legs. Warm hands trailed up the back of her thighs and under the skirt of her dress.

"Why are you wearing clothing?" he grumbled.

"I don't heal my patients in the nude," she chuckled.

"Consider it," he growled, reaching for the hem of her dress and tugging up.

Teari pulled the dress over her head the rest of the way and dropped it on the floor as he nuzzled her stomach, licking and nipping at her skin. His hands were dipping into the back of her panties and tugging them down her legs.

"Angel," he whispered, taking her in. "You are a sight for sore eyes."

"Do you need me to heal those as well?" Teari's fingers threaded into his hair, gripped and tipped his head back as she leaned closer and kissed him.

Chel's hands were everywhere, exploring, and when they trailed to the vee between her thighs, sinking into her softness, that was all he could take.

"I can see just fine," he murmured.

In one swift movement Teari was on her back and

Chel was above her; his boxers had disappeared and he grabbed her thighs, pulling her to the edge of the bed to meet him.

"Chel?" Teari asked, making sure he was there and not completely consumed by the Bloodlust.

He glanced up. "Angel. I'm going to fuck you like you've been dreaming of since that night."

Teari bit her lip and nodded. "Ok," she agreed.

He pushed her thighs up and sank into her. Teari's head pressed back into the mattress as he moved, hands on her hips, squeezing the softness there. Then his mouth was on her skin. Her hands moved to his shoulders, searching for a way to hold on. It was pointless, really. She felt the scrape of his teeth against the underside of her breast then the wetness of his mouth on her nipple. Teari moaned, feeling the sharpness of her own teeth pressing against the inside of her mouth. She licked her lips as their hips rocked together in slow motions.

He was kissing her, then licking her neck, then sucking the soft skin over her collarbone. He tested her resolve with his teeth.

"Yes," Teari gasped.

He nipped the space below her ear. "Are you giving me permission to bite? Last time you told me I'd had enough blood."

"Yes." He twisted his hips just right to make her whimper. "Please."

"Will you bite back, Angel?"

Teari rolled her tongue over her teeth. It had been so long since she had blood. "Maybe."

Chel moved and rolled; suddenly Teari was on top, astride his hips, tension coiling in her belly. Chel sat up, hand sliding into the hair at the nape of her neck. He pulled her head to the side, revealing the column of her neck. She pulled him close, pressed skin to his lips, felt the flutter of his lashes against her neck, then the pinch of teeth. And she was gone. Her body shivered and stars filled her vision. The thirst came and for the first time in a long time, she didn't ignore it. She pressed her mouth to his shoulder, then her teeth to his skin until sweet blood filled her mouth.

CHAPTER 48

Chel woke to cold sheets and the sound of the surf.

For a tight second, his pulse hammered like he was back in Purgatory; alone, abandoned, staring at the mist that would never clear.

"Teari?"

The beach house was quiet. His breath caught on the thought that maybe she'd gone again and that the last twenty-four hours had been a dream his mind had conjured out of need and salt air. He was halfway out of bed when the door creaked open.

"Easy," she said, stepping inside with a bag of medical supplies cradled in her arms. Her hair was windblown, cheeks flushed from the ocean air. "You didn't think I'd run off, did you?"

Chel sank back against the pillows, relief loosening his chest. "I've had worse mornings."

She set the bag on the nightstand and began pulling out rolls of bandages, antiseptic, and fresh gauze. "You'll have worse if you try getting up again. You're still half-stitched together."

Chel grunted but didn't argue. He let her work—careful hands, precise movements, the faint scent of the sea still clinging to her skin. Every press of her fingers grounded him more than he wanted to admit.

After a few minutes she spoke, her voice quieter than the rustle of the bandages. "Do you... hate me now?"

His brow furrowed. "Why would I—"

"Because of what my father made me do," she interrupted, eyes fixed on the gauze she was wrapping. "Sending the young souls away. Hiding his... trysts with human women. You know what that meant for them. For their families." Her throat worked as if she was swallowing glass. "I carried out his orders. You've seen me at my worst, Chel. I can't expect you to—"

He caught her wrists, halting her work. "Stop."

She finally met his gaze.

"You were forced into it," he said, steady and low. "I know you. You'd never choose that. And I know what it's like when someone with power twists your choices until there's nothing left but obedience." His eyes softened, though his voice didn't waver. "If you need to hear it... I forgive you. But you don't need it. Because it was never your sin to be guilty for."

Her lips parted, but she didn't speak.

"I've been taken advantage of, Teari. I can spot it a

mile away. You were protecting yourself in a no-win game. That doesn't make you like him. It makes you the furthest from it."

For a long moment, she stayed silent, searching his face. Then she leaned in, closing the small space between them. Her mouth met his; warm, tentative at first, then firmer, like she was sealing his words into her.

"Thank you," she whispered. "Thank you for freeing me of him. I've never felt so free in my whole life."

He let his hands slide down her arms, keeping her close. "You're stuck with me now, Angel."

Her faint smile answered him before the waves filled the quiet again.

She stayed close after the kiss, her forehead resting lightly against his, her hands still tangled in his.

When she finally eased back, she didn't say anything. She just picked up the roll of bandages again and resumed where she'd left off.

Chel let his head fall against the headboard, watching her work. The morning light filtered through the slats of the blinds, striping the sheets in gold and shadow. Her touch was steady and each careful movement seemed to pull him farther from the cold, hollow edges of Purgatory's memory and stitched his soul closer to his bones.

He closed his eyes, letting her work. For the first time in weeks, he allowed himself to believe he was in a place that was kind of like home.

She didn't rush or speak unless she needed to shift him or ask if something hurt. The silence was comfortable, stretching between them like a warm blanket instead of a chasm.

He realized, somewhere in the quiet, that he'd stopped bracing for the sound of a door closing. Stopped scanning the space for signs she was about to disappear again. She was here. Still here.

When she finished, she smoothed her palms down the fresh wrap on his ribs, almost as if she were making sure he was real.

"Better?" she asked softly.

He caught her hand before she could pull away. "Better," he confirmed.

For a moment, neither of them moved. The waves outside rolled in and out, and the gulls calling faintly overhead.

Chel thought about the danger still circling them, the whispers about the child of an Archangel, the kind of threats that didn't stop at death. It sat heavy in his chest, but he didn't speak it aloud. Not yet. Not when her hands were warm on him, not when her eyes held that quiet steadiness he'd missed for too long.

"I have a question," Chel whispered, tugging her close.

Teari waited, eyes widening, fearing the worst.

"You are my wife."

"That's not a question." She smiled.

"I want to make it real."

She nodded. "One day it will be official. Now that I

took over my father's kingdom, I'm sure Babylon will have something to say about this."

"I'll kill them." He kissed her quickly. "You are mine. I've waited long enough."

She patted his chest. "Yes. I am yours. But please don't kill them."

Chel closed his eyes, satisfied and the quiet stretched until Teari finally broke it.

"I want to show you something," she said, her voice low but carrying that flicker of purpose he knew meant she'd been thinking about it for a while.

Chel opened one eye. "Show me?"

"We'll need to go to the Peabody Library."

He sat up a little straighter, studying her. "Is this work or curiosity?"

"Both," she said, already sliding off the bed to grab her boots. "Come on. Get dressed."

He swung his legs over the side of the bed, wincing just enough to make her pause. He waved her off, reaching for his shirt. "If we're going all the way into the city, we should stop for breakfast somewhere."

She snorted, pulling her hair into a loose knot. "You've learned *nothing*, have you?"

"What?" he asked, feigning innocence.

"After your last round of diner food, you were sick for days. You're still not fully healed."

He started to argue, but she turned toward the kitchen and came back holding two frozen breakfast sandwiches. She waved them in the air like proof of victory.

"Microwave magic," she declared.

Chel stared at the sad little plastic-wrapped sandwiches. "I wait months to eat real food again, and this is what I get?"

"They're good," she said with mock offense, tossing them into the microwave. "And safe."

He leaned against the counter, arms crossed. "I was picturing a plate of eggs and toast at a real table. Coffee that doesn't taste like ash."

"You had plenty of refreshments last night," she said over her shoulder, her tone laced with mischief. "Was that not good enough for you?"

He froze for half a beat, watching the sly curve of her mouth as she turned back toward him.

"Angel, that's different," he said, voice dropping lower as his dark eyes scanned her body.

She handed him the steaming sandwich. "Mm-hm. Eat your breakfast, Hellion."

He took it with a muttered grumble but couldn't stop the small, unwilling smile tugging at his mouth.

CHAPTER 49

———

TEARI STEPPED THROUGH THE PORTAL AND into the quiet alley beside Peabody Library, her boots landing softly on the cobblestones. Leaves were falling. Golden light bled through the oak leaves above, dappled and warm. The autumn air was crisp, and Teari realized why Rue loved this season so much. The promise of change was in the air and it was a bit magical.

She stood there for a moment, squinting into the sun. Her hand hovered over her chest.

"Are you going to make it?" Chel whispered in her ear.

She shivered. "I was just thinking something feels off."

Chel took her hand. "Let's investigate, Angel."

The last time she'd been here, Jasper had walked her down to the Saturday market where Yelena worked part-time selling handcrafted jewelry. The girl had smiled. She'd laughed. She was safe.

But now, the air crackled with something foreign. A creature was here. A twinge of doom filled her stomach just like when her father would call her incessantly.

She walked to the back door of the Library and knocked.

"Jasper?" she called softly, pushing the door open.

No answer.

Chel stepped inside first.

The library was dim. They walked through the hallways until they arrived in the main room with the fireplace where Jasper spent most of his time.

A book lay splayed open on the floor beside the sofa. A shattered glass glittered on the floor. There was no blood. No scuffle. But Teari's heart plummeted. It looked like he'd left in a hurry, dropped his drink, and ran.

"She wasn't just reborn. She was placed. Watched over. Protected."

Yes, the Angel had been waiting at the Peabody Library for years. He had been waiting for Yelena. He was her Guardian. She could sense that something was happening. Teari swallowed and stepped outside. Her eyes swept the tree line, the edge of the river in the distance, scanning for any trace of movement, any sound. Nothing. There was stillness in the streets like the moment after a scream when everything goes still.

There went that surprise.

"I've got a bad feeling about this." Teari pulled her

phone from her coat pocket and tried Jasper first. It went straight to voicemail.

A cold breeze swept through the trees, brushing her hair back from her face.

She turned her gaze skyward.

"Meg," she whispered, "I think we have a problem."

"The library is empty," Chel said. "And I'd appreciate it if you wouldn't take off next time."

Teari frowned at him.

She held up her phone as it rang. "This is for us. Meg?"

"Yes."

"Something has happened here. Chel and I stopped by Peabody Library and Jasper is gone. It looks like he left in a hurry."

"Okay," Meg said. "I cannot send any more reinforcements. A Hellion should do."

"Just one?" Teari asked, glancing at Chel. "He's injured."

Meg's voice shouted, "Tighten your boot laces, Hellion! You're all she's got."

Chel made a face. "That was bizarre."

A small *meow* echoed off the sidewalk.

Chel turned to a black cat trotting toward them.

"Is that... Lucipurr?" Teari asked.

Chel bent and the black cat went straight for him, nuzzling his hand and arm then twining between his ankles.

Lucipurr purred, then turned and trotted toward the street, pausing every few steps to glance back at them.

"Do you think...?" Teari started.

"Can't hurt to find out," Chel muttered, already falling into step behind the cat.

The trail wound through two side streets, then into an older part of the city where brick buildings sagged under the weight of time. Lucipurr slipped through a gap in a chain-link fence, vanishing into the shadow of a looming warehouse.

Chel ducked after him, Teari close behind. That's when he spotted the still figure by the corner. Broad-shouldered, and a bit too tall for most men. Jasper.

He didn't even flinch at their approach, his gaze locked on the darkened windows above.

"What's in there?" Chel asked.

Jasper's mouth was grim. "Trouble."

Chel's attention sharpened. "What kind of trouble?"

Jasper didn't look at him, still studying the building's shadowed windows. "The kind that slithered out of the wrong realm. I've been tracking them for days. Thought I had time to move Yelena someplace safer." His jaw tightened. "I was wrong."

Teari stepped closer. "You think she's inside?"

"I don't think." Jasper's voice was low, sure. "I know. The creatures that took her work for someone older. Someone who doesn't just cross realms, he collects from them."

Chel's gaze slid from Jasper to the warehouse's dark

facade. It was the creature from the books Evelyn had shown him. "The Magpie."

Jasper's wings shifted at the name. "If that's what you want to call him."

The silence between them stretched until Teari exhaled sharply. "Well... this wasn't part of the plan."

Chel's head turned, slow. "What plan?"

She hesitated, then gave a small, rueful smile. "I brought you to see your sister." She gestured toward the looming warehouse. "We're here instead."

Chel let out a short, humorless laugh. He looked back toward the warehouse, his posture settling into the kind of stillness Teari had learned meant violence was coming. "Alright. Let's go get our girl."

Jasper's eyes narrowed. "We'll have to be quick. He doesn't keep to one place for long."

Lucipurr, who'd been waiting by the fence, flicked his tail and padded toward the warehouse door like he was leading the charge.

Chapter 50

The warehouse door groaned as Jasper eased it open, just enough for them to slip inside.

Chel's senses lit instantly. He tasted rust and salt in the air and something faintly metallic that didn't belong on the Earthen plane. The air was damp, stale, and carried the wrong kind of quiet.

Lucipurr darted ahead, tail high, weaving between stacks of abandoned crates. His paws were soft on the concrete.

They moved through the shadows until the floor beneath them shifted from dust to damp stone. Chel's eyes adjusted, tracing the dim lantern-light leaking from down a corridor. He could hear soft movements in the distance, chains shifting, the ragged rhythm of breathing from too many lungs.

The room they entered wasn't what he expected. It wasn't a dungeon, but it might as well have been. Each "cell" was cordoned off with bars or glass. There were small enclosures that kept the inhabitants contained, but... cared for. Real beds. Tables with food. Neat stacks of folded clothing.

In each cell were creatures he'd never seen before or only heard about in old demon stories.

A man with tattered wings, feathers molting in uneven patches. A young woman whose skin shimmered with scales when the light touched her. A child who looked human, until her shadow moved independently of her body.

Chel's jaw clenched. "He's not just taking them... he's curating them."

Jasper's face was grim. "These are creatures we don't even have names for anymore."

Teari pressed closer to the bars of one cell, watching an old man trace shapes into the air. They were sigils she recognized from Rue's ancient Enochian texts. "This... this is what Rue and Evelyn found in those books."

Chel gave a tight nod. "The Magpie isn't just collecting trophies. He's building something. Or waiting for something." His gaze hardened. "And he thinks Yelena is part of it."

Lucipurr's ears twitched. A door at the far end of the room creaked open, and a shadow spilled across them.

Jasper reached for his blade. "That's him."

The footsteps were unhurried, almost lazy, but each one carried the kind of weight that made Chel's skin crawl.

The figure who emerged from the shadows was tall and narrow, draped in black and silver that shimmered faintly in the low light. His hair was the color of tarnished coins, swept back to reveal sharp cheekbones and eyes that glittered like wet obsidian. A long coat brushed the ground, stitched through with strange patterns that seemed to shift when Chel tried to focus on them.

"Well," the Magpie drawled, voice like silk. "I thought I felt a few uninvited guests scurrying about."

Chel took a half-step forward, angling himself so Teari was slightly behind him. "You've taken something that doesn't belong to you."

The Magpie's gaze swept over him with idle curiosity, lingering an instant too long as though searching for the seams of Chel's skin. A knowing smile touched his lips.

"Many things here do not 'belong,' Hellion," he replied, gesturing languidly toward the cells. "That is the point of a collection. Every piece is rare. Precious. Chosen. And you should taste their blood."

Teari's voice was sharp. "Yelena is not a thing."

The Magpie's smile widened, cold and foxlike. "And that is precisely why she is so valuable. The right bloodline. The right... resonance. You should thank me for keeping her safe."

Jasper's hand tightened on his blade. "Safe? You've got creatures in cages."

"They are not harmed," the Magpie said smoothly, moving toward a cell that held a woman with pale, shifting eyes. "Fed. Clothed. Sheltered from realms that would devour them whole. Realms that just might kill them." He tilted his head at the woman behind the glass. "Each of them has a story. A lineage worth preserving. You'd be surprised how many the Veil forgets—or hides."

Chel caught the way Teari stiffened. She understood the undertone. This wasn't random. He was hunting bloodlines.

The Magpie stopped before them, so close Chel could see the faint shimmer of runes etched into the leather of his gloves. "If you've come to take the girl, I'm afraid she's... unavailable. But do stay. I so rarely have visitors with taste."

He was watching Teari like she was a precious painting in a museum.

The Magpie turned without waiting for an answer, his coat sweeping the dust as he moved deeper into the warehouse's belly. "Come along," he called over his shoulder, the sing-song cadence in his voice making it sound less like an invitation and more like a dare.

Chel exchanged a glance with Teari, then followed. Jasper fell into step on her other side, his eyes sweeping every shadow. The air grew heavier the farther they went, the smell of old stone and something faintly metallic filling their lungs.

They passed cell after cell. Each was holding something that made Chel's gut knot. A man with silver-veined skin sat cross-legged on the floor, unmoving. A young girl with horns curling like a ram's sat stroking her hair, though her vacant eyes never left the far wall.

"These are just...," Teari murmured, but her voice had gone flat.

Chel heard the strain beneath it.

"They are treasures," the Magpie corrected lightly, his fingers brushing the bars of a cell as if he were petting a favored pet. "Some rescued. Some acquired. All of them rare." He stopped in front of a narrow corridor, gesturing with his free hand. "And here is the one you've been sniffing after."

Yelena stood behind a wall of reinforced glass, her hair loose around her shoulders, eyes wide but sharp. When she saw Teari, she pressed her palms against the barrier. Her eyes landed on Jasper, recognition sparking. "You."

The Magpie clicked his tongue. "Careful, little songbird. Words travel here."

Chel stepped closer, ignoring him. "Are you hurt?"

Yelena shook her head, but her gaze darted toward the other cells.

The Magpie's smile thinned, though he didn't deny it. "It's not so hard to follow a thread, once you learn how it weaves." His eyes shifted to Teari. "Some threads shine brighter than others."

Chel moved in front of her, every instinct screaming. "Not for you."

The Magpie's laugh was low and pleasant, and that

made it worse. "Not today. But one day, Hellion, everyone with the right blood will belong to me."

He tilted his head toward Yelena's cell. "You'd best decide if you want her free because everything has a price. And I'm always willing to upgrade my treasures."

Jasper stepped forward before Chel could say a word, his wings folding tight against his back. "What's the price?"

The Magpie didn't hesitate. "A trade." His gaze drifted until it landed on Teari.

Chel's hand twitched toward the hilt at his hip. "Not happening."

The Magpie's smile curved, knowing and cruel. "Why not? She's a rare thread. Beautiful, too. A child of an Archangel... there are whole realms that would burn for the chance to bind her."

Teari stiffened beside him, but her chin lifted, steady.

"I'll go," Jasper cut in. His voice was calm, but the tension in his jaw betrayed him. "I'm bound to the girl's protection. That's my oath. If you must have a trade, take me."

The Magpie's eyes narrowed, the playfulness thinning from his voice. "You? An Angel bound by rules and guilt? Your kind is far too noisy to keep. And you're not nearly as rare as you think. You are more trouble than you're worth."

Jasper didn't blink. "You'll get me without a fight. You'll never get her without one. And I've trained as a healer. I'm not completely useless."

The Magpie tilted his head as if considering, then let his gaze drift to Chel. "Then perhaps... you. You've already been through Purgatory once. I'd wager you wouldn't survive a second time. Old Hellion. Your soul is barely attached. And... you're one of the old ones, a Hellion from before Lucifer's defeat." The Magpie began to pace, circling Chel in an arc.

Chel kept moving so the Magpie could not get close to Teari, whom he was shielding.

Chel said nothing, but his jaw locked tight.

"Yes, I have been keeping track of what happens on all realms."

Jasper stepped forward again, his voice hardening. "It's me or no one."

A long, quiet moment passed. The Magpie's black eyes gleamed, as if weighing the taste of the offer. "Perhaps," he said finally, though there was no promise in his tone. "But not today. I find it more... entertaining to wait."

Chel's grip on his weapon tightened, but he forced himself to remain still. The Magpie's gaze had returned to Teari like a hook sinking deeper.

Chel didn't miss the way the Magpie's words wrapped around her name. And for the first time since walking out of the ocean, Chel felt the old restlessness stir in his blood because he knew—with bone-deep certainty— that whatever game the Magpie was playing, Teari was already part of it whether she knew it or not.

The Magpie flicked his wrist and the door to Yelena's cell opened.

Teari reached for the girl and tugged her close. "Let's get out of here," she said to Chel.

The Hellion nodded and glanced to Jasper. The Angel was already moving to Yelena's side.

The Magpie watched them leave, a simple smile spread across his face.

"That was entirely too easy," Teari muttered under her breath.

"Yup." Chel glanced down and noticed Lucipurr had joined them again. "Follow the cat out of here."

"It was a set up," Jasper warned.

The air outside the warehouse was damp and heavy, carrying the faint tang of rust and rain. Jasper lingered behind to keep watch, but Chel caught Teari's arm the moment they were far enough from the Magpie's reach.

"Are you not afraid?" His voice was low, edged with something sharper than anger.

She blinked at him, feigning ignorance. "What?"

"You heard him. He didn't want Jasper. He didn't want me. He wanted you." Chel's hand slid down her arm, smoothing over the scars below her elbows, until his fingers found her wrist. "You think I'm just going to ignore that?"

Her expression softened, but there was an irritating calm to it. "It's not me," she said with a shrug. "Whatever he's after, he's wrong. I'm fine."

Chel's jaw flexed. "Teari—"

"He said those things to get under our skin," she interrupted, turning toward the cracked sidewalk that led them back to the street.

"He got under mine," Chel growled. "That's the problem."

She glanced back over her shoulder. "Then maybe don't let him."

He followed, but his eyes kept sweeping the shadows, every sense sharpened. The Magpie's voice still gnawed at the edges of his thoughts, curling around one undeniable truth. Teari could tell him she was fine all she wanted. That didn't change the fact that someone out there had just marked her.

CHAPTER 51

EARLIER...

THE ANGELS, HUMAN, AND HELLIONS HAD GONE ahead, their bootsteps loud and clumsy and echoing in the dark. Lucipurr padded after them, tail twitching in agitation, his paws making no sound on the cracked stone floor. To them, he was just a cat. To him, they were fragile creatures, like glass jars rattling down a cliffside. He doubted they even realized how close they were to shattering.

Good thing they had him. He wondered how half of them even survived before he came along.

Lucipurr's nose twitched. The Magpie's stink clung to the air and it smelled like old dust and older feathers. Eternal rot. That thing had been collecting since before even Lucipurr had memory, and his memory stretched far beyond Rue's short life, beyond her mother's life, and beyond the wars and the deception that had infiltrated the realms.

He slipped between shadows, into the places between where no one could see him unless he wanted them to. The cages hummed there; half in this realm, half in another, bars stretched from reality into dream. Humans, Angels, demons and other creatures–each prisoner was locked not just by steel but by threads of the Veil itself. Their eyes followed him, but none spoke. They could sense he wasn't quite there. He dabbled on the edges, half in and half out.

Lucipurr's whiskers twitched. He was searching for someone, but he was the only one that knew what to look for. Too much time had passed. No one knew that others like him existed. Lucipurr realized that Rue and the others didn't exactly know what he was. He didn't speak their language so he didn't have the ability to explain. And while he'd watched Rue and Evelyn and that little blonde librarian named Layla search and pour over old books, they'd never found any information about his kind. He doubted they would. That horse might know something. But Lucipurr was quick to stay hidden when that White creature was around.

Once, long ago, there had been others like him; cats that prowled between the realms, guardians of travelers and soul-tethers. They were ethereal companions born when the Veil was younger, stronger, less corrupted, and it's threads were sparkly and clean. They had wandered together through the dream-shadows, weaving between the heartbeats of mortals, curling on the shoulders of kings. But one by one, they had vanished. Taken. Stolen. Killed. Collected. Skinned. Eaten.

And Lucipurr knew who had taken them.

While the Hellion and the Angels spoke with the Magpie, Lucipurr had disappeared into the shadows. His tail lashed as he padded closer to a long corridor where cages stood stacked to the ceiling. The Hellion was barely seeing a spec of the Magpie's collection.

A flicker of fur caught his eye, black as midnight, but thinner, ragged. A faint glow shimmered in its eyes—eyes like his.

He pressed closer to the bars, heart clawing in his chest.

"Little brother?" he whispered, though his mouth made no sound. The words were vibration in the dark, carried on shadow.

The figure inside the cage did not stir, but only blinked once, slowly, as though dreaming. He was bound in chains not of iron but of thought, tethered to the Magpie's cruel design. The Magpie knew this brother could escape with a lick of darkness and so he was cruelly bound to this in-between realm.

Lucipurr's ears flattened. He had been searching for so long. Every time he curled in Rue's lap, every time he purred into her sleepless nights, it was with the weight of knowing one of his kin was still out there, trapped. He'd been searching for them for years.

Lucipurr paced outside of the cell, intelligent eyes

searching for a way to get in without getting snatched up. Filaments of the Veil were waving in the air, some strapped over Little Brother, some reaching toward Lucipurr. They whipped closer. No. This wasn't going to work. It was too dangerous. He needed to find help, possibly a creature with opposable thumbs.

The Magpie had stolen too much; souls, fragments of realms, and creatures older than the Archangels themselves.

The Hellion and the Angels were speaking again. They'd collected the girl.

"I will be back for you, Little brother," Lucipurr sent the message. The one like him blinked and a whisker twitched.

Lucipurr pulled back to return to them, melting into shadow then through it. He would not tell them. Not yet. Rue was his tether, his anchor, the one creature who kept him from unraveling into the in-between. He would not burden her with this pain until he had claws deep in the Magpie's throat.

He trotted after the Hellion and the Angels and the girl, tail high, a black slip of defiance in the dark. They thought he was guiding them out. Perhaps he was. But he was also leading himself back; back to the day when the cages would break, when his kin would walk free again.

And on that day, the Magpie would finally learn what it meant for shadows to have teeth.

Chapter 52

The Peabody Library was a flurry of activity after Chel, Teari, Yelena, and Jasper returned.

Lucipurr had disappeared during the walk back.

Jasper rushed them into the building and began pouring fresh salt across the thresholds. He pulled a marker from his pocket and began strengthening the runes.

It didn't take long for more to arrive.

A knock on the door echoed.

Teari gripped Yelena's hand and drew her close. Chel stepped in front of them, guarding.

"It's going to be okay," Teari whispered to the girl.

Yelena nodded. "I know."

Chel glanced at them from the corner of his eye.

"We'll explain everything soon," Teari said.

Yelena nodded, eyes wide.

There was a vibration in the air. Something powerful was on the other side.

Jasper gripped the gilded door handle and pulled. A breeze of cool air whipped in, followed by a few fallen autumn leaves.

"I guess we are having a meeting of the minds," a familiar voice said. "Jasper, may we enter?"

Jasper stepped back, motioning to the fresh line of salt across the threshold of the door. "Don't disrupt it," he warned.

It was Meg.

And the Raven King.

And... the White Horse.

More followed. Rue, Dacre, Evelyn, Remington, Layla, Thrush, Gabriel, Shay, Jed. And lastly, Nero.

Teari was staring at Thrush and the realization occurred, he had wings. She could see his wings on the Earthen plane.

"Oh no," Teari muttered.

Slowly, The Raven King's giant black wings appeared, Chel's Hellion wings came next. Teari glanced over her shoulder. White wings. She looked to Gabriel. More white wings.

The White Horse was pacing, watching all of them. Dark eyes flicking from creature to creature. Jasper crossed the room and went to Yelena's side. Even his white wings were visible.

That could only mean one thing: the Veil between realms was thinning.

"I'll make this quick because I have always believed that so many powerful beings should never be in the same place at once." The White Horse focused on Meg and Sparrow. "Something is happening and it's spreading over to my realm. You demolished the Black Mansion?"

"It's been burned," Meg stepped forward. "But there's more. Layers underneath that we didn't know about." Meg motioned to the girls: Rue, Evelyn and Layla. They moved to a long table, their mates had been carrying large books. They set them down and opened them. "The girls discovered something."

The White Horse stepped forward to gaze at the books. "There's more than this," she said. "Many have been lost and hidden and destroyed."

"Tell her Rue." Meg motioned to the largest of the books.

Rue cleared her throat and tucked a piece of long, dark hair behind her ear. "We have been doing a lot of research about the history of the realms and we found something. Something with the Black Mansion at the core of it all."

The White Horse blinked.

Nero moved next to her.

"Something or someone was banished to its own realm, a prison realm of sorts."

Evelyn unfolded a large piece of parchment and laid it out. It was the blueprints of the Black Mansion.

"Underneath the Black Mansion, there were ley lines into other realms." Rue turned an aged page from one of the books and pointed at an image and ancient runes. "We have been trying to decipher all of this but the language is odd. It's not quite Enochian or Hellspeak. It's something in-between." Rue glanced at the White Horse. "There is a Magpie, a creature that was banished."

Yelena shivered remembering the cells and the creatures she had seen when the Magpie had her.

"It was an ancient Archangel," Gabriel said. "I had to throat punch a few colleagues but I got some information out of them. They cast him out and imprisoned him. But it seemed he made some deals, he found ancient magic, he created his own tunnels into the realms."

"And so you dig up what has been hidden." The White Horse looked at Jed then Teari then Meg as she spoke. "There is much more information you need to find to set this straight and strengthen the Veil again." She focused on Chel. "Hellion. Will you join my alliance?"

Chel's face went slack. He looked to Meg.

Meg smiled and nodded.

"Of course," Chel said. He looked to Teari.

The White Horse nodded and knocked her teeth together. "You will be a Guardian of the gulf portal. You will keep my realm safe from whatever comes through that portal until the Veil strengthens."

A shiver went through Chel. "It is my honor. I would like to bring my Angel and have her there with me."

Teari made a small gasp. Gabriel's blue eyes caught hers, but he didn't appear worried.

The White Horse tipped her head to the side and watched Teari with one large dark eye. "Angel? She is a Queen."

Chel cleared his throat. "She is."

"Angel, Queen of the fallen Archangel Michael's kingdom, will you join my alliance?" the White Horse asked.

Teari looked to Gabriel. He mouthed, "Say yes."

"Yes," Teari said.

"Good. You may visit your mate as you wish and help him watch over the gulf portal but do not forget you have a kingdom to rule. Perhaps converse with the Raven King on how to handle this."

"I will." Teari glanced to Sparrow but his features were impassive.

The White Horse's gaze fell upon Yelena. She blinked. "Finish your schooling."

"I'd like her to stay with me," Chel said, motioning to his sister.

"No. She stays with Guardian Angel." The White Horse tipped her nose toward Jasper. Then she looked around the room. "She stays here with him. You cannot return to your previous living quarters. It's not safe."

Yelena went pale. "I..." she couldn't find words.

"I will watch over her, as I always have," Jasper said, taking a step closer to Yelena.

The White Horse focused on Meg and Sparrow next. "Thank you." Her gaze rolled over everyone in the room.

The White Horse glanced from wall to wall. Then she looked at Rue. "Where is your cat?"

Rue frowned, "Lucipurr? He's at our house, sleeping."

"No, there he is." The White Horse was staring at the shadows behind a bookshelf. "Come out, cat."

Lucipurr stepped out of the shadows, tail waving.

"You'll have some explaining to do," the White Horse whispered.

Lucipurr let out an innocent *meow*.

The runes began glowing. Salt grit sparkled across the thresholds. Jasper stood with Yelena at the circulation desk, murmuring reassurances as he re-inked runes into the oak and pointed to the ones she needed to learn.

A tremor shivered through the stacks.

Chel's head snapped up. Teari felt it too as the air went taut, humming like a plucked wire.

"Hold," Jasper warned, wings half-flaring.

The salt line at the front doors hissed. Something pressed against the ward from the other side. It was testing, searching for an entrance, and then slipped through a hairline crack where the gilding had worn thin. It hit the marble like spilled ink and unfurled on itself, a hunched shadow with jointed limbs and eyes like wet coal.

Yelena sucked in a breath. "That is one of the creatures that took me from my apartment."

Teari moved without thinking, drawing her close.

Chel stepped in front of both of them, shoulders braced, dagger up.

Across the room, Thrush startled, wings flaring sharp and bright before he wrestled them still. The Raven King swore under his breath, hand lifting, blade humming with power. Each male stepped in front of their mate instinctively.

"Let me," Lucipurr said, it sounded like a simple meow to everyone else.

Nero's hooves tapped the floor and he sucked in a breath, ready to release fire if the kitten failed.

The little black cat slipped from behind a shelf and padded straight toward the thing. It tilted its head at him, a hiss peeling off its teeth. Lucipurr's tail twitched once. The lights flickered. For an instant he wasn't there at all, he was a seam of darkness unzipping the floor and then he was on the creature's back, sinking claws into it.

The shadow folded in on itself, shrieking without sound. Lucipurr sank deeper. He bit with tiny fangs. The thing collapsed, then evaporated, the smell of rust dropping from the air.

Silence returned in stages: the tick of radiators, the wind at the stained glass, Yelena's breath hitching against Jasper's shoulder.

The White Horse paced once, hooves ringing faintly against nothing, then stilled. "If one can slip through, more will try."

Meg's gaze cut to Chel. "Guardian."

Chel nodded. "I'm on the gulf before sunrise."

The White Horse's dark eye moved from face to face, ending on Teari. "Keep your wards strong, Queen. That thing came for you. The Veil will close again, but not if you pretend it isn't tearing. That goes for all of you. I cannot have the dead walking in this realm again. The humans barely recovered from the last incident."

Teari inclined her head. "We're not pretending."

Sparrow's black wings curled in, the room exhaled, and the council began to move again—assignments dispatched, books shut, thresholds re-salted.

Lucipurr sat primly by the front mat, licking one paw like he hadn't just eaten a nightmare. Dacre smiled before nudging Rue's shoulder, "That was interesting, little dark princess."

Rue's eyes were wide in disbelief.

She crouched and picked up her kitten, holding him close against her chest.

"How did you find that creature?" the White Horse asked.

"My brother brought him to me," Rue motioned to Remington.

"I found him at the beach house," Remm said.

CHAPTER 53

The beach house breathed with the tide. Night had peeled away to a soft, pearly morning; gulls sketched white arcs above the dunes.

Chel leaned in the bedroom doorway, watching Teari pull a sundress over her head as sun skimmed her cheek. He should have been sleeping. He should have been anywhere but here yet here was the only place he wanted to be once the grip of Purgatory let go. Here with her.

"We'll have to split time," she said, fastening a button. "The Archangels in Babylon are going to be in an uproar."

"Let them talk." He crossed to her, careful of the healing ribs and stitched wounds, but truth be told he felt a lot better these past few days. "Jed is going to help me rig the beach. If anything tries to get through, I'll feel the pull."

"That's a lot of ground to cover for one Hellion," she said, a small smile cutting through the worry.

"Guardian and Hellion. Come here, Angel." He reached for her.

He traced the scar below her left elbow. "I don't want you to go back. They'll come for you." He made himself say it. "If they can't take Yelena, they'll try a brighter key. The Magpie already promised."

Her mouth twitched—stubbornness, humor, maybe both. "Good luck to them. I have Babylon, a Hellion, and more."

"I'm serious."

"So am I." She stepped in, palms sliding up his chest. "I'm not a girl hiding in my father's kingdom anymore. I'm not alone. They want a soul. They'll find death. I was of Gabriel's Legion for years. I fought beside you in the war against Lucifer. I can handle myself, Hellion."

He let out the breath he didn't know he was holding. "I just got you back."

"I'll be here." She tipped his face down and kissed him.

"I want you here," he admitted against her mouth, a wry smile there.

"I'm here now, Guardian." She kissed him again, softer. "And when Heaven screams, I'll come back to the beach. When the gulf stirs, you'll come to the sky. We meet in the middle."

"Every month," he said. "Like we promised."

"Or sooner," she said, threading her fingers through

his. "Sooner is allowed." She was looking him up and down. "Sooner is always gonna happen if that's how you're going to dress. I don't want these locals cozying up to you."

"I'll kill them." He was serious.

"We don't kill humans. The White Horse will have your head."

They stood a long time at the open window, the gulf shining like hammered metal, the horizon calm only because two people had decided to hold it steady.

EPILOGUE

Rue slept curled on her side, one hand flung across the quilt, ink smudged at the edge of her palm where she'd fallen asleep over a translation. The lamp hummed. Outside, night held its breath.

On the dresser, Lucipurr lifted his head.

The house's corners were too dark tonight. The shadows stretched a fraction too long, threads in the baseboards humming. He slid off the wood and onto the floor without touching it, a slip of darkness gliding to the window.

He stepped through his reflection and into another realm.

Here, the world forgot its edges. The Magpie's lair bled into train tunnels and caved halls and the under-ribs of old cathedrals. Lucipurr knew the way by scent and memory. The familiar dust, feathers, oil, the faint copper of long-kept cages.

Where the warehouse had stood, there was ruin. Bars bent. Glass webbed. The hum of wards gone thin. He padded through the wreckage, tail low, listening.

A sound answered. Not a voice, not a cry, it was closer to a ripple. He followed it to a small, narrow cell partly unmade by whatever fight had torn this place open. This was a memory–not real. He still saw it, none-theless.

Inside, a black cat lay curled, ribs showing through fur like drawn wire, eyes a dim starshine. "Little brother, where did he take you?" Lucipurr asked.

Lucipurr pressed his forehead to the glass that wasn't there anymore and breathed slow, letting the Between know he was watching. *Not tonight.* The Magpie had shifted his collection, moved the delicate pieces some-where deeper. Coward.

Behind Lucipurr, the dark stirred. He showed his teeth. The stir subsided.

"Soon," he told the empty cell.

He crossed realms again, slipped back through the seam of the window into Rue's room. The lamp still hummed. Dacre's eyes were open, watching Lucipurr without a word. He'd been doing that ever since Lucipurr's cover had been blown at the Peabody Library.

Rue murmured something in her sleep and rolled closer to the warm space where he always curled.

Lucipurr leapt onto the quilt, circled once, and settled against her stomach. Her hand, without waking, found the back of his neck and scratched the place that made his purr rumble low.

He stared at the door, eyes a thin green crescent.

The Magpie was patient. So was he.

When the cages opened for good, shadows would have teeth. And he would be there first.

A Note

Thank You

To every reader who picked up *These Thorns are Sharpest*—whether you've been with me since the first Veil of Shadows book or you just stumbled across my work on TikTok at 2 a.m. THANK YOU! You are the reason this world keeps growing. Every like, share, review, late-night DM, and "OMG..." message fuels my dark little writer heart. And I love responding with: "I wonder what's going to happen next?!"

To my incredible BookTok family: Mellystarr, massiel reads, ShadowDaddy/D, Linda, Kim.d.f.reads, Tameka, Tracy, Cass Marie, Shania, littlekick, sweetpea26_26, Del (I'm still thinking about that alpha rescue, after all this time!), thatgalbritt, punkachoo, Short.n.sweet, Shannon, curious_kitten, momma Deb, SarLitten, Raye, Platinum_VERA, OkayLucy, DivaSoldierFoster, jennifer-7746, Whit, Brianne, Mikayla, Brandi B, Ken,

Like.A.Diamond, Mystery Book Bundles, Sam/Dillon, DeyaReads, Jessica, Oopsiedaisies, Sarah, Letty, Chantel, Megs, Mama Guti, Bookinit, AuthorAnnette S, Patty.M.G, Ivan.n.honey, Janet Marie Freels, Andrea, White Booktok, and sooooo many more!! You all make promoting vampires, morally gray chaos, and slow-burn romance a joy.

To my ARC readers on Booksirens: Thank you, thank you. I love getting your first reviews and thoughts.

To my editor, Kristy: you catch the things I miss and all those extra commas, sharpen every shadow, and somehow know when I've been holding back on a scene. Thank you for pushing me to make each book better than the last.

To my family: you've listened to my rambling lore dumps, tolerated my writing marathons, my Livestreams, and never once questioned why I'm Googling things like "how to unlive an Archangel?" You're my safe place and my chaos crew, and I love you for it.

Here's to more books, more worlds, and more late nights chasing the stories that refuse to let us sleep.

I'm still smiling about the night you all got me to 1 million likes during the livestream!

Let the Vampires Bite,
  Meredith

About the Author

M. R. Pritchard delves into the profound clash between good and evil, the mystical realms of gods and monsters, and the intricate transformations of ordinary people into beings of immense power. Her gripping narratives often unfold within the haunting backdrop of apocalyptic or post-apocalyptic landscapes, offering a unique blend of suspense and wonder.

M. R. Pritchard is a two-time Kindle Scout winning author, her short story "Glitch" has been featured in the 2017 winter edition of THE FIRST LINE literary journal. Her short story "Moon Lord" has been featured in Chronicle Worlds: Half Way Home (Part of the Future Chronicles) and will be time capsuled on the moon on the Lunar Codex in 2024.

Visit her website MRPritchard.com and Subscribe. You'll get subscriber only content, deleted scenes, updates, special previews of new projects, and book deals.

Looking to buy direct? Visit MidnightLedgerbooks (dot) com to get signed books, early releases, and extras.

www.ingramcontent.com/pod-product-compliance
Lightning Source LLC
Chambersburg PA
CBHW021230190726
48289CB00005B/1259